Also by James Lee Burke

LAY DOWN MY
SWORD AND SHIELD

LAY DOWN MY
SWORD AND SHIELD

A NOVEL BY
JAMES LEE BURKE

HYPERION
NEW YORK

ISBN 0-7868-8950-0

Designed by Nicholas A. Bernini

10 9 8 7 6 5 4 3 2 1

This book is for my father,
James L. Burke, Sr.
who taught me most of the good things
I know about

LAY DOWN MY
SWORD AND SHIELD

ONE

Almost ninety years ago during the Sutton-Taylor feud, John Wesley Hardin drilled a half dozen .44 pistol balls into one of the wood columns on my front porch. My grandfather, Old Hack, lived in the house then, and he used to described how Wes Hardin had ridden drunk all night from San Antonio when he had heard that Hack had promised to lock him in jail if he ever came back into DeWitt County again. The sun had just risen, and it was raining slightly when Hardin rode into the yard, his black suit streaked with mud, horse sweat, and whiskey; he had a shotgun tied across his saddle horn with a strip of leather and his navy Colt was already cocked in his hand.

"You, Hack! Get out here. And don't bring none

of your Lincoln niggers with you or I'll kill them, too."

(My grandfather was sheriff and justice of the peace, and the Reconstruction government had forced him to take on two Negro federal soldiers as deputies. Of the forty-two men that Hardin eventually killed, many were Negroes, whom he hated as much as he did carpetbaggers and law officers.)

Hardin began shooting at the front porch, cocking and firing while the horse reared and pitched sideways with each explosion in its ears. Wes's face was red with whiskey, his eyes were dilated, and when the horse whirled in a circle he whipped the pistol down between its ears. He emptied the rest of the chambers, the fire and black powder smoke roaring from the barrel, and all six shots hit the wood column in a neat vertical line.

Hack had been up early that morning with one of his mares that was in foal, and when he saw Wes Hardin through the barn window he took the Winchester from the leather saddle scabbard nailed against the wall and waited for Wes to empty his pistol. Then he stepped out into the lot, his cotton nightshirt tucked inside his trousers, blood and membrane on his hands and forearms, and pumped a shell into the chamber. Wes jerked around back-

wards in the saddle when he heard the action work
behind him.

"You goddamn sonofabitch," Hack said. "Start to
untie that shotgun and I'll put a new asshole in the
middle of your face."

Hardin laid his pistol against his thigh, and
turned his horse in a half circle.

"You come up behind me, do you?" he said. "Get
your pistol and let me reload and I'll pay them nigger deputies for burying you."

"I told you not to come back to DeWitt. Now
you shot up my house and probably run off half
my Mexicans. I'm going to put you in jail and wrap
chains all over you, then I'm taking you into my
court for attempted assault on a law officer. Move
off that horse."

Wes looked steadily at Hack, his killer's eyes intent and frozen as though he were staring into a
flame. Then he brought his boots out of the stir-
rups, slashed his spurs into the horse's sides, and
bent low over the neck with his fingers in the mane
as the horse charged towards the front gate. But
Hack leaped forward at the same time and swung
the Winchester barrel down with both hands on
Hardin's head and knocked him sideways out of the
saddle into the mud. There was a three-inch split
in his scalp at the base of the hairline, and when

he tried to raise himself to his feet, Hack kicked
him squarely in the face twice with his boot heel.
Then he put him in the back of a vegetable wagon,
locked his wrists in manacles, tied trace chains
around his body and nailed the end links to the
floorboards.

And that's how John Wesley Hardin went to jail
in DeWitt County, Texas. He never came back to
fight Hack again, and no other law officer ever got
the better of him, except John Selman, who drove
a pistol ball through his eye in an El Paso saloon
in 1895.

As I stood there on my front porch that hot,
breathless July day, leaning against the column with
the six bullet holes, now worn and smooth, I could
see Hack's whitewashed marker under the pin oaks
in the Holland family cemetery. The trees were still
in the heat, the leaves filmed with dust, and the
shade was dappled on the headstones. Four generations of my family were buried there: Son Holland, a Tennessee mountain man from the
Cumberlands who came to Texas in 1835 and
fought at the battle of San Jacinto for Texas' in-
dependence, was a friend of Sam Houston, later
received twelve hundred acres from the Texas Re-
public, and died of old age while impressing horses
for the Confederacy; Hack's two older brothers,
who rode with the Texas cavalry under General

Hood at the battle of Atlanta; Great Uncle Tip, who made the first drive up the Chisholm Trail and married an Indian squaw; Sidney, a Baptist preacher and alcoholic, who always carried two revolvers and a derringer and killed six men; Winfro, murdered in a brothel during the Sutton-Taylor feud, his body dragged on a rope back and forth in front of the house by drunken cowboys; Jefferson, who had two years' business college in Austin and decided to compete with the King and XIT ranches in the cattle market and lost six hundred acres of Holland land as a result; and Sam, my father—Hackberry's son—a genteel man with a rheumatic heart, a one-time southern historian at the University of Texas and later a United States congressman during the New Deal, and finally a suicide.

Out beyond the cemetery the low, green hills sloped down towards the river, which was now low and brown, and the crests were covered with blackjack, live oak, and mesquite. The cotton in the fields was in bloom, the rows evenly spaced and stretched out straight as a rifle shot, and the tomatoes had come out big and red in the early summer showers. The sun flashed brilliantly on the windmill blades, now idle in the still air, and in the distance the clapboard and shingle homes of the Mexican farm workers looked like flattened matchboxes in the heat. My three natural-gas wells pumped monotonously up and down, the pipes on the well heads dripping moisture from the intense cold inside, and occasionally I could smell the slightly nauseating odor of crude gas. The wells were located in the middle of the cotton acreage, the derricks long since torn down, and the cotton rows were cut back from the well heads in surgically perfect squares, which always suggested to me a pastoral reverence towards the Texas oil industry.

The front lane was spread with white gravel, the adjoining fields planted with Bermuda grass, and white wood fences ran both the length of the lane and the main road where my property ended. The lawn was mowed and clipped, watered each day by a Negro man whom my wife hired to take care of the rose gardens, and there were magnolia and orange trees on each side of the porch. The main portion of the house had been built by Hackberry in 1876, although the logs of Son Holland's original cabin were in our kitchen walls, and it had changed little since. My wife had added a latticework verandah on the second story, with large ferns in earthen pots, and a screened-in side porch where we used to eat iced-tea dinners on summer evenings. After we began to take our meals separately, the porch was used as a cocktail bar for her lawn parties, complete with a professional bartender in a white jacket who shaved ice into mint julep glasses for the

Daughters of the Confederacy, the Junior League, and the Texas Democratic Women's Club.

But regardless of the Sunday afternoon lawn parties, the political women with their hard eyes and cool drinks, the white boxes filled with roses, the air-conditioning units in the windows, it was still Old Hack's place, and sometimes at night when I was alone in the library the house seemed to creak with his angry presence.

I suppose that's why I always felt that I was a guest in the house rather than its owner. Even though I was named for Hack, I never had the gunfighter blood that ran in the Holland family. I was a Navy hospital corpsman during the Korean War and spent three months in Seoul passing out penicillin tablets for clap until I was finally sent up to the firing line, and I was there only six days before I was shot through both calves and captured by the Chinese. So my one attempt at Hack's gunfighter ethic was aborted, and I spent thirty-two months in three P.O.W. camps. However, I'll tell you more later about my war record, my wound and purple heart, and my testimony at a turncoat's court-martial, since they all became part of my credentials as a Democratic candidate for Congress.

I lit a cigar and walked down the glaring white lane to where my car was parked in the shade of an oak tree. I had showered and changed clothes a

half hour before, but already my shirt and coat were
damp, and the sun broke against my dark glasses
like a hot green scorch. I sat back in the leather
seat of the Cadillac and turned on the ignition and
the air conditioner, and for just a moment, as the
stale warm air blew through the vents, I could smell
the concentrated odor of the gas wells, that scent
of four thousand dollars a month guaranteed in-
come from Texaco, Inc. I dropped the car into low,
pushed slowly down on the accelerator, and I felt
all three hundred fifty horses throb up smoothly
through the bottom of my boot. The gravel pinged
under the fenders, and I rumbled over the cattle
guard onto the main road, then pushed the accelerator to the floor and listened to the tires whine
over the soft tar surfacing. My white fences
whipped by the windows, clicking like broken
sticks against the corner of my eye, and I steered
with three fingers ninety miles an hour around the
chuck holes and depressions, biting gently down on
my cigar and watching the shadows on the fields
race with me towards San Antonio and Houston.
Several times when drunk I had driven one hundred
and twenty miles an hour at night over the same
road, hillbilly and gospel music from Del Rio thundering out of the radio, and the next morning I
would sweat through those whiskey hangovers and
see yellow flashes of light in my mind, the Cadillac

rolling over in the field, the white fence gaping among the shattered boards, and I would be inside, bleeding blackly between the steering wheel and the crushed roof.

But sober I drove with magic in my hands, an air-cooled omnipotence encircling me as the road sucked under the long frame of my automobile.

As I neared Yoakum I unscrewed the cap of my whiskey flask and took a drink. The white ranch houses and the barns, the cattle and horses in the fields, the acres of cotton, and the solitary oak trees rolled by me. The sun reflected in a white flash off the hood of the car, and ahead the road seemed to swim in the heat. A thin breeze had started to blow, and dust devils spun along the dry edge of the corn fields. On the top of a slope the blades of a wind-mill turned into the breeze and began spinning rapidly; then the water sluiced out in a long white spray into the trough. At the edge of town I passed the rows of Negro and Mexican shacks, all alike even though some of them were built decades apart, all weathered gray, the porches collapsing, tarpaper nailed in uneven shapes on the roofs, the dirt yards littered with broken toys, tangled wire, dirty children, plastic Clorox bottles, and garbage set out to rot in boxes. In the back, old cars with rusted engines and spider-webbed windows sat among the weeds, faded overalls and denim shirts hung on the washlines, and the scrub brush that grew in the gravel along the railroad bed was streaked black by passing locomotives.

I sipped again from the flask and put it in the glove compartment. It was Saturday, and Yoakum was crowded with ranchers and farmers, women in cotton-print dresses, Mexican and Negro field workers, pickup trucks and battered cars, and young boys on the corner in lacquered straw hats and starched blue jeans that were as stiff as cardboard. On Main Street the old high sidewalks had iron tethering rings set in them, and the wood colonnade, built in 1900, extended over the walk from the brick storefronts. Old men in white shirts with clip-on bow ties sat in the shade, spitting tobacco juice on the concrete and looking out at the traffic with their narrow, sunburned faces. At the end of the street was the stucco and log jail where my grandfather had locked up Wes Hardin. It was set back in a lot filled with weeds, and the roof and one of the walls had caved in. The broken timbers and powdered stone lay in a heap on the floor, and kids had smashed beer bottles against the bars and had left used contraceptives in the corners. But on one wall you could still read the worn inscription that an inmate had scratched there with a nail in 1880: *J. W. Hardin says he will kill Hack Holland for nigger meat.*

I had always wondered if Hack ever worried about Hardin breaking out of prison, or about Hardin's relatives catching him in the back with a shotgun. But evidently he was never afraid of anything, because when Hardin was released from prison after fourteen years Hack sent him a telegram that read: *"Your cousins say you still want to gun me. If this is true I will send you a train ticket to San Antonio and we can meet briefly at the depot."*

Through law school at Baylor I used one of Hack's .44 Colts as a paperweight. The bluing had worn off the metal, and the mahogany grips were cracked, but the spring and hammer still worked and the heavy cylinder would rotate properly in place when I cocked it. After I started law practice with my brother in Austin, I hung the pistol on my office wall next to a 1925 picture of Hack as an old man, with my father in a white straw hat. I had my law degree and Phi Beta Kappa certificate framed in glass on the wall, also; but the gun, Hack's creased face and long white bobbed hair dominated the office.

It was almost two o'clock and over one hundred degrees when I reached San Antonio. The skyline was rigid in the heat, and on the hills above the city I could see the white stucco homes and red-tiled roofs of the rich with their terraced gardens and mimosa trees. I turned into the Mexican district and drove through blocks of secondhand clothing stores, Baptist missions, finance companies, and pawnshops. Slender pachucos in pegged slacks and maroon shirts buttoned at the cuff, with oiled hair combed back in ducktails, leaned idly against the front of pool halls and wino bars.

I pulled into the Mission Motel, a dirty white building constructed to look like the Alamo. There were arches and small bell towers along an outer wall that faced the street. Cracked earthen jars, containing dead plants, stood in an imitation courtyard in front of the office. The bricks in the courtyard had settled from the rains and Johnson grass grew between the cracks. I took a room that I'd had before, a plaster-of-Paris box with a double bed (an electric, coin-operated vibrating machine built in), a threadworn carpet, walls painted canvas yellow, and a bucket of ice and two thick restaurant glasses placed on the dresser. I cut the seal on a bottle of Jack Daniels and poured a glass half full over ice. I sat on the edge of the bed, lit a cigar, and drank the whiskey slowly for five minutes. The red curtains were pulled across the window, but I could still see the hot circle of the sun in the sky. I finished the glass and had another. Then I felt it begin to take me. I had always liked to drink, and I'd found that during the drinking process the best feeling came right before you knew you were drunk, that lucid moment of control and perception when all the doors in your mind spring open and the mysteries suddenly reduce to a simple equation.

I dialed an unlisted number given to me three years ago by R.C. Richardson, a Dallas oilman whom I'd kept out of prison after he defrauded the government of fifty thousand dollars on a farm subsidy. He had written out a ten-thousand-dollar check on my office desk, his huge stomach hanging over his cowboy belt, and handed me his business card with the number penciled on the back.

"I don't know if lawyers like Mexican chili, but you won't find none better than this," he said.

He was crude, but he was right in that it was one of the best call-girl services in Texas—expensive, select, and professional for that ethic. I always felt that the money and organization must have come from the Mafia in Galveston, because none of the girls or the woman who answered the phone seemed to be afraid that the client might be a cop.

The woman on the phone sounded like a voice from an answering service. There was no inflection, accent, or tonal quality that you could identify with a region or with anyone whom you had ever met. I used to imagine what she might have looked like. She must have answered calls from hundreds of men in motel rooms and empty houses, their voices nervous, slightly drunk, hoarse with embarrassment and passion, cautious in fear of rejection. I wondered if those countless confessions of need and inadequacy had given her a devil's insight into the respectable world, or if she was merely a mindless drone. I couldn't identify her with the image of a fat, bleached madam with glass rings on her fingers, who would be altogether too human for the voice over the phone. Finally, I had come to think of her as a hard, asexual spinster, thin and colorless, who must have developed a quiet and cynical sense of power in her ability to manipulate the sex lives of others without any involvement on her part.

As always she was discreet and subtly indirect in asking me what type of girl I wanted and for what services. And as always I made a point of leaving my motel registration name—R.C. Richardson.

I hung up the phone and poured another whiskey over ice. Thirty minutes later the girl arrived in a taxi. She was Mexican, tall, well dressed in expensive clothes, and she had a delicate quality to her carriage. Her black hair was combed over her shoulders, and her white complexion would have been perfect except for two small pits in one cheek. She had high breasts and a good ass, and her legs were well formed against her tight skirt. She smiled at me and I saw that one of her back teeth was missing.

"You want a whiskey and water?" I said.

"It's too hot now. I'm not supposed to drink in the afternoon, anyway," she said. She sat in a chair, took a cigarette from her purse, and lit it.

"Have one just the same." I poured a shot into a second glass.

"It won't make me do anything extra for you, Mr. Richardson."

"People in Dallas call me R.C. You can use my name in the Petroleum Club and it's better than a Diners card."

"I don't think you'll get your money's worth if you drink much more," she said.

"Watch. I'm a real gunfighter when I get loaded."

I stood up and took off my shirt and tie. The whiskey had started to hum in my head.

"You should pay me before we start," she said. She smoked and looked straight ahead.

My white linen coat hung on the back of a chair. I took my billfold from the inside pocket and counted out seventy-five dollars on the dresser top.

"Does any of your organization come out of Galveston?" I said.

"We don't learn about those things."

"You must meet some of the juice behind it. An occasional Italian hood wearing sunglasses and a sharkskin suit."

"Your date is for two hours, Mr. Richardson."

"Take a drink. What about that voice on the phone? Has she ever been laid herself?"

The girl set her cigarette on the dresser edge, slipped her shoes off, and rolled her hose down. I drank a long swallow from my glass.

"Maybe she's Lucky Luciano's grandmother smoking a reefer into the receiver," I said.

"You must not get a chance to talk much."

She stood up, put her arms around my neck, and pressed her stomach hard against me. I could smell the perfume in her hair. She moved the flat of her hand down my back and bit my lip lightly with her eyes closed.

"Don't you think we should start?" she said.

I kissed her mouth and could taste the whiskey on my own breath.

"Why don't you have a drink?" I said. "I don't like a woman to wither under me because of Jack Daniels."

"You're married, aren't you?" She smiled and worked her fingers under my belt.

"I just don't enjoy women who look like they're in pain when you bend over them. It's part of my R.C. Richardson genteel ethic."

"You must be a strange man to live with."

"Give me a try sometime."

She pushed her stomach into me again, then

dropped her arms and finished undressing. She had a wonderful body, the kind you rarely see in whores, with high breasts and brown nipples, long legs tanned on the edge of some gangster's swimming pool, a flat stomach kept in form by twenty-five sit-ups a night, the buttocks pale right below the bathing-suit line, and a small pachuco cross with three rays tattooed inside one thigh.

I took off my trousers and shorts and laid them across the top of the chair. I picked up my cigar from the ashtray and looked into the full-length mirror on the closet door. At age thirty-five I had gained fifteen pounds since I played varsity baseball as a sophomore at Baylor. I had a little fat above the thigh bones, the veins in my legs were purple under the skin, and my hair had receded a little at the part; but otherwise I was as trim as I had been when I shut out almost every team in the Southwestern Conference. There was no fat in my chest or stomach, and there was still a ridge of muscle in the back part of my upper left arm from two years of throwing a Carl Hubbell screwball. My shoulders had grown slightly stooped, but I still stood over six feet barefooted, and the bit of gray in my sand-colored hair made me look more like a mature courtroom lawyer than an aging man. Then there was my war wound, two holes in each calf, white and scarred over, placed in an even, diagonal line

as though they had been driven there by an archer's
arrow.

We made love on the bed for an hour, stopping
only for me to pour another glass. My head was
swimming with whiskey, my heart was beating, and
my skin felt hot to my own touch. The floor was
unlevel when I walked to the bottle on the dresser,
and my breathing became heavier and more hoarse
in my throat. We went through all the positions
which she knew and all the experiments I could
think of, re-creating the fantasies of adolescent
masturbation. She was a good whore. She affected
passion without being deliberately obvious, and she
tensed her body and widened her legs at the right
moment. After the third time when I didn't think I
could go again she bent over my stomach and
kissed me and used her hands until I was ready to
enter her. She was soft inside, and she hadn't been
at her trade enough years yet to enlarge too much.
She raised herself on her elbows so that her breasts
hung close to my face, and constricted the muscles
in her stomach and twisted one thigh sideways each
time we moved until I began to feel it swell inside
me, then build in force like a large stone rolling
downhill over the lip of a canyon, and burst away
outside of me with the empty tranquility of an
opium dream.

Then I fell into an exhausted whiskey stupor.

The dust in the air looked like weevil worms turning in the shaft of sunlight that struck against the
Jack Daniels bottle. The girl got up off the bed and
began dressing, and a few moments later I heard
the door click shut after her. I was sweating heavily,
even in the air conditioning, and I leaned my head
over the edge of the bed to make the room stop
spinning. There were flashes of color behind my
closed eyes, and obscene echoes of the things I had
said to the girl when the stone began to roll downhill. My throat and mouth were dry from the whiskey and heavy breathing, the veins in my head
started to dilate with hangover, and I wanted to get
into the shower and sit on the floor under the cold
water until I washed all the heat out of my body;
but instead I fell deeper into a delirium and then
the dream began.

I had many dreams left over from Korea. Sometimes I would dig a grave in frozen ground while
Sergeant Tien Kwong stood over me with his burpgun, occasionally jabbing the short barrel into my
neck, his eyes flat with hatred. At other times the
sergeant and I would return to the colonel's interrogation room, where I sat in a straight-backed
chair and looked at nothing and said nothing until
the sergeant brought my head down on his knee
and broke my nose. Or sometimes I was alone, naked in the center of the compound, where we were

allowed to wash under the water spigot and scrub the lice out of the seams of our clothing once a week. And each time I went there and turned the rusted iron valve I saw the words embossed on the surface—*Manufactured in Akron, Ohio.*

But this afternoon I was back in "the Shooting Gallery," a very special place for me, because it was there that my six days on the firing line ended. That afternoon had been quiet, and we had moved into a dry irrigation ditch that bordered a two-mile plain of rice farms with bare, artillery-scarred foot-hills on the far side. In the twilight I could see the shattered trees and torn craters from the 105's, and one hill, from which the North Koreans had started an attack, had been burned black with napalm strikes. We had heard that the First Marine Divi-sion had made contact with some Chinese at the Choshin, but our area was thought to be secure. They had two miles of open space to cross before they could reach us, and we had strung wire and mines outside our perimeter, although it was con-sidered unnecessary because the North Koreans didn't have enough troops in the hills to pull a straight-on offensive. At seven-thirty the search-lights went on and illuminated the rice fields and devastated slopes; then the nightly bugles and meg-aphone lectures against American capitalism started. The reverberating cacophony and the unnatural white light on the hills and corrugated rice fields seemed like an experiment in insanity held on the moon's surface. Sometimes the North Koreans would fail to pick up the phonograph needle and the record would scratch out static for several minutes, echoing down off the hills like someone raking his fingernails across a blackboard. Then the searchlights would change angle and sweep across the sky, reflecting momentarily on the clouds, and settle on another distant hilltop pocked with brown holes.

I sat with my back against the ditch and tried to sleep. My blanket was draped around me like iron in the cold, and my feet ached inside my boots. I had gotten wet that afternoon crossing a rice paddy, and grains of ice had started to form inside my clothes. Even with my stocking cap pulled low under my helmet, my ears felt as though they had been beaten with boards. In the distance I heard one of our tanks clanking down a road; then a .30 caliber machine gun began firing far off on our right flank. "What's that fucking asshole doing?" a corporal next to me said. He was a tall hillbilly boy from north Alabama. His blanket was pulled up over his helmet, and he had cut away his glove around the first finger of his right hand. I had a small bottle of codeine in my pack, and I started to take it out for a drink. It didn't taste as good as

whiskey, but it warmed you inside like canned heat.
The machine gun fell silent a moment, then began
firing again with longer bursts, followed by a B.A.R.
and the irregular popping of small-arms fire. "What
the hell is going on?" the corporal said. He raised
up on his knees with his M-1 in his hands. Suddenly, flares began bursting in the sky, burning in
white halos above the corrugated fields. The corporal's face was as pale as candlewax in the light,
his lips tight and bloodless.

The first mortar rounds struck outside our wire
and exploded the mines we had strung earlier. Yellow and orange flames erupted out of the earth and
flicked around the strands of concertina wire. I
could feel the suck of hot air from the vacuum, my
ears roared with the thunder of freight trains crash-
ing into one another, and the wall of the ditch
slammed into my head like a sledge. The rim of my
helmet had cut a neat slit across my nose, and I
could taste the blood draining in a wet streak over
my mouth. Somewhere down the line, among the
shower of rocks and frozen earth, the tremors reverberating through the ground, the locomotive engines blowing apart, I heard a Marine shout, a
prolonged voice rising out of a furnace,
"DOOOOOOOOOOOC!" I started to crawl
along the floor of the ditch on my hands and knees,
then the Chinese corrected their angle of fire and

marched the barrage right down the center of our line.

Somehow I had believed that if I ever bought one it would come as a result of some choice I had made; that I would be killed after some positive act of my own—no matter how unconscious or reckless—but there would still be a type of control in my death. However, now I knew that I was going to die in the middle of a fire-storm. I had no more chance of resisting my death than if God crashed His fist down on top of me. The shells burst in jagged intervals along the ditch, blowing men and weapons in every direction. The corporal was suddenly frozen in an explosion of light and dirt behind him. His mouth and eyes were wide, his helmet pitted and torn with shrapnel. He seemed to pirouette in slow motion, the weight of his tall body resting inside one boot, then he fell backwards across me. The blood ran from his stocking cap like pieces of string over his face. He opened and closed his mouth with a wet, sucking sound, the saliva thick on his tongue. He coughed once, quietly and deep in his throat; then his eyes fixed on a phosphorescent flare burning above us.

Moments later the fire-storm ended, almost too quickly, because it seemed that nothing that intense and murderous could ever end, that it would perpetuate itself indefinitely with its own cataclysmic force. I pushed the corporal off me, my ears ringing in the silence (or what seemed like silence, since automatic weapons had begun firing again on both sides of us). The corporal's helmet rolled off his head, and I saw a long incision, like a scalpel cut, across the crown of his skull. The dead were strewn in unnatural positions along the ditch, some of them half-buried in mounds of dirt from the caved-in walls, their bodies twisted and broken as though they had been dropped from airplanes. The faces of the wounded were white with shock and concussion. Down the line a man was screaming.

"Are you hit, Doc?" It was the first lieutenant. He carried his carbine in one hand. His left arm hung limply by his side.

"I'm all right." Our voices sounded far away from me.

"Get ready to move the wounded out of here. The right flank is getting their ass knocked off. We're supposed to get artillery in five minutes and pull."

"You're bleeding pretty heavy, Lieutenant."

"Get every man moving you can. We're going to have gooks coming up our ass."

However, the artillery cover never came, and we were overrun fifteen minutes later. Our automatic weapons men killed Chinese by the hundreds as they advanced across the rice fields. We packed snow on the barrels of the .30 caliber machine guns to keep them from melting, and the bottom of the ditch was littered with spent shell casings and empty ammunition boxes. The dead lay in quilted rows as far as I could see. They moved forward and died, then another wave took their place. The bugles began blowing again, potato mashers exploded in our wire, and every time a weapon locked empty or a Marine was hit they moved closer to the ditch. Our only tank was burning behind us, the lieutenant was shot through the mouth, and all of our N.C.O.'s were dead. We fired our last rounds, fixed bayonets in a silly Alamo gesture, and then the Chinese swarmed over us.

They ran along the edge of the ditch, firing point-blank into us with their burpguns. They shot the dead and the living alike, in the hysterical relief that comes with the victory of living through an attack. Their weapons weren't designed for accuracy, but they could dump almost a full clip into a man who was closer than twenty feet. For the first time in my life I ran from an enemy. I dropped the handles of a stretcher with a wounded Marine on it and ran across the bodies, the ammunition boxes, the bent bazookas, the knocked-out machine guns, the lieutenant spitting blood and parts of teeth on his coat, and suddenly I saw a young Chinese boy, not over seventeen, his thin, yellow face pinched with cold, standing above me in tennis shoes and quilted clothes. I guess (as I remember it) that I threw my arms out in front of me to prevent that spray of flame and bullets from entering my face and chest, but the gesture was unnecessary because he was a poor marksman and he never got above my knees. I felt a pain like a shaft of ice through both legs, and I toppled over as though a bad comic had just kicked me deftly across the shins.

My Korean recall, born out of Jack Daniels and sexual exhaustion, ended here. I awoke at six-thirty, sweating, my head thick with afternoon whiskey. For a half hour I sat on the shower tile under the cold water, chewing an unlit cigar. The white indentions in my calves felt like rubber under my thumb.

CHAPTER

TWO

The Shamrock-Hilton Hotel in Houston was crowded that night with Democrats from all over Texas. They came in party loyalty almost seven hundred strong—the daughters of forgotten wars, the state committee from Austin, the A.F.L.-C.I.O. fat boys, the oil-depletion wheelers, manicured newspaper publishers, slick public relations men, millionaire women dressed in Neiman-Marcus clothes with Piney Woods accents, young lawyers on their way up in state politics (each of them with a clear eye, hard grip, and a square, cologned jaw like Fearless Fosdick), the ten-percenters, the new rich who bought their children's way into Randolph-Macon, the ranchers with a bright eye on the agriculture subsidy, a few semi-acceptable Mafia characters from Galveston, several ex-hacks, doormen, flunkies, and baggage carriers from Lyndon's entourage, three Hollywood movie stars who had been born in Texas, an astronaut, one crippled commander of the Veterans of the Spanish-American War who sat in a wheelchair, an alcoholic baseball player who used to pitch for the Houston Buffaloes before he went up to the Cardinals, some highly paid prostitutes, an Air Force general who has probably won a footnote in military history for his dedication in the fire-bombing of Dresden, and United States Senator Allen B. Dowling.

I had driven from San Antonio in two and one half hours, highballing wide-open like a blue shot through small towns and farm communities, while drunken cowboys drinking beer in front of saloons stared at me in disbelief. I pulled into the white circular drive of the Shamrock and waited in the line of cars for the band of uniformed Negro porters to take over my luggage, my Cadillac, and even my attempt to open a door by myself. They moved about with the quick, electric motion of rubberbands snapping, their teeth white, their faces black and cordial, obsequious and yet confidently efficient. I imagined that they could have cut all our throats with pleasure. They reminded me of Negro troops in Korea when they were dealing with Mr. Skins, a white officer. They could go about a job in a way that deserved group citations, and at the same time insult an officer and laugh in his face without doing anything for which they could be reprimanded unless the officer wanted to appear a public fool.

I idled the car up to the glass doors at the entrance; one Negro pulled open the car door for me, another got behind the wheel, and a third took my suitcase from the trunk. I handed out one-dollar tips to each of them (with the stupid feeling of an artificial situation that you have when you pay a shoeshine boy), and followed the third porter into the hotel. And I wondered, looking at his gray, uniformed back, the muscles stiff and flat under the cloth, *Would you really like to tick a razor across my jugular, you uprooted descendant of Ham, divested of your heritage, dropped clumsily and illiterate into a south Texas cotton patch, where you could labor and exhaust yourself and kind through the next several generations on tenant shares? Yes, I guess you could, with a neat, sharp corner of the blade that you would draw gingerly along the vein.*

But I still had a fair edge on from the Jack Daniels, the Mexican girl, and the dream, and I imagine that is why I suddenly had such strange insights into that black mind walking before me.

I gave my name at the desk and was told that my wife had taken a suite of rooms on the tenth floor. She and my brother Bailey had come to

Houston yesterday when the convention started, and I was supposed to join them today at noon for lunch on the terrace with several of the oil-depletion boys who had all types of money to sink into a young congressman's career. However, I didn't have to speak before the convention until ten that night, and I didn't think that I could take a full day of laughing conversation, racial jokes, polite gin by the swimming pool, and powdered, middle-aged oil wives who whispered banal remarks like slivers of glass in my ear. I had met all of them before in Dallas, Austin, Fort Worth, and El Paso, and they were always true to themselves, regardless of the place or occasion. The men wore their same Oshman western suits and low-topped boots, the diamond rings from Zale's that looked out of place on their fat hands, the string ties or open-neck sports shirts that directed attention away from the swift eyes and the broken veins in the cheeks. They spoke of huge finance with indifference, but I knew that their groins tingled with pleasure at the same time. Their women liked me because I was young and good-looking, successful as a lawyer, tanned from playing in fashionable tennis courts, and with an inner steeled effort I could clink the ice in my glass and look pleasant and easy while they told about all the trivial problems in their insipid lives (in this respect I was very self-disciplined, because

I always knew when to excuse myself and walk
away before the inner rigidity broke apart).

Besides, I really didn't need them to be elected
congressional representative from my district. The
Holland name and my father's reputation would as-
sure almost any member of my family a political
position if he wanted it. Also, people still remembered when I returned from the war as a wounded
hospital corpsman, dressed in Marine tropicals with
a walking cane, an ex-P.O.W. who had resisted
brainwashing for thirty-two months while other
American troops were signing confessions, inform-
ing on each other, and defecting to the Chinese.

Finally, my Republican opponent was a seedy
racist, so fanatical even in his business dealings that
his insurance agency failed. At different times he
had belonged to the John Birch and Paul Revere
societies, the Independent Million, the White Cit-
izens League, and the Dixiecrat Party. He was a
mean and obnoxious drunk, a bully towards his wife
and children, and I don't know why the Republi-
cans let him run, except for the fact that he could
always raise money from fools like himself and they
hadn't won an election in DeWitt since Reconstruction, anyway.

Verisa had taken a five-room suite with a cocktail
bar, deep rugs, oil paintings on the walls, potted
rubber plants, and a porch that overlooked the

swimming pool far below. The porter set my suitcase down and closed the door behind me. I could
see the anger in Verisa's eyes. She sat on the couch
in a white evening gown, her legs crossed tightly,
with the tip of one high-heeled shoe pointed into
the coffee table. Her auburn hair was brushed to a
metallic shine, and her skin looked as bloodless and
smooth as marble. If I had been closer to her I
could have smelled the touch of perfume behind
her ears, the powdered breasts, the hinted scent of
her sex, a light taste of gin on her breath. She
looked at me briefly, then turned her eyes away and
lit a cigarette. The toe of the shoe flicked momentarily into a carved design in the side of the table.
She was always able to hold her anger in well. She
had learned part of that at Randolph-Macon and
the rest from living with me. She could reduce flying rage to a hot cigarette ash or a few whispered
and rushed words in the corner of a cocktail party,
or maybe one burst of heat after we were home;
but the pointed flick of the shoe was a fleshy bite
into my genitals for seven years of marriage, broken
young-girl dreams, her embarrassment when I
brought oil-field workers or soldiers from Fort Sam
Houston to the country club, my drunken discus-
sions in the middle of the night about my Korean
War guilt, and for the stoic and futile resignation

she had adopted, out of all her social disappointments, in hopes of becoming the wife of a Texas congressman on his way to the Senate and that opulent world of power which goes far beyond any of the things you can buy or destroy with money.

"Hack, don't you give a goddamn?" she said quietly, still looking straight ahead.

"What did I miss?"

"A day of my making excuses for you, and right now I'm rather sick of it."

"Lunch by the pool with the Dallas aristocracy can't be that awful."

"I'm not in a flippant mood, Hack. I don't enjoy apologizing or lying for you, and I don't like sitting three hours by myself with boorish business people."

"Those are the cultured boys with the money. The fellows who oil all the wheels and make Frankenstein run properly."

I went to the bar and poured a double shot of whiskey over ice. It clicked pleasantly on the edge of the afternoon drunk, and I felt even more serene in the sexual confidence which I always had towards Verisa after whoring.

"I don't know where you've been, but I suspect it was one of your Okie motel affairs."

"I had to meet R.C. Richardson in Austin."

"How much do you pay them? Do they go down on you? That's what they call it in the trade, isn't it?"

"It's something like that."

"They must be lovely girls. Do they perform any other special things for you?"

"Right now R.C.'s working on a deal to patent hoof and mouth disease. He has federal contracts for Viet Nam that run in millions."

"Your girl friends probably have had some nice diseases of their own."

"Let it go, Verisa."

"Oh, I shouldn't say anything to you? Is that it? I should spend a day of congenial conversation with people who chew on toothpicks, and then meet you pleasantly at the door after you return from screwing a Mexican whore."

Something inside me flinched at her accuracy. I poured a short drink into the bottom of the glass.

"I bet you've gone to bed with me, not knowing whether they had given you one of their diseases," she said.

She was really tightening the iron boot now.

"Do you want a highball? I'm going to change clothes."

"Oh Christ, you've probably done it," she said, and put her fingers over her mouth.

"I never did that to you."

"You probably don't even remember. You have to wait two weeks to know, don't you?"

"You're letting it walk away with you." But she was right. I didn't remember.

"It happened to a girl I knew in college, but she was a dumpy thing who did it in the back seats of cars with Marines and sailors. I didn't believe it ever happened with your husband."

"Pull off it. You're working towards a real bad conclusion."

"I wonder that you didn't give me sulfa tablets."

I fixed her a drink with a squeeze of lemon and set it on the table in front of her.

"I'm sorry that you got strung out today," I said. "I thought Bailey would take you to lunch if I didn't make it."

"Tell me if you really did it to me."

"Look, it was a shitty day for you. I should have been here to eat lunch with those bastards, or I should have called Bailey and told him to take care of it. But I'm going to change clothes now. We should go downstairs in a few minutes."

"You must have a very special clock to go by. It starts to work correctly when you feel the corner at your back."

"You ought to drink your highball."

"Why don't you drink it? It makes you more electric and charming in public," she said.

"You've gotten it out pretty far in a short time."

"I might stretch it out so far that you ache."

"Isn't this just spent effort? If you want to believe that you've won the ballgame in the ninth inning, go ahead. Or maybe you would like me to kiss your ass in apology."

"You've done that without a need for apologizing. An analyst would have a wonderful time with you."

"I won't go into embarrassing descriptions, but as I recall you enjoyed every little piece of it."

"Yes, I remember those sweet experiences. You tried to enact all the things you had learned in a Japanese whorehouse while you slobbered about two boys who died in a Chinese prison camp."

"You better shut it off in a hurry."

"What was the boy's name from San Angelo and the Negro sergeant from Georgia?"

"You don't listen when I tell you something, do you?"

"It's just a little bit of recall from things you brought up. Didn't you say they were buried in a latrine? In your words, to lend more American fertilizer to the Korean rice crop."

"You're fucking in the wrong direction."

"My, Captain Marvel with his favorite drunk word."

"This isn't your style. So step back real quick before you find yourself in a bad place."

"Are you going to hit me? That would make a perfect punctuation mark in my day."

"Just don't bend it anymore."

"Don't walk away, Hack. If you blow this for us, I'll divorce you and sue for the home. Then I'll repay you in the most fitting way I can think of. I'll cover that historical cemetery of yours with concrete."

I took the bottle of whiskey and my glass from the bar and slammed the bedroom door behind me. I could feel the anger beating in my head and the veins swelling in my throat. I seldom became angry about anything, but this time she had reached inside me hard and had gotten a good piece between her nails. I drank out of the bottle twice and started to change clothes. My face was flushed with heat in the mirror. I kicked my trousers against the wall and pulled off my shirt, stripping the buttons. I stood in my underwear and had another drink, this time with measured sips. The whiskey began to flatten out inside me, and I felt a single drop of perspiration run down off an eyebrow. Hold it in, sonofabitch, I thought. The Lone Ranger never blows his Kool-Aid. You just give the sheriff a silver bullet and let Tonto pour you a drink. But Verisa had really been off her style this time. She had collected a valise of surgical tools during the day for an entry into all my vital organs. In fact, I didn't know whether to mark this to her debit or credit. As I said, in the past she could always load all of her outrage into a quiet hypodermic needle, thrust subtly into the right place (her best probe, the one she used after I had done something especially painful to that private part of her soul, was to go limp and indifferent under me, her arms spread back on the pillows, during my disabling moment of climax).

I had one more drink, just enough to go over the back of the tongue, then brushed my teeth, took three aspirins and two vitamin pills, and rinsed out my whiskey breath with Listerine. I dressed in an Italian silk shirt, a dark tie, a pressed white suit, and rubbed the polish smooth on my boots with a damp towel. I lit a cigar and breathed out the smoke in the mirror. You're all right, Masked Man, I thought.

I heard Verisa open the front door, then the voices of Bailey and Senator Dowling.

"Hack," Verisa said, tapping her fingernails lightly on my door. I knew she had already gone into her transformation as the pleasant wife of a congressional candidate. It was amazing how fast it could take place.

I stepped out of the bedroom and shook hands with the Senator.

"How are you, Hack?" he said, his face healthy and cheerful. He was fifty-five years old, but his handshake was still hard and his wrist strong. He was six inches shorter than I, solidly built, his shoulders pulled straight back, and his white hair trimmed close to the scalp. His acetylene-blue eyes were bright and quick, impossible to penetrate, and you knew after he glanced confidently into your face that his lack of height was no disadvantage to him. He had the small, hard chest of a professional soldier, and his tailored suit didn't have a fold or a bulge in it. He wore dentures, and they caused him to lisp slightly with his Texas accent, but otherwise he was solid. Also, Senator Dowling had managed to remain a strong southern figure through five administrations. He had been on many sides over the years, and he always walked out of the ballpark with the winning team (and therein lay his gift, the ability to sense change before anyone else got a whiff of it). He was put into Congress by a one-million-acre southwest Texas corporation ranch in 1940, and in the next two years he paid off his obligations by sponsoring large subsidies for growing nothing on arid land. Then he represented the oil interests, the franchised utility companies, and

the Houston and Dallas industries up on antitrust
suits. He assured his constituents that he was a seg-
regationist until the Kennedy administration, then
he backed one of the first civil rights bills. In the
meantime he acquired a three-thousand-acre ranch
in the hill country north of Austin, and stock in
almost every major corporation in Texas with a defense contract.

"Fine, Senator. How have you been?" I said.

"Good. Relaxing at the ranch. Fishing and playing tennis a little bit before the campaign."

"Hack, fix the Senator a drink," Verisa said.

"Thank you. A half jigger and some soda will be
fine," he said.

"You should try the bass in Hack's ponds," Bailey
said. He sat in one of the tall bar chairs with his
arm over the back. Good old Bailey, I thought. He
could always come through with an inane remark at
the right time. He looked like my twin, except five
years older and fifteen pounds heavier, with wrin-
kles in his forehead and neck. Bailey was a practical
man who worried about all the wrong things.

"I'd hoped to talk with you earlier today," the
Senator said, and looked straight into my face with
those acetylene-blue eyes.

"I had to stop over in Austin with a client. Maybe
we can talk after my speech," I said.

"Verisa says you're having people up for drinks later. I'd rather we have some time between ourselves."

"Hack, we're invited for breakfast at the River Oaks Country Club in the morning," Bailey said. "Maybe the Senator can join us. You all can talk, and then we'll play some doubles."

"That sounds fine," the Senator said. "I could use a couple of sets against an ex-Baylor pitcher."

The sonofabitch, I thought.

"My opponent hasn't somehow organized his ragtail legions, has he?"

"Oh no, no. I don't think we need to spend too much time on this gentleman." He laughed with his healthy smile. "I wanted to talk with you about several things that will come later in Washington. Your father helped me a great deal when I was first elected to Congress, and I learned then that it's invaluable to have an experienced friend."

I handed him his highball glass with the half jigger and soda. He had learned to be a cautious person with liquor, and I knew he wouldn't finish the glass I had given him.

"Well, I appreciate it, Senator. But I don't know how good my Baylor arm will be on the court," I said, biting down inside myself.

"Hack is defensive tonight," Verisa said.

"He should be," the Senator said. His eyes took on a deeper blue with his smile.

"I have a weak serve, but I'm hell on defending the net," I said. "One flash of the wrist and I drive tennis balls into concrete."

"We had better go downstairs pretty soon," Bailey said. His face was flat, but his discomfort showed in the nervous tic of his fingers on his trouser leg.

"I don't expect that our audience will disappear," the Senator said. "They usually have their way of waiting, as a U.S. Senator sometimes does."

Sorry, you bastard. I'm all out of sackcloth and ashes tonight, I thought. I set my cigar in the ashtray and poured an inch of Jack Daniels into a glass. Bailey's face began to tighten in the silence. Verisa's eyes waited on me, her lips pinched slightly, but I held out. I sipped the whiskey and drew in on the cigar as though the conversation were far removed from me.

"Would you like to drive with us out to the country club in the morning?" Bailey said.

"Thanks. I'll find my way there. From what I understand, Hack drives like he's trying to put A. J. Foyt back in the grease pit," the Senator said.

"I wouldn't try to beat a Texas boy at his own game, Senator."

"It depends on what type of game." His eyes crinkled at me.

"I have a pretty good shutout record in my field."

"I remember, Hack. I watched you pitch twice. But as I recall you used to have a little trouble with a lefthanded batter."

"Sometimes you have to bear down a little more."

He took a thin swallow of his highball and placed the glass on the bar, his expression assured and pleasant, then looked casually at his watch.

"Bailey's probably right. We should go downstairs. I'll drop up later for a few minutes and say hello to your guests," he said, and put his hand on the small of my back. "Then tomorrow we'll see what type of tennis game we can work out."

I saw the ease come back into Verisa's face, and Bailey stood up stiffly as though he had just been unstrapped from an electric chair. I took my typewritten speech in its leather folder from my suitcase, and we walked down the carpeted corridor towards the elevator like an amiable family of four.

The dining tables in the Shamrock Room were filled. The silver, the crystalware, the white tablecloths, the spangled evening gowns and decanters of wine reflected softly under the lights. The Senator introduced me from the rostrum, and the rows of faces became hushed and polite. Even the fat

boys from the oil interests, in their string ties and
cowboy boots, looked quietly deferential. I read
them my twenty-minute speech of non-language
and they applauded thirteen times. Whenever I approached some vague conclusion, pointed at nothing, I could see their eyes grow more intent, their
heads nodding slightly, as some private anger with
the nation, the universe, or themselves found a con-
sensus in my empty statements, then the hands
would begin clapping. They had found a burning
spokesman to represent all the outraged goodguys.
I was tight enough to be unconscious of my
speech's stupidity, and after a while I even felt that
I might be saying something meaningful. They rose
to their feet when I finished. I shook dozens of
hands, smiled with country boy humility at the
compliments, and invited half the dining room to
Verisa's cocktail party.

The party was a success in every way. Verisa was
able to become the radiant wife of a congressional
candidate, moving with detached pleasantness between groups of people (the society editors from
The Houston Post and *The Chronicle* both agreed the
next day that Mrs. Holland was one of the most
lovely hostesses to appear in Texas politics in a
long time). And I was able to make a doubleheader
out of the evening: I managed to get drunk twice
in one day. The Negro waiters put a fresh whiskey

and water in my hand every time I flicked my eyes in their direction, and within two hours Mr. Hyde had begun to prowl obscenely through the hallways of my mind. The room was so crowded by midnight that the air conditioning couldn't clear the smoke, and the noise brought complaints from the floors above and below us. People whom I had never seen before drank three cases of bourbon and Scotch, ate four hundred dollars' worth of catered food, burned cigar holes in the carpet, charged thirty-minute long-distance calls to my room, and threw glasses and bottles off the terrace into the swimming pool. Someone wheeled in the commander from the Veterans of the Spanish-American War, who sat stupefied in one corner, staring out at the bedlam from his atrophied, withered face, until a sentimental W.W. II veteran decided to take him on a careening ride through the corridor. The alcoholic baseball pitcher and I argued about how to throw a crippling beanball, one of the society editors threw up in the bathroom and had to be put in bed by Verisa, and the fire-bomber of Dresden unzipped the back of a woman's evening dress.

I insulted the astronaut and his wife, who left after a polite five-minute interval, then two of the Negro bartenders quit when an oil broker made a racial remark to them. I took over the bar and poured all the remaining bourbon, gin, and Scotch

into a punch bowl, and insisted that everyone in
the room have a drink. This resulted in four more
people passed out, a clogged toilet, and a group
plan to open up the dining room for steak and eggs.
Someone brought in a hillbilly singer from a nightclub, who propositioned Verisa, and the Air Force
general drank six glasses from the punch bowl and
urinated off the balcony. By four A.M. the room was
totally destroyed. All the furniture was either
burned or broken, the floor was littered with cigar
and cigarette butts, the French doors were smashed,
the potted plants overturned, and the electric plug
in the drink mixed had short-circuited and melted
into the wall socket. (Later, I received an eight-
hundred-dollar repair bill from the Shamrock-
Hilton, and I kindly forwarded it to the Texas
Democratic Committee in Austin.)

At five A.M. the last of the guests supported each
other out the door, while Verisa accepted their incoherent compliments and told them to visit us at
the ranch (she was still radiant, even through her
fatigue). I lay down on the bed next to the society
editor, and as the false dawn glowed on the horizon
and touched the room with its gray light, she rolled
her head towards me, her mouth wide with snoring,
her face oval and white, and I thought *Good night,
good night, sweet Desdemona*, and I fell once more into
Mr. Hyde's world.

• • •

The clay tennis courts at the country club were green and freshly chalked under a hot, blue sky. I sat at a marble-topped table with Bailey under the shade trees, sipping a glass of tomato juice and vodka, while Verisa and the Senator whocked the ball back and forth across the net. Behind the courts the sun shattered off the swimming pool, and children in dripping swimsuits lined up on the diving board. In the distance the smooth green contours of the golf course arched away through the oak trees, and the sandtraps looked like ground white crystal in the light. My hangover was bad. I was sweating unnaturally, shaking inside like a tuning fork vibrating to the wrong chord, and I felt a hard pressure band across one side of my head. My tennis shorts and polo shirt were already wet, although I hadn't been on the court yet, and the vodka wouldn't take hold. Bailey kept talking about our law practice in Austin, my failure to come into the office regularly, and my rudeness to the Senator. His words were like pieces of broken china in my head. He spoke from some abstraction inside himself, looking into my eyes occasionally, his face earnest with the dumb innocence of a nondrinker talking to a man with a bleeding hangover. I lit a cigar, tried to concentrate on the tennis game, and had another vodka and tomato juice.

"It's insane to do these things to yourself," he said. "You're hungover three days out of seven, you go into court with your fingers shaking, and in the meantime other people are picking up after you."

"Are you picking up after me, Bailey?"

"What do you think I did yesterday? And last night you insulted a half dozen people within fifteen minutes."

"I thought I only got the astronaut." I wiped the sweat off my forehead on my sleeve and drained the vodka and tomato juice.

"You want to get blasted again?"

"I might unless the conversation changes."

"It's goddamn insane. You can be in office in a few months. The youngest congressman from the state. After one or two terms you can do anything you want in Texas."

"I know those things."

"Then why don't you act like you have a goddamn mind?"

I held my glass up to the waiter for another drink.

"You count on too much from people," Bailey said.

"Will you go to hell or shut up for about five minutes?"

"You can get angry, but I'm right in what I say."

"Bailey, would you get away from me a few minutes?"

"You see what that booze does?"

"Goddamn it, go swimming or chase golf balls if you like. Believe me, I'm up to my eyes with it."

He stood up, his face slightly hurt and angry, and walked across the clipped grass to the clubhouse. I knew that in a half hour he would be back as though nothing had been said, and then later he would start to bore in again. Bailey was a good boy, but he was simply unteachable.

The Senator moved about the court like a man twenty years younger than his age. I have to admit that he looked good out there. The matted gray hair on his chest and his thick, muscular shoulders glistened with sweat, and he whocked the ball in a white streak across the net. For a short man he had a fine driving serve, and his backhand was always accurate and strong. He had a good eye for court distance, and most of his shots just skimmed the top of the net and hit in a low bounce on the clay. Verisa was a good tennis player, but he took her in two easy sets. The Senator was a competitor, and his gentlemanly affectation ended when he entered the games.

They joined me at the table, and the waiter served us a cold lunch of pickled shrimp on cracked

ice. For the next hour I listened to the Senator's
advice on my campaign, the upcoming year in
Congress, and contributions from several oil companies (the checks, which already amounted to over
sixty-five thousand dollars, had all been deposited
by Bailey in a special account in Austin). Then I
was told indirectly, with compassion, to avoid public statements on civil rights, at least while in Texas,
and that I shouldn't lean too far towards labor, since
as a Democrat I could already count on their vote.
I nodded my head and listened as intelligently as
possible, but my hangover wouldn't let go and few
of his sentences seemed to have any relationship to
one another. Actually, more than any instruction in
Texas politics, he wanted to exact penance from
me because of yesterday, and I was in the perfect
condition for it—a mental cripple.

"Next week I plan to visit the wounded Viet Nam
veterans in Walter Reed," he said. "I think it might
be good for you to come along."

"Why's that?"

"You were wounded yourself in Korea. I think
the boys like to know that they have congressmen
who understand what they've been through."

"I'm afraid I had enough of V.A. hospitals, Senator," I said.

"We'll be there an hour or so. Then you'll be
back home the same night."

"I better pass."

"Go on, Hack. Bailey will be at the office," Verisa said.

"No, I don't—"

"You need a trip. Enjoy it," Bailey said. He had come back from the clubhouse fresh with resolve.

"I spent two months in the V.A. in '53 and I really—" I was smiling in my best convivial way.

"This type of exposure is important to you, Hack," the Senator said.

Fuck it, I thought. "All right, Senator. I'll be glad to."

We finished lunch and played a set of doubles. Verisa and I stood the Senator and Bailey, and the sweat rolled down my face and chest in rivulets. My timing was bad, my movements uncoordinated, and I drove most of my serves into the bottom of the net. My head was thundering from the heat and exertion. The air seemed so humid that it was like steam on my skin. If Bailey hadn't been such a bad player we would have lost the set six games straight, but Verisa managed to keep us only one game behind. I was even proud of her. In her short white tennis skirt and cap with a green visor she was the loveliest thing on the courts. Her legs and shoulders were freckled with suntan, her auburn hair wet and shining on the back of her neck, and you could get a good look at her fine ass when she bent over with her serve.

We went into the final game five to four, and I
wanted to beat the Senator very badly. He played
confidently, controlling the backline with an easy
sweep of his racket in either direction. His thick
eyebrows were heavy with perspiration, and his
blue eyes refracted a mean success every time he
drove the ball into my shoelaces.

However, I soon learned that the Senator's re-
venge for yesterday wasn't complete yet. I moved
up to the net for the final point, Verisa served, and
Bailey returned the ball in an easy, high-arching
lob. I whocked it with all the strength in my shoulder straight into the Senator. The game should
have been over and the set tied, but the Senator
caught my drive with one short, forearm chop of
the racket, and smashed the ball murderously into
my face. My sunglasses broke on the court, my eyes
watered uncontrollably, and I felt the blood running from my nose. Through the tears I could see
him walking quickly towards me, his face gathered
in concern, but there was victory in his eyes.

Later, Verisa drove us back to the hotel while I
held a blood-flecked towel filled with ice cubes to
my nose. The bridge was already swollen, and there
was a sickening taste in the back of my throat. I
tilted my head back on the seat and looked with
one eye out the window at the stream of angry
traffic along South Main. At the court the Senator

had apologized in his most empathic manner, the tennis pro arrived with a first-aid kit and tried to push cotton balls up my nose, a Negro waiter put another vodka and tomato juice on the table and left, and now Bailey sat in the backseat talking about going to the hospital for an X-ray.

"Do you think it's broken?" Verisa said.

"No, he just flattened it a little. A warning," I said. My words were nasal and smothered under the towel.

"It was an accident," Bailey said. "You cut the ball right into him."

"Why don't you get off the goodguymanship ethic? Leave the Boy Scouts for a while, at least till we get to the hotel," I said. "He was out to tear my head off."

"That's hangover paranoia."

"Oh, shit," I said.

"How many U.S. Senators would spend their time trying to help a thirty-five-year-old lawyer's political career?"

"Don't you know a sonofabitch when you see one?"

"You're constructing things to fit some strange frame of reference in your own mind."

"You're an amateur, Bailey. You better learn to recognize sophisticated viciousness."

"You're really thinking foolishly."

"I don't care if you want to look at the world like Little Orphan Annie. But right now I feel like someone took a shit in my head, my nose is full of blood, and if you say anything more I'm going to call the Senator from the hotel and give him my best delivery."

"You better take us to Herman Hospital," Bailey said.

"I've had my nose broken before and I know what it feels like. Just turn it off for a few more blocks."

"I'll have the hotel doctor come to the room," Verisa said.

"Forget that, too," I said. "I'm driving down to the Valley this afternoon. Just as soon as I can get six aspirins down and a double shot of Jack Daniels."

"You're going to the Valley!" Verisa said. Her head turned sharply at me.

"I got a letter from a Mexican fellow I was in Korea with. He got involved in some trouble with this farm labor union, and he's in the county jail waiting to go up to prison on a five-year sentence."

"What am I supposed to do in the meantime?" she said.

"Ride back home with Bailey or take a flight. You don't like to drive with me, anyway."

"So I'm left with the pleasant experience of explaining the condition of the room to the management. Is that it?" she said. "I imagine that by this time the cleaning woman has run down the hall in hysterics."

"Ignore them. We didn't do the damage. They know what to expect when they contract for a convention. Particularly when it's composed of lunatics."

"It's lovely of you to leave me with these things."

"All right. I'll talk with the manager on the way out. I'll drip a few drops of blood on his desk, talk with him cordially, and then I'll tell him to go to hell."

"You do what you want, Hack," she said. "Get drunk for a week in the Valley, go across the border and find a sweet two-dollar girl, indulge all your disgusting obsessions."

She turned the car into the hotel drive, and a doorman stepped out to the edge of the walk under the canopy. I rubbed the dampness of the towel over my face.

"I have to go see this man," I said. "He was a good friend to me when I went on the line. I was so goddamned scared I couldn't paste a Band-Aid on a scratch."

"Just don't talk about it," she said. "Drive down the road and forget anything else. That's the way you do things best."

"Listen a minute. I don't enjoy driving three hun-

dred miles in one-hundred-degree heat with a
hangover and a bloody nose. But this man has five
years hard time to do because of a scuffle on a
picket line. He doesn't have a goddamn cent and
he can't get a white lawyer to file an appeal for
him. Next week he'll be chopping cotton on the
prison farm and there won't be a thing I can do for
him."

"We can call the A.C.L.U. You don't have to go
down there today," Bailey said.

"No, you go on, Hack," she said. "It would be
too terrible for you to live through one day of putting things together without beginning another adventure."

"Okay, piss on it," I said. "I'll catch air in a few
minutes, and you can go back to the ranch and
serve cocktails to the D.A.R. Then next week we
can take a trip to Walter Reed and shake hands
with the basket cases. A war-time V.A. ward should
be included on all bus tours. You can meet the
dummies in their wheelchairs and the guys without
human faces. It's a balling scene."

Bailey lit his pipe in the backseat and Verisa's
eyes were brilliant with anger as the doorman
stepped around the front of the car. I lowered the
window and dumped the cracked ice in the towel
onto the concrete.

People stared at me in the lobby as I walked

towards the elevator with the towel under my nose. I still wore my tennis shorts and canvas shoes, with a sports coat over my blood-streaked polo shirt. Verisa and Bailey walked on each side of me as impervious as granite. Upstairs, I showered and changed into a pair of cream slacks and a soft, maroon shirt, ordered a bottle of Jack Daniels from the bar, and ate a half dozen aspirin in the bathroom. I could hear Verisa making reservations on an afternoon flight to San Antonio. I looked in the mirror at my swollen nose, a slightly puffed upper lip, and the white discoloration in my face, and I decided to leave the whiskey doubleheaders to Grover Alexander or some other better lefthander than I. A bellboy brought the bottle; I took one drink out of it and closed the suitcase. I started to speak to Verisa, but she put a cigarette in her mouth and looked out through the smashed French doors at the oil wells pumping in the distance.

CHAPTER

THREE

The late sun was red on the hills above the Rio Grande. The river was almost dry in places, dividing around bleached sandbars, and in the twilight the water had turned scarlet. On the other side, in Mexico, there were adobe huts and wooden shacks along the banks, and buzzards circled high in the sky. I turned off the air conditioner, rolled down the windows, and let the warm air blow through the car. In the first quick rush of wind I could smell the sweet ripeness of the whole Valley: the citrus groves, the tomato and watermelon fields, the rows of cotton and corn, the manure, and pastures of bluebonnets. The windmills were spinning, and cattle moved lazily towards the troughs. A single scorch of cloud stretched across the sun, which now seemed to grow in size as it dipped into the

hills. The base of the pin oaks and blackjack trees
grew darker, then the bottom rim of the sky glowed
with flame.

I had mended from my hangover during the long
drive, and I felt the numb serenity of a longtime
dying man who had just received an unexpected
extension of life. Then, in that cool moment of reflection, I wondered why I always drank twice as
much when I had to make ritual appearances, or
why I had gone to Houston in the first place, since
my talk before a few hundred semiliterate oil men
had little to do with my probable election, anyway;
or lastly, why I had ever entered politics and the
world of Senator Allen B. Dowling.

I could guess at the answers to the first two questions, which weren't of particular consequence, except that I didn't want another hangover and defeat
at the tennis court like I'd had this morning; but
the answer to the third question worked its way
through the soft tissue and dropped like an ugly,
sharp-edged black diamond into a bright space in
the center of my mind. Inside, under all the cynicism, the irreverence towards the icons and totems,
my insults to astronauts and country club women,
I wanted a part of the power at the top.

I tried to believe that my motive was to atone
for Verisa's spent dreams, or that I wanted to equal
my father in his law and congressional career, or at

least that I was simply an ironic man who felt he could do as good a job as comic-page segregationists; or maybe at worst I was just a pragmatist with knowledge of the money to be made in the dealings between the federal government and the oil interests. But that black diamond had blood crusted on its edges, and I knew that I had the same weaknesses as Verisa and the Senator; I wanted power itself, the tribal recognition that went with it, and that small key to its complexities carried secretly in my watchpocket.

I accelerated the Cadillac through the low hills towards Pueblo Verde. The evening had started to cool, the sky deepened to dark purple, and the last of the sun's afterglow burned into itself in a gathering fire at one small point on the horizon. I didn't care for these moments of reflection, even though they came with the cool release from hangover, and I had learned long ago that solitude and introspection always bring you to Mr. Hyde's cage. Every jailer knows that an inmate would rather take a beating with a garden hose than go to solitary, where the snakes start coming out of hibernation and the voices from years ago thunder through long tunnels. The North Koreans and the Chinese knew the same trick, too. The broken noses and smashed fingertips, or even digging your own grave under Sergeant Tien Kwong's burpgun, weren't nearly as effective as six weeks in a dirt hole with an iron sewer grate over your head. There you could concentrate on your guilt for forgotten sins, your inadequacy as a man, your lack of courage when you dropped a wounded Marine on a stretcher and ran, your resentment towards a dying Australian who was always given the largest portion of rice in the shack; or you could look up through the iron slits in the grate at the Chinese sentry who watched you while you squatted like a dog and defecated into a helmet.

So Socrates and his know-thyself ethic were full of shit, I thought, or he never spent time in solitary before he drank the hemlock or drove down a south Texas road on a clear summer evening with Mr. Hyde sitting in the passenger's seat.

The main street in Pueblo Verde was almost empty, the wood frame buildings along the high sidewalks locked and darkened. A few old cars and pickup trucks were parked in front of a beer tavern with an insect-encrusted neon sign buzzing above a broken screen door. In the Sunday night quiet I could hear the hillbilly music from the jukebox and the laughter of a half dozen high school kids smoking cigarettes under the oaks in the courthouse square.

The hotel was a two-story wood building with flaking white paint and a latticed verandah. The

letters on the ROOMS FOR GUESTS sign were blis-
tered and faded, and the small lobby, with a plastic
television set in one corner and wilted flowers in
dime-store vases, smelled like dust and old wallpaper. I signed the register while the desk clerk
looked over my shoulder at my Cadillac parked in
front, then I could feel his eyes become more intent
on the side of my face.

"Will you have somebody wake me at seven in
the morning?" I said.

"You're getting on the road early, huh?"

"No, I'll be in town."

"Oh." His narrow gray face continued to watch
me as I followed the Negro hired man with my bag
towards the staircase.

My room overlooked the street and the trees on
the courthouse lawn. I sent the Negro to the tavern
for six bottles of Jax, pulled off my shirt, and turned
on the overhead wooden fan. It was probably too
late to visit the jail, and also I was too spent to
argue with night-duty cops. I sat in a straw armchair
with my feet in the open window and pried the cap
off a beer with my pocketknife. The foam boiled
over the top and ran down cold on my chest. I
tilted the bottle and drank it straight to the bottom.
I could still feel the highway rushing under my automobile, the mesquite and blackjack sweeping behind me, and I drank two more beers, tasting each

cool swallow slowly. Then a breeze began to blow through the window, a train whistle echoed beyond the dark hills, and I fell asleep in the chair with a half-empty bottle held against my bare stomach.

At first I felt only the swaying motion of the boxcar and the vibration of the wheels clicking across the switches. Then I heard my own voice, loud with urgency, telling me to wake up before it started. But it was too late, or that alter-self inside was inept in turning off the right valve, because I now saw the drawn faces of the other men crowded in the boxcar with me. Outside in the night the snow was driving almost parallel to the ground, there was a slick of ice on the floor of the car, and some of the men had already been stripped of their boots by the Chinese. Their feet were beginning to discolor with the first stages of frostbite, and by morning the skin would be an ugly yellow and purple, the toes swollen into balloons. I watched a Greek urinate on his feet, then dry them carefully and rewrap them with his scarf. The wounds in my calves throbbed with each pitch of the car, and the blood had run down into my socks and frozen. But I had been lucky. The Chinese had machine-gunned all our wounded before we were loaded on the train, and I would have been shot, too, except that I had managed to keep limping forward in the line between two Marines. Before the guard slammed the boxcar door and bolted it, I looked out into the snow at the bodies of the men who had been thrown begging in front of the burpguns. Their mouths and eyes were still wide with disbelief and protest, their hair flecked with snow like old men.

In the next fifteen hours the train stopped three times, and each time we heard a boxcar door slide open, hysterical shouts in English and Chinese, and the firing of burpguns. Whenever the train slowed we became a community of fear as each of us listened, motionless, to the decreasing metallic clack of the wheels. Once, while pulled off on a siding, we heard several guards crunching outside in the snow, then they stopped in front of our boxcar. They talked for a minute, laughed, and one of them slid back the iron bolt on the door. I looked dumbly into the black eyes of the Greek who had urinated on his feet, and the heart-racing fear and desperate question mark in his face seemed to join us together in a quick moment of recognition. Then another train roared by us a few feet away, its whistle screaming in our ears, and our boxcar jolted forward, knocking us backward into one another. We heard the bolt slam into place and the guards running towards the caboose.

By morning the car was rancid with excrement and urine. We had no water, and several men broke ice from the floor with their boots and melted it in a helmet over a dozen cigarette lighters. It tasted like wheat chaff, sweat, and manure. The snow had stopped blowing and the sun shone through the cracks in the walls. The light broke in strips on our bodies, and the stench from the corner began to grow more intense. During the night I had been unable to stand up and urinate through a crack in the car wall, and I had to let it run warmly down my thighs. My own odor sickened me. I wondered if the Jews who had been freighted to extermination camps in eastern Europe ever felt the same self-hating, cynical disgust at their condition, lying in their own excretions, or if they tried to tear the boards out of the walls with their fingernails and catch one SS guard around the throat with probing thumbs. My feeling was that they went to their deaths like tired people lined up before a movie which no one wanted to see, revulsed by themselves and the human condition, their naked bodies already shining with the iridescence of the dead.

I woke into the hot morning with a dark area of warm beer in my lap. Two Negro trusties from the jail, the white letter *P* Cloroxed on the backs of their denim shirts, were watering the courthouse lawn. The wet grass was shiny with light, and the shade of the oaks was like a deep bruise on the sidewalks. At the edge of the square there was an open-air fruit market, with canvas stretched on poles over the bins, and Mexican farmhands were unloading cantaloupes and rattlesnake melons from the bed of a stake truck. The sky was clear blue, and the shadows from a few pink clouds moved over the hills.

I dressed in my linen suit with a blue silk shirt and walked down the main street to a cafe. I had a breakfast steak with two fried eggs on top, then smoked a cigar and drank coffee until the courthouse opened. Even though I could feel the July heat rising, it was still a beautiful day, the orchards at the foot of the hills were bursting with green and gold, I was free from the weekend's whiskey, and I didn't want to visit the jail. Most people think that the life of a criminal lawyer is a romantic venture, but it's usually a sordid affair at best. I had never liked dealing with redneck cops, bailbondsmen, county judges with high school educations, or talking with clients at two A.M. in a drunk tank.

I crossed the street to the courthouse and went to the sheriff's office in the back of the building. By the office door there was a glass memorial case filled with junk from the World Wars and Korea— German helmets, bayonets, a Mauser rifle without a bolt, an American Legion medal, canteens, a .30 caliber machine gun with an exploded barrel, and a Chinese bugle. A deputy in a khaki uniform sat

behind an army surplus desk, filling out forms with
a short pencil. He was lean all over, tall, and his
crewcut, glistening head was pale from wearing a
hat in the sun. His fingers were crimped over the
pencil as he worked out each sentence in printed
and longhand letters. His shirt was damp around
the shoulders, and his long arms were burned
brown and wrinkled with veins.

"Can I help you?" he said without looking up.

"I'd like to see Arturo Gomez."

He put the pencil down and turned his face up
at me. His green, yellow-flecked eyes were flat, his
face expressionless.

"Who are you?"

"My name's Hackberry Holland. I'm a lawyer."

"You ain't his."

"He's a friend of mine from the service."

"Well, visiting hour is at two o'clock."

"I have to go back to Austin this morning. I'd
appreciate it if I could talk with him a few minutes."

The deputy turned the pencil in a circle on the
desk top with his finger. There was a hard knot of
muscle in the back of his arm.

"You working with these Mexican union people?"

"No."

"You just drove down from Austin to see a friend
in jail?"

"That's right."

"It won't help him none. He's going up to the state farm Wednesday. And I expect there might be a few more with him soon."

"I wouldn't know about that." I bent over and tipped my cigar ashes into the spittoon, then waited for the deputy to continue the statement which he had prepared long ago for strangers, slick lawyers, and nigger and Mexican lovers.

"You can take it for what it's worth, Mr. Holland, but these Mexicans was stirred up by agitators from the outside. They can make fair wages in the field any time they want to work, but they stay drunk on wine half the time or sit in the welfare office." His yellow-flecked eyes looked into my face. "Then those union organizers started telling them they could get twice as much money by shutting down the harvest. Just let the cotton and grapefruit rot and they're all going to be nigger-rich. People around here is pretty fed up with it, and it's lucky that a couple of them California Mexicans haven't been drug behind a car yet."

"As I said, I'm not representing anyone."

"It's against the rule, but I'll take you down to see Gomez a minute. I just thought you ought to know we ain't pushing these people into a corner they didn't build for themselves."

I followed him down a staircase into the basement of the building. The rigid angles in his body, the rolled khaki sleeves, and the flush of anger in his neck reminded me of several drill instructors whom I had met at Parris Island. They all had the same intense dedication to perverse abstractions which had been created for them by someone else.

The basement of the courthouse, the jail, had been constructed with large blocks of limestone, sawed and chiseled and set with mortar in uneven squares. The corridor was lighted by two bulbs screwed into sockets on the ceiling, and the cells looked like caves cut back into the rock with iron doors on them. The stone was damp with humidity, and the air was rank with disinfectant, D.D.T., urine, and tobacco smoke. Each of the iron doors had a row of holes perforated in the top, and a slit and apron for a food tray. At the end of the corridor was a large room, with two wide barred doors that swung open like gates, and overhead on the rock in broken white letters were the words *Negro Male*. I could see the spark of hand-rolled cigarettes in the dark, and smell the odor of stale sweat and synthetic wine. There was a wire-screen cage built against one wall, with a small table and two wooden chairs inside. The deputy unlocked the door and opened it.

"Wait in here and I'll bring him out," he said. He walked back down the corridor and slipped the bolt on one of the cells. He had to use both hands to pull the door open.

Art stepped out into the light, his pupils contracted to small black dots. His denim jail issue was too big for him and his hair hung down over his ears. He was barefoot, his shirt and trousers were unbuttoned, and his thin frame was stooped as he walked towards the cage, as though the rock ceiling was crushing down on him. He had a cigarette in an empty space where a tooth had been, and there was a cobweb scar on the edge of one eye. He had started to get jailhouse pallor, and the two pachuco tattoos on his hands looked like they had just been cut into the skin with brilliant purple ink. I hadn't seen him in five years, when he was contracting tomato harvests in DeWitt County, but it seemed that everything in him had shrunken inwards, hard and brittle as bone. The deputy closed the cage door on us and locked it.

"You can talk ten minutes," he said, and walked back down the corridor. The light gleamed on his shaved head.

"What about it, Hack? You want to play Russian roulette with me?" Art said, and smiled with the cigarette in his teeth. His long fingers were spread out on the table top.

"How in the hell did you go up for assault because of a picket-line arrest?"

"What happened and what I got tried for ain't the same thing. The Texas Rangers moved in on our picket line because they said we wasn't fifty feet apart. They knocked a couple of our people down, and when I yelled about it they put the arm on me. I pushed this one fat bastard on his ass, and he got up and beat the shit out of me with a blackjack. Man, they're real bad people when they turn loose. I can still see that guy swinging down on me. His eyes was sticking out of his head. He must have saved it up for a long time."

"What did your lawyer do in the trial?"

"He was appointed by the court. He lives right here in the county and he wanted me to plead guilty. I told him to go fuck himself, so he chewed on his pipe for three days, cross-examined one witness, and shook hands with me after the judge gave me five years.

"Look, Hack, I know I'm leaning on you for a favor, but I want to beat this shit. Our union's got a chance if we don't get broke up. We got a few people in Austin on our side, and some of the locals are afraid enough of the chicano vote that they might come around if we stay solid. But our treasury's broke and I got nobody but kids to organize the pickets and boycotts while I'm in the pen. And I'll tell you straight I don't want to build no five years. Four cents a day chopping cotton ain't good pay." He smiled again, and took the cigarette from his lips and put it out on the bottom of the table.

"All right, I'll try to file an appeal. It takes time, but maybe with luck I can spring you on bond."

He took another cigarette from his shirt pocket, popped a kitchen match on his thumbnail, and lit it. The scar tissue around his eye was yellow in the flame. "A year ago I was ready to charge the hill with a bayonet in my teeth. Corporal Gomez going over the top like gangbusters with a flamethrower. I was ready to build life in the pen for our union, but three months in lockdown here, man, it leaves a dent. Every night when that bastard sticks a plate of grits and fried baloney through the slit I say hello to his fingernails."

"You know what you're doing is crazy, don't you?"

"Why? Because we're tired of getting shit on?"

"These people have lived one way for a hundred and fifty years," I said. "You can't make them change with a picket sign."

His face sharpened, and his yellow-stained fingers pressed down on the cigarette.

"Yeah, we been eating their shit for just about that long. But we ain't going that route no more. We got more people than the anglos, and this land belonged to us before their white ass ever got on it."

"You can't alter historical injustice in the present. You're only putting yourself and your people up against an executioner's wall."

"You can jive about all that college bullshit you want, but we been picking your cotton for six cents a pound. You ever do stoop labor? Your back feels like a ball of fire by noon, and at night you got to sleep on the floor to iron out your spine. All you anglos are so fucking innocent. You got the answers counted out in your palm like pennies. You march off every Christmas and hand out food baskets to the niggers and greaseballs, and then for the next twelve months you congratulate yourself on your Christianity."

He drew in on the cigarette and pushed his long black hair out of his face. He looked at the table and breathed the smoke out between his lips. "Okay, man, I'm sorry. I sit in my cell all day and think, and I don't get to talk with nobody except the hack. So I just made you my dart board."

"Forget it," I said.

"But learn something about our union before you start to piss on us."

"All right."

"Like maybe we ain't just a bunch of uppity niggers."

"The deputy's going to be back in a minute."

"Look, watch out for that motherfucker. The

other night one of the blacks started screaming in the tank with the d.t.'s, and he kicked him in the head. I think he's a Bircher, and the guys in here say he's got a bad conduct discharge from the Corps for crippling a guy in the brig."

"Okay, let's finish before he gets back. Were there any Mexicans on the jury?"

"What world do you live in, man?"

"We can use jury selection in an appeal, even though I'd rather hang them on the charge itself. I'll have to get a transcript of the trial and talk with your lawyer."

"Don't fool with him. I told you he wouldn't pour water on me if I was burning. He's a little fat guy with a bald head, he owns five hundred acres of blackland, and he thinks I was brainwashed in Korea. When I asked him about an appeal he chewed on his pipe and farted."

"What's his name?"

"That's Mister Cecil Wayne Posey. His office is right across the street."

"Why didn't you write me before the trial?"

"I don't like to bruise old friends."

"Well, you sure picked a shitty time to bring in a relief pitcher."

"You're a good man, Hack. I trust your arm."

I heard the stairway door slam and the deputy walking down the stone corridor in his brogans.

"I'll be back tomorrow," I said. "You want anything?"

"No, just watch after yourself in town. They're pissed, and that southern accent of yours won't help you none when they find out you're working with our union."

"I don't think they'll roll a congressional candidate around too hard."

"I mean it, Hack. They don't give a damn who you are. We stepped on their balls with a golf shoe. There ain't been any Klan activity here since the 1920's, and last week they burned a cross on an island in the middle of the river. You better keep your head down, buddy."

Art lit another cigarette off the butt while the deputy unlocked the cage.

"Tomorrow," I said.

"Yeah, stay solid, cousin."

I looked at the black soles of his bare feet as the deputy led him back to his cell. The deputy clanged the door shut, shot the bolt, and stared at me with a fixed gaze while I tore the cellophane wrapper off a cigar. I bit the end off and spit it on the floor. I could feel his hot eyes reaching me through the wire screen. He rattled his change in one pocket with his hand.

"You want to get out of here this morning, Mr. Holland?" he said.

● ● ●

Upstairs by the office door a girl leaned against the wall with a carton of cigarettes in her hand. She wore sandals, bleached bluejeans, and a maroon blouse tied in a knot under her breasts. She had on large, amber sunglasses, hoop earrings, and a thin strand of Indian beads around her neck. Her skin was brown, her body lithe and relaxed, and her curly brown hair was burned on the ends by the sun. Her eyes were indifferent through her glasses as she looked at me and the deputy.

"Would you give these to Art Gomez, please?" she said. Her voice was level, withdrawn, almost without tone.

The deputy took the carton of cigarettes and dropped it in his desk drawer without answering. He sat down in his chair and began to sharpen a pencil with his pocketknife into the wastebasket. I knew that each stroke of that knife was cutting into his own resentment at the restraint his job forced upon him in dealing with a hippie girl and a slick, outside lawyer. He bent over his traffic forms, his knuckles white on the pencil, and began to print out his report as though we were not there.

The girl walked back towards the entrance. There was a pale line of skin above the back of her bluejeans, and her ass had the natural, easy rhythm that most women try to learn for a lifetime. Everything in her was smooth and loose, and her motion had the type of cool unconcern that bothers you in some vague place in the back of your mind.

"Hello," I said.

She turned around, framed in the square of yellow light through the entrance, and looked at me. She wore no makeup, and in the black shadow over her face she looked like a nun in church suddenly disturbed from prayer.

"I expect you work with Art's union. My name's Hack Holland. I'm trying to file an appeal for Art before he goes up to prison."

She remained immobile in the light.

"I'd like to meet some of the people in your union," I said.

"What for?"

"Because I don't know anybody in this town and I might need a little help."

"There's nothing we can do for you."

"Why don't you give me a chance to see?"

"You're wasting your time, man."

"I'd like to see Art out in the next light-year, and from what I understand so far I can't expect any help from his lawyer, the court, or the clerk of records. So I can either wander around town a few more days and talk with people like the deputy in there or cowboys in the beer joint, or I can meet someone who'll tell me what happened on that picket line."

"We told what happened."

"You told it in a local trial court that was prejudiced. I'm going to take the case to the Court of Criminal Appeals in Austin."

"What's your thing with Art?"

"We were in Korea together."

"You can't do any good for him. The A.C.L.U. has had our cases in Austin before."

"Maybe I'm a better lawyer," I said.

"Believe it, man, you've got a bum trip in mind."

"I believe in the banzai ethic. At least I'll leave a dark burn across the sky when I go down."

"You ought to find a better way to pay back army debts."

"I was a Navy corpsman, and I paid off all my debts in Band-Aids before I was discharged."

She turned back into the light to walk outside.

"Do you want a ride?" I said.

"I'll walk."

"You don't want to miss a good experience with the most arrested driver in Texas. Besides, I need some directions."

"Stay away from our union headquarters if you want to help Art."

"I don't expect that we'll all end up in the penitentiary if I drive you home."

We walked down the courthouse sidewalk under the shade of the oak trees to my automobile. The sun had risen high in the sky, and the tar surfacing on the street was hot and soft under our feet. The heat shimmered off the concrete walk in front of the hotel.

We drove into the Negro and Mexican section back of town. The dirt roads were baked hard as rock, and clouds of dust swept up behind my car. The unpainted wood shacks were pushed into one another at odd angles, the ditches strewn with garbage, and the outhouses were built of discarded boards, R.C. Cola signs, and tarpaper.

"I have to see Art's lawyer after I drop you off, but I'll come back a little later," I said.

"I thought you didn't expect any help from him."

"I don't, but maybe I can use inadequate defense as a reason for appeal."

She took a package of cigarettes from her bluejeans pocket and lit one. I glanced at the smooth curve of her breasts as she pushed the package back in her pocket.

"You're pretty sure I've got a loser, aren't you?" I said.

"I just don't think you know very much about the county you're working in."

"So you're up against some cotton growers who don't want to pay union scale, and a few part-time

Klansmen. And you've met a redneck deputy sheriff who probably rents his brains by the week. That doesn't change the law or trial procedure."

"Wow. You must walk into court with a copy of *The National Review* between your teeth."

"I've had eight years of law practice, babe, and I haven't lost many cases."

"I don't believe you've dealt very much with union farm workers, either."

"I've spent all my life in Texas. I don't expect to find out anything very new about it in this case."

"Don't you realize the rules in your court don't apply to us? Art's jury brought in a guilty verdict in fifteen minutes, and later the foreman said it took them that long because they sent out for some cold drinks."

"All right, I can use things just like that in the appeal."

"I'm not kidding you, man; lose some of those comic-book attitudes if you want to do anything for him," she said.

"You really know how to turn on the burner, don't you?"

"I'm just telling you about the bag you're trying to pick up."

"You're a hard girl."

"Do I get that free with the ride home?" The sunlight through the window was bright on the

burned ends of her hair. She had her arm back on
the seat while she smoked, and I could see the
whiteness at the top of her breasts.

"You're not from Texas. What are you doing
here, anyway?"

"Would you like to flip through the celluloid
windows in my wallet?"

"It's just a question."

"It seems like an expensive trip home."

"Maybe I should put on my chauffeur's cap, and
you can sit in the back seat and I'll close the glass
behind me."

"I was a graduate student in social work at Berkeley. I got tired of writing abstract papers about hungry people so I joined the Third World and came
out to your lovely state."

I hit a chuckhole in the road and felt the car
slam down on its springs. The dust was so heavy
that it had started to filter through the air-
conditioning system. Two Negro children were
running along the edge of a ditch, throwing stones
at an emaciated dog scabbed over with mange. The
road reached a deadend in front of a converted
general store with a sign above the door that read:
United Farm Workers Local 476. The glass display windows were yellow and pocked with BB holes, and
filmed with dirt on the inside and outside. Strips of
Montgomery Ward brick had been nailed over the

rotted boards in the walls, the steps had collapsed, cinder blocks were propped under one side of the building to keep it from sagging, and I could almost hear the flies humming around the outhouse in back. A boy of about nineteen, barefoot and without a shirt, sat on the front porch playing a twelve-string Gibson guitar.

"Don't wrinkle your eyes at it, man," she said. "We're lucky we could rent anything in this town."

"I didn't say a thing."

"I could hear the tumblers click over in your head. You've got the middle class hygiene thing. Anything except green lawns and red brick sends you running up the street."

"That's a lot of shit."

"Okay. Thanks for the ride."

She closed the door and walked down the dusty path to the building. I watched the motion of her hips and her full thighs as she stepped up on the porch, then I turned the Cadillac in a circle and headed back towards town.

I went to Mister Cecil Wayne Posey's office and was told by his junior partner that I could find him at home. His ranch was all blackland, lined with rows of cotton and corn and orange trees. A dozen Mexicans and Negroes were hoeing in the cotton, and horses stood in the groves of live oak trees on the low hills. The large, one-story house had new white paint and a wide screened-in porch, and poplar trees were planted along the front lane. There were two great red barns in back with lightning rods and weather vanes on the peaks, a windmill pumping water into a trough, and rolls of barbed wire and cords of cedar posts stacked against a tractor shed.

As I walked up the lane I heard a woodpecker rattling against a dead limb in the heat. Mr. Posey rose from his round-backed wicker chair on the porch and shook hands. The lower portion of his stomach was swollen all the way across the front of his pants. His skin was soft, pudgy to the touch, and his head was almost completely bald except for a few short gray hairs. His eyes were colorless, and his voice had the bland quality of oatmeal. He reminded me of a miniature, upended white whale. When he sat down the watch in his pocket bulged against the cloth like a hard biscuit.

A Negro maid in a lace-trimmed apron served us iced tea with mint leaves and slices of lemon on a silver service, then I began quietly to press Mr. Posey for his reasons in not filing an appeal for Art. Actually, my questions, or even my presence there, would probably be considered a violation of professionalism among attorneys, since I was indirectly implying that he had been negligent in the case; but the flicker of insult never showed in his eyes, and if his tone or the pale expression around his mouth indicated anything, it was simply that I was an idealistic young lawyer who had embarked on a fool's errand. He lowered his face into the tea glass when he drank, and momentarily the moisture gave his lips a streak of color.

"I didn't feel there was basis for appeal, Mr. Holland," he said. "I originally advised Art to plead guilty in hopes of a reduced charge, but he refused, and I doubt if the Court of Criminal Appeals will consider the case of a man who was convicted on the testimony of four Texas Rangers and two bystanders. He did hit the officer twice before he was restrained, and that's the essential and inalterable fact of the case."

"Who were these bystanders?"

"Two county workmen who were operating a grading machine on the road when the arrests were made."

I looked at him incredulously.

"Did you feel these men were objective witnesses?" I said.

"They had no interest in the issue. They merely stated what they saw."

"I understand that most of the people on the picket line testified, also."

"Unfortunately, most of them have been in local court before, and I'm afraid that their statements were overly familiar to the jury. One young man admitted to the district attorney that he'd been three hundred yards away from the arrest, but he was sure that Art hadn't struck the officer. It's difficult to contest a conviction on evidence of that sort, Mr. Holland."

His face bent into the iced tea glass again, and a drop of perspiration rolled off his temple down his fat cheek. He shifted his buttocks in the wicker chair and crossed his legs. His massive, soft thighs stretched the crease in his slacks flat.

"Art's been organizing a farm workers' union in this county for the past year. Do you believe any members of the jury had preconceived feelings towards him?"

"None that would affect the indictment against him. He was tried for assaulting a Texas Ranger, not for his involvement in a Mexican union."

I borrowed a match from Mr. Posey and lit a cigar. I looked at him through the curl of flame and smoke and wondered if he had any conception of his irresponsibility in allowing his client to be sentenced to five years in a case that would be considered laughable by a law school moot court.

He put his empty pipe in the center of his teeth, drew in with a wet rattling sound, and farted softly in the back of the chair. I finished my tea, shook hands and thanked him for his help, and walked down the gravel path to my automobile under the trees. Behind me I heard him snap the metal latch into place on the screen door.

I drove back to town and had lunch and two beers at the cafe, then spent an hour in the clerk of records office while an aged secretary made a Xerox copy of the trial transcript for me. There was no breeze through the windows, my sunglasses filmed with moisture in the humidity, and the electric fans did nothing but blow drafts of hot air across the room. The deputy sheriff came in once to drop a pile of his penciled reports on the clerk's desk, and as he walked past me he stared into my face without speaking.

I spent the rest of the afternoon in the hotel, with my feet propped in the window, reading the transcript and sipping whiskey poured over ice. The flies droned dully in the stillness, and occasionally I would hear the hillbilly music from the beer tavern. Across the square the sun slanted on the rows of watermelons and cantaloupes in the open-air fruit market.

The transcript was an incredible record to read. The trial might have been constructed out of mismatched parts from an absurd movie script about legal procedure. There had been no challenge of the jurors, each of the Texas Rangers contradicted the others, a Baptist minister testified that many of

the union members were Communists, and the two
county workmen said they had seen a Mexican attack a Ranger, although they had been eating their
lunch in the back of a truck a half mile down the
road at the time. The three witnesses for the defense were sliced to pieces by the district attorney.
They were led into discrediting statements about
their own testimony, forced into stumbling admis-
sions about their involvement in revolution, and referred to sixteen times as outside agitators. And
Cecil Wayne Posey never raised an objection. Nor-
mally, any two pages torn at random from such a
comic scenario would be grounds for appeal, but
under Texas law the appeal has to be made in local
court within ten days of sentencing, unless good
cause is shown for an extension, and since Mr. Posey's refusal to continue the case had virtually guaranteed that his client would go to prison, I would
have to start the whole process over again in Austin.

It was dusk outside now. I threw the transcript
in my suitcase, took a cold bath, and shaved, with
a glass of whiskey on top of the lavatory. As a rule
I didn't try to correct the inadequacies inherent in
any system, but in this case I thought I would send
a letter to the Texas Bar Association about Mr. Posey. Yes, Mr. Posey should receive some official
recognition for his work, I thought, as I drew the

razor blade down in a clean swath through the shaving cream on my cheek.

I ate a steak for supper and drove back to the union headquarters in the Mexican district. There were thunderclouds and heat lightning in the west, an electric flash all the way across the horizon, and then a distant, dry rumble. The air tasted like brass in my mouth. Parts of the dirt road had been sprinkled with garden hoses to wet down the dust, and the cicadas in the trees were deafening with their late evening noise. Fireflies glowed like points of flame in the gathering dusk, and across the river in old Mexico the adobe huts on the mud flat wavered in the light of outdoor cookfires. High up in the sky, caught in the sun's last afterglow, a buzzard floated motionlessly like a black scratch on a tin surface.

I parked the car in front of the union headquarters and walked up the path to the wooden steps. The boy with the Gibson twelve-string still sat on the porch. He had three steel picks on his fingers and a half gallon bottle of dago red next to him. His bare feet were covered with dust, and there were tattoos on each arm. He chorded the guitar and didn't turn his head towards me.

"She's inside, man," he said.

"Do I knock or let myself in?"

"Just do it."

I tapped with my knuckle on the screen and waited. I heard dishes rattling in a pan in the back of the building.

"Hey Rie, that guy's back," the boy shouted over his shoulder.

A moment later the girl walked through a back hallway towards me. Her arms were wet up to the elbow. She had splashed water on her blouse, and her breasts stood out against the cloth.

"Man, like you really want to meet us, don't you?" she said, pushing open the screen with the back of her wrist.

"I decided against watching television in the hotel lobby this evening."

"Come in the kitchen. I have to finish the dishes."

The flowered wallpaper in the main room was yellowed and peeling in rotted strips, coated with mold and glue. United Farm Workers signs, pop art posters of Che Guevara and Lyndon Johnson on a motorcycle, and underground newspapers were thumbtacked over the exposed sections of boarding in the walls. A store-window manikin lay on top of the old grocery counter with an empty wine bottle balanced on her stomach. A mobile made of beer-bottle necks clinked in the breeze from an oscillating fan that rattled against the wire guard each time it completed a turn. The single lightbulb suspended from the ceiling gave the whole room a hard yellow cast that hurt the eyes.

I followed her through the hallway into the kitchen. Her brown hips moved as smoothly as water turning in the current. Two young girls, a college boy, and a Negro man were scraping dishes into a garbage can and rinsing them under an iron pump. Through the back window I could see the last red touch of the sun on a sandbar in the middle of the Rio Grande.

"We had a neighborhood dinner tonight," the girl from Berkeley said. "There's some tortillas and beans in the icebox or you can get a dish towel."

"You have a charge account with the supermarket?"

"We get the day-old stuff from the Mexican produce stands," she said.

"I think I'll just have a whiskey and water if you'll give me a glass." I took my silver flask from my coat pocket.

"Help yourself," she said.

I offered the flask to the others.

"You got it, brother," the Negro said.

He picked up a tin cup from the sideboard and held it in front of me. His bald, creased head and round black face shone in the half-light. Four of his front teeth were missing, and the others were yellow with snuff. I poured a shot in his cup and then splashed some water in my glass from the pump. I could taste the rust in it.

"So what would you like to find out about the United Farm Workers?" the girl said.

"Nothing. I read the trial transcript and talked with Mr. Posey this afternoon. The conviction won't hold."

The Negro laughed with the cup held before his lips. The college boy straightened up from the garbage can and looked at me as though I had dropped through a hole in the ceiling.

"You believe that?" the Negro said. He was still smiling.

"Yes."

"I mean, you ain't bullshitting? You're coming on for real?" the college boy said. He wore bluejeans and a faded yellow and white University of Texas T-shirt.

"That's right, pal," I said.

The Negro laughed again and went back to work scraping plates. The two young girls were also smiling.

"Who you working for, man?" the boy said.

"Judge Roy Bean. I float up and down the Pecos River for him on an inner tube."

"Don't get strung out," the girl said.

"What am I, the visiting straight man around here?"

The girl dried her hands on a towel and took a bottle of Jax out of the icebox. "Come on out front," she said.

"We wasn't trying to give you no truck. We ain't got bad things here," the Negro said. He grinned at me with his broken, yellow teeth.

In the front room the girl sat in a straight-backed chair, with one leg pulled up on the seat, her arm propped across her knee, and drank out of the beer bottle. Behind her on the wall was a poster with a rectangular, outspread bird on it and the single word *HUELGA*.

"They're kids, and they don't know if you're putting them on or if you're a private detective working for their parents," she said. "The black guy has been in the movement since the Progressive Labor Party days, and he's heard a lot of jiveass lawyers talk about appeals."

"I guess I just don't like people to work out their problems on my head."

"I told you this afternoon about coming down here."

"Maybe I should have worn my iron helmet and flack jacket."

"They don't have any bad will towards you. They're good people."

"I'm paranoid and suspicious by nature."

"That's part of the middle-class syndrome, too. It goes along with the hygiene thing."

"Goddamn, I picked a hell of a ballgame to relieve in. Between you, Cecil Wayne Posey, and that
deputy at the jail I feel like I'm standing ten feet
from the plate and lobbing volley balls at King
Kong."

She took the bottle from her lips and laughed,
and her almond eyes were suddenly full of light.
She touched away the foam from the corner of her
mouth with two fingers.

"I should have put on my Groucho Marx clothes
this evening," I said. "You know, an hour or so of
Zeppo and the gang throwing pies while your people go up to the pen."

I finished my drink, and the minerals and iron
rust in the water tasted like a gladiator's final toast
in the back of my throat.

"You're out of sight," she said.

I poured a thin shot over the orange flecks in the
bottom of the glass and drank it down. The smoky,
charcoal-filtered taste of undiluted Jack Daniels,
born out of Tennessee limestone springs and rick-
yards of hickory, rolled down inside me with the
lightness of heated air, then I began to feel the
amber caution signal flashing somewhere behind
my forehead.

"Yeah, I'm a walking freak show. The next time
I'll appear with my whole act. Seals blowing horns,

monkeys riding unicycles, jugglers, clowns with exploding bombs in their pants."

"Wow, you really let it hang out," she said. Her
wet eyes were bright with refractions of light.

"It comes free with the ride home." I poured the
rest of the whiskey into my glass. "Come on, let's
drink."

"What do you do when you're not defending ex–
Korean War buddies?" she said.

"I work for the money boys. Oil corporation
suits, swindles against the government, the Billy Sol
account. I also run for Congress part time."

"You're putting me on."

"Buy a copy of *The Austin American* November 5.
I'll be smiling at you on the front page."

"If you're not jiving, you must be an unbelievable
guy."

"You want to talk about my geek act some more?"
I said.

"I mean what do you expect? You drop in here
from outer space and come on like H. L. Hunt and
W. C. Fields at the same time."

"I was put together from discarded parts." I finished my glass, and the amber light flashed red and
began to beat violently.

"Tell me, really, why did you come here tonight?"

"I already told you. Television ruptures the blood vessels in my eyes."

The Negro, the two girls, and the college boy walked out from the kitchen.

"There's a man who likes to drink," I said.

"You been reading my mail," the Negro said.

"How about a case of Jax and a bottle of Jack Daniels?" I took a twenty-dollar bill from my wallet.

"We got a few more people coming over tonight," he said.

"Get two cases. Take my car."

"It's just down the road. I'd get busted for grand auto in that Cadillac, anyway."

He took the twenty-dollar bill and stuck it in the pocket of his denim shirt.

"You ain't going to tip me later, are you?" he said.

"I left my planter's hat in the car."

He laughed and his round black face and brown eyes glistened with good humor. "You're all right," he said, and went out the screen door with the college boy.

"You always do this on a case?" the girl said.

"No. I usually don't drink with the people I know. Most of them belong to the ethic of R.C. Richardson and the Dallas Petroleum Club. They like to throw glasses and urinate off hotel balconies. They also like to feel waitresses under the table. R. C. Richardson is a very unique guy. In the last fifteen years he's taken the state and the federal government for a little less than one million dollars. He wears yellow cowboy boots, striped western pants, a string tie, and he has a one-hundred-pound stomach that completely covers his hand-tooled belt. Three days a week he sits in the Kiwanis and Rotary and Chamber of Commerce luncheons and belches on his boiled weenies and sauerkraut, and then rises like a soldier and says the pledge of allegiance with his hand over his heart. But actually, the guy has class. The others around him are clandestine in their midnight dealings and worm's-eye view of the world. They don't have his sincere feeling for vulgarity."

"He must be an interesting man to work for," she said.

"Do you have another beer in the icebox?"

"This is the last one. Take it."

"I never take a girl's last drink. It shows a lack of gentility."

"You are from outer space."

I could feel the blood tingling in my hands and face. My scalp started to sweat from the whiskey.

"What's your name, anyway?" I bit the end off a cigar.

"Rie Velasquez."

"You're not Mexican."

"No."

"So what are you?" I reached over and took the beer bottle out of her hand.

"My father was Spanish. He came from Spain during the Civil War."

I let the beer and foam roll down my throat over the dry taste of the whiskey and cigar smoke.

"Hence, you joined the Third World Liberation Front. The gasoline and dynamite gang."

"You ought to change your brand of bourbon."

"Right or wrong? Didn't they incinerate a few college buildings in the last year?"

"Don't you think that sounds a bit dumb?"

"Bullshit. Ten of those people could have a whole city in flames within twenty-four hours."

She took a cigarette from the pack in her blue-jeans and lit it. She pinched the end between her lips as she drew in on the smoke.

"What type of bag do you think we operate out of, man?" she said. "Did you see any kerosene rags and coal oil hidden under the porch? You believe we all came down here because of your tourist brochures about the scenic loveliness of the Texas desert?"

"I just don't buy that revolution shit."

"Why don't you read something about the United Farm Workers? They don't have anything to do with revolution. They're tired of being niggers in somebody's watermelon patch."

"Yow!" the Negro yelled, as he kicked open the

screen door with a case of beer on one shoulder and a block of ice wrapped in newspaper on the other. "Man, we got it. Spodiodi and brew. We're in tall cotton tonight, brothers."

The college boy carried the second case of beer, and the boy with the guitar had already cut the seal on the bottle of Jack Daniels. They put the two cases on the old grocery counter, and the Negro chopped up the ice with a butcher knife and spread it over the bottles. He opened the first bottle by putting the cap against the edge of the counter and striking downward quickly with the flat of his hand. The white foam showered up over his head and splattered on the floor. He covered the lip of the bottle with his mouth and drank until it was almost empty. The beer streamed down his chin into the matted black hair on his chest.

"Lord, you can't beat that," he said.

I took the whiskey and poured three inches into my glass.

"You'll drive nails through your stomach like that. Put a little brew on top of it," the Negro said. He slapped another cap off on the edge of the counter and handed the bottle to me.

"Use this and avoid the slashed hand shot," Rie said, and threw an opener to the college boy.

Eight Mexican field hands, all dressed in faded denim clothes, overalls, straw hats, and work shoes, came through the screen door in single file as though they had been lined up at a bus stop. They were pot-bellied and short, thin and stooped, tattooed with pachuco crosses and hung with religious medals, scarred and stitched, some of them missing fingers, sunburned almost black, with trousers bagging in the rear and their Indian hair wet and combed straight back over the head.

They had a pint of Old Stag and a gallon milk bottle filled with blackberry wine. The Negro began passing out the Jax, and an hour later the room roared with mariachi songs and Apache screams.

"Let me try that guitar, buddy," I said to the boy from the front porch. He sat on the floor with his back against the wall and a glass of wine and whiskey between his legs. His face was bloodless and his eyes couldn't fix on my face. I put the strap of the twelve-string around my neck and tried to pick out "The Wreck of Old '97," but my fingers felt as though a needle and thread had been drawn through all my knuckles. Then I tried "The Wildwood Flower" and "John Hardy," and each time I began over again I hit more wrong notes or came up on the wrong fret. I smoked somebody's cigarette out of an ashtray, finished my drink, and then started an easy Jimmie Rodgers run that I had learned to pick when I was sixteen. It was worse than before, and I laid the guitar face down on the counter among the scores of empty beer bottles.

"I bet you blow a good one when you're cool," Rie said. She was sitting in the chair next to me with a small glass of wine in her hand. Her legs were crossed, and the indentation across her stomach and the white line of skin above her bluejeans made something drop inside me.

"Give me an hour and I'll boil them cabbages down," I said.

"Do it tomorrow morning."

"I'm going to streak out of here like the fireball mail tomorrow morning. My Cadillac and I are going to melt the asphalt between here and Austin." Someone put the whiskey bottle in my hand, and I took two large swallows and chased it with beer.

"You must have a real dragon inside," Rie said.

"No, I deal with Captain Hyde. That bastard and I have been together almost fifteen years. However, when he starts acting like an asshole I unscrew my head and throw it in the Rio Grande a couple of times."

"No kidding, pull it back in, man," she said.

"I thought you were a hip girl. You're giving me the concerned eye of a Baptist reformer now."

"I think you're probably a madman."

"You ought to see me and John Wesley Hardin

drunk in the streets of Yoakum. He rides on the
fender of my Cadillac, busting parking meters and
stoplights with a revolver in each hand."

The noise became louder. All the beer, whiskey,
and wine were gone, and I gave one of the Mexican
field hands another twenty dollars to go to the tavern.
The twelve-string guitar was passed from hand to
hand, tuned in a half dozen discords, two strings
broken, and finally dropped in a corner. Someone
suggested a knife-throwing contest, and a bread cut-
ter, two bowies, a rippled-bladed Italian stiletto, my
pocket knife, a hand ax, and a meat cleaver were flung
into the wall until the boards were split and shattered
and knocked through on the ground outside.

The room was beginning to tip and blur in front
of my eyes. I was smoking a dead cigar butt that I
had frayed under my boot heel a few minutes earlier.

"Spodiodi, man. It's the only thing. You got to
put them snakes back in the basket," the Negro said
in my face. His eyes were red, and his breath was
sour with wine.

"I don't deal in snakes."

"Man, they're crawling through your face."

I knew that I had an answer for him, but the
words wouldn't rise out of the echoes and flashes
of light in my head.

"Shit, let's go down to the river. This place is
hotter than a brick kiln," I said.

"It's all that corn," the Negro said.

"Come on, Judge Roy Bean is holding court in his inner tube," I said, and pulled Rie up from her chair by the hand.

"Hey, man," she said.

I carried the bottle of whiskey by the neck and pulled her through the hallway into the kitchen. The Negro followed us with a beer in each hand and a half dozen bottles stuck down in his trousers. We walked down the bare slope towards the mud flat. The moon was full and white as ivory in a breathless sky. A rusted Ford coupe with no glass in the windows sat half-submerged in the river. The current eddied and swirled through the gaping window in back and coursed over the top of the seats and the steering wheel. The moon's reflection rippled across the water's brown surface, and I could see the sharp backs of garfish turning by the sandbars. Behind us the Mexican field hands were still singing. The Negro finished one beer and threw the bottle arching high over the river.

"Yow!" he yelled.

"Goddamn, look at it. There's Mexico," I said. "Fifty yards and you can drop right through the bottom of the twentieth century."

Rie sat down on a rotted log with her bare feet in the water. The moonlight turned the burned tips of her hair to points of silver.

"A whole land full of bandit ghosts and Indian legends," I said. "You just step through the hole in the hedge, and there's Pancho Villa splashing across the river with pistols and bandoliers hanging all over him. Zapata cutting down *Federales* with his machete. Illiterate peasants executing French kings. Cortez destroying an entire culture."

"There's diphtheria in the well water of those adobe huts, too," Rie said.

"You're like every goddamn Marxist I ever met. No humor or sense of romance."

"Quit shouting."

"Isn't that straight?" I said. "It's the revolutionary mind. You can't realize that man is more a clown than a Satan. You approach everything with a sullen mind and try to convert buffoons into Machiavelli."

"Oh for God's sake, man."

I took a drink out of the bottle. The whiskey splashed over my mouth.

"You goddamn people don't know what human evil is. One of these days you and I are going to have some Chinese tea and talk about the Bean Camp together. I'll also give you a couple of footnotes on Pak's Palace and No Name Valley."

I felt the ground shift under my feet, and I thought I was going to fall. I put my arm on her shoulder to keep my balance.

"There's mudcat nesting in that car. I know how

to get them, too," the Negro said. He took off his shirt and shoes, and laid the remaining bottles of beer in an even line on the bank. "You just swim your hand under the water and back that shovel-mouth into a corner and catch him real fast inside the gill. Come on, brother. I'm going to teach you how to fish like black people."

He waded out into the river up to his hips and pulled open the rusted car door with both hands. The moon's reflection off the water made his black body glow.

"He does this when he gets drunk," Rie said. "You can do it, too, if you want me to take both of you down to the county hospital tonight."

"That's just what a yankee would say. Don't you know that colored people catch fish when white people couldn't bring them up with a telephone crank?"

I sat down on the mud flat and pulled off my boots. I felt the water soak through the seat of my trousers.

"He had eight stitches the last time he hand-fished in that car," she said.

"I don't believe it. That sounds like more Marxist-yankee bullshit."

I walked out into the river, and the warm, muddy current swirled around my waist and my feet sunk into the silt. The Negro was bent over the top of the front seat with both his arms submerged to the shoulder. His face was concentrated, his eyes looking into nothing, as though his fingers were touching some vital and delicate part of the universe.

"She's backed up and fanning right next to the trunk. She's got young ones under her," he said.

"Watch her fins."

"She'll open up in a minute to get a piece of my finger, then I'll grab a whole handful of meat inside her gill."

He ducked forward, the surface of the water shook and quivered momentarily, and then he drew one hand back with a ragged cut between the thumb and forefinger. The drops of blood squeezed out through the bruised edges of the skin and ran down his wrist. He closed his eyes in pain and sucked the cut.

"I told you to—" Then I heard the sirens rolling in a low moan down the dusty street in front of the union building.

"Shit," Rie said from the river bank.

I turned around and saw the revolving blue and yellow lights on top of three police cars, winking and flashing in the dark.

"The Man done arrived," the Negro said, with his cut hand still held before his mouth.

Sheriff's deputies and city police went through

the front door of the building, walked around the sides with flashlights, looked in the outhouse, and then focused two car spotlights on us in the river. The electric white glare made my eyes water.

"You people walk towards me with your hands on top of your head!" a voice shouted from behind the light.

"Them dudes can reach out from a long way, can't they?" the Negro said. He flopped both his arms over his bald head and started wading out of the river. The light broke around his body as though he had been carved out of burnt iron.

For some drunk reason I closed the car door carefully in the current and lifted the handle upward into place.

"On your head, punk!" the voice shouted.

"Fuck you," I said.

Suddenly, both of the arcs were turned directly into my face, and the Negro disappeared from my vision in one brilliant explosion of light.

"Don't screw with them, Hack. Get out of there," Rie said from the darkness.

I waded out of the shallows with one hand over my eyes. My face burned with the heat from the lights.

"I give you warning. Get them over your head."

"I told you to go fuck yourself, too." I tripped on

the mudbank and fell on my elbows. My forearms and one side of my face were covered with wet sand. Rie tried to pick me up by the back of my shirt.

"They'll kill you, Hack. Get up and walk. It's just a disturbing the peace bust. We'll be out in the morning," she said.

A sheriff's car, with both spotlights burning, drove down the embankment on the hard ground, bounced over a log, and turned to a stop in front of me. As the beams of light changed angle I saw the Mexican field hands lined up against the building, with their arms outstretched before them and their legs widespread, while two policemen shook them down.

The whip aerial on the car rocked back and forth, and the deputy from the jail opened the driver's door and walked towards me. I stood up and put a wet cigar in my mouth. My clothes were filled with sand and mud, and my hair felt like paint on top of my head. His .357 Magnum and the cartridges in his leather belt glinted in the moonlight. There was a line of perspiration down the front of his shirt, and his package of cigarettes stuck up at an angle under the flap of his pocket, which struck me at the time as an odd thing for a military man. His jawbones were as tight as his crewcut scalp.

"I figured that was you, Mr. Holland, and I didn't

want nobody dropping the hammer on you for some wetback crossing the river," he said.

"What have you got? Disturbing the peace? Disorderly conduct?"

"We got all kinds of things. I expect if we look around here a while we might find some dope."

"Why don't you let these people alone? There wasn't any complaint from this neighborhood."

"Get in the car, please, miss," he said to Rie.

"Look, she was out here. She didn't have anything to do with that drunk party."

He opened the back door of the automobile and took Rie by the elbow.

"Just keep your peckerwood hands in your pockets a minute," I said.

"What?"

"You heard me, motherfucker."

"Mr. Holland, you can drive out of here tonight in that Cadillac of yours and I'll forget about that. The next time you want to help out the niggers and the wetbacks you just write out a check to the Community Chest and stay out of this county."

"I'll be all right. Go to Austin tomorrow and put it in for Art," she said. She sat in the back seat behind the wire-mesh screen.

"Let her out," I said.

"You really want to push it, Mr. Holland?"

"Yeah, I do. From what I understand you have a b.c.d. from the Marine Corps and you do most of your law enforcement on helpless winos in a drunk tank. So why don't you get off the bad ass act?"

"You're under arrest. I don't expect you're going to get out of our jail very soon, either."

"You're fucking with the Lone Ranger, too, peckerwood," I said.

He brought his billy out of his back pocket and caught me right above the temple. A shotgun shell exploded in my head, and I fell against the car door and hit the ground on my hands and knees. He kicked me once in the stomach, and my breath rushed out of me as though someone had opened a large hole in the middle of my chest. The inside of my mouth was coated with sand, my eyes bulged, and I started to vomit, then his boot cut across the back of my head with the easy swing of a football player kicking an extra point.

CHAPTER

FOUR

Sometime in the early morning hours I woke up on the stone floor of a cell in the bottom of the courthouse. The cell was almost completely black, except for the dim circles of light through the row of holes in the top of the door. Moisture covered the walls, and the toilet in the corner had overflowed. I pulled myself up on the iron bunk and touched the huge swelling above my temple. It was as tight as a baseball, and the blood had congealed in my hair. My head was filled with distant bugles and claps of thunder, and I felt the cell tilt on its axis and try to pitch me off the bunk into the pool of water by the toilet. Then I vomited between my legs.

I raised my head slowly, my eyes throbbing and the sweat running down my face. I found a dry

kitchen match in my shirt pocket and popped it on
my thumbnail. I held the flame over my wristwatch
and saw the smashed crystal and the hands frozen
at five after one. My white pants were still wet and
streaked with mud, and my shirt was torn off one
shoulder. I stumbled against the door and leaned
my face down to the food slit.

"Hey, one of you sons of bitches better—" But
my voice broke with the effort of shouting. I tried
again, and my words sounded foolish in the stillness.

"Cool that shit, man," a Negro voice said from
down the corridor.

I lay back on the tick mattress with my arm
across my eyes. I could smell the urine and stale
wine in the cloth, and I imagined that there were
lice laying their strings of white eggs along the
seams, but I was too sick to care. I slept in delirious
intervals, never sure if I was really asleep or dream-
ing, and my nightmare monsters sat with spread
cheeks on my feet and grinned at me with their
obscene faces. They appeared in all shapes and
sizes of deformity: hunched backs, slanted eyes,
split tongues, and lipless mouths. Major Pak was
there with his fanatical scream and the electrician's
pliers in his clenched hand, the guards in the Bean
Camp who let our wounded freeze to death to save
fuel, and then Sergeant Tien Kwong leaned over

me and inserted the end of his burpgun into my mouth and said, smiling, "You suck. We give you boiled egg."

A deputy slipped the bolt on my cell and pulled open the door. I winced in the light and turned my face towards his silhouette. His stomach hung over his cartridge belt. Behind him a Negro trusty was pushing a food cart stacked with tin plates and a tall stainless-steel container of grits.

"You can go now, Mr. Holland, but the sheriff wants to talk with you a few minutes first," the deputy said.

"Where's the man who brought me in?"

"He's off duty."

"What's his name?" My head ached when I sat up on the bunk.

"You better talk with the sheriff."

I got to my feet and stepped out into the corridor. The Negro trusty was ladling spoonfuls of grits and fried baloney into tin plates and setting them on the iron aprons of the cell doors. The uneven stone on the floor hurt my bare feet, and my right eye, which had started to stretch tight from the swelling in my temple, watered in the hard yellow light. The deputy and I went down the corridor and up the stairs to the sheriff's office. The fat in his hips and stomach flopped inside his shirt each time he took a step. His black hair was oiled and pasted down flat across his balding pate, and he used the handrail on the staircase as though he were pulling a massive weight uphill.

The sheriff sat behind his desk with a handrolled cigarette between his lips, and my billfold, pocketknife, and muddy boots in front of him. He wore steel-rimmed glasses, and his ears peeled out from the sides of his head. His face was full of red knots and bumps, a large brown mole on his chin, and his gray hair was mowed right into the scalp, but his flat blue eyes cut through the rest of it like a welder's torch. He put the cigarette out between his fingers in the wastebasket, and started to roll another one from a package of Virginia Extra in his pocket. The tips of his teeth were rotted with nicotine. He curved the cigarette paper under his forefinger and didn't look at me when he spoke.

"My deputy wanted to charge you with attempted assault on a law officer, but I ain't going to do that," he said. He spread the tobacco evenly in the paper and licked down the edge. "I'm just going to ask you to go down the road, and that'll be the end of it."

"Your man is pretty good with his feet and a billy."

"I reckon that's what happens when you threaten a law officer, don't it?" He put the cigarette in his mouth and turned towards me in his swivel chair.

"I don't suppose that I could bring a charge against him here, but I have a feeling the F.B.I. might be interested in a civil rights violation."

"You don't seem to understand what I'm saying, Mr. Holland. I got my deputy's report right here, co-signed by a city patrolman, and it says you were drunk, resisting arrest, and swinging at an officer with your fists. Now maybe you think that don't mean anything because you're an Austin lawyer, but that ain't worth piss on a rock around here."

"You're not dealing with a wetback or a college kid, either." My head felt as though it were filled with water. Through the window I could see the sun striking across the tree tops.

"I know exactly what I'm dealing with. I been sheriff here seven years and I seen them like you by the truckload. You come in from the outside and walk around like your shit don't stink. I don't know what you're doing with them union people, and I don't really give a goddamn, but you better keep out of my jail. The deputy went easy with you last night, and that's pretty hard for him to do when he runs up against your kind. But the next time I'm going to turn him loose."

"You might also tell your trained sonofabitch that he won't catch me drunk on my hands and knees again, and in the meantime he ought to contact a public defender because I have a notion that he'll need one soon."

The sheriff struck a match on the arm of the chair and lit his cigarette. He puffed on it several times and flicked the match towards the spittoon. The knots and bumps on his face had turned a deeper red.

"I'm just about to take you back to lockdown and leave you there till you find some other smart-ass lawyer to get you out."

"No, you're not, because you've already been through my wallet and you saw a couple of cards in there with names of men who could have a sheriff dropped right off the party ticket."

"I'll tell you something. Tonight I'm going out on patrol myself, and if I catch you anywhere in the county you're going to get educated downstairs and piss blood before you're through. Pick up your stuff and get out of here."

"What's the bail on the others?"

"Twenty-five dollars a head, and you can have all the niggers and pepper-bellies and hippies you want. Then I'll get my trusties to hose down the cells."

I picked up my billfold from his desk and put four one-hundred-dollar bills before him.

"That ought to cover it, and some of your water bill, too," I said.

He figured on a scratch pad with a broken pencil for a moment, smoking the saliva-stained cigarette between his lips.

"No, we owe you fifty dollars, Mr. Holland, and we want to be sure you get everything coming to you." He opened his desk drawer and counted out the money from a cash box and handed it to me. "Just sign the receipt and you can collect the whole bunch of them and play sticky finger in that union hall till tonight, then I'll be down there and we can talk it over again if you're still around."

"I don't believe you'll be that anxious to talk when you and your deputy and I meet again."

"I'm going to let them people out myself. Don't be here when I get back," he said. He stood up and dropped his cigarette into the spittoon. His flat blue eyes, staring out of that red, knotted face, looked like whorls of swimming color without pupils. He stuck his shirt inside his trousers with the flat of his hand and walked past me with the khaki stiffness of a man who had once more restored structure to his universe.

I sat down in a chair and put my boots on. They were filled with small rocks and mud, and when I stood up again I felt the dizziness and nausea start. I wiped the sweat off my face with my shirt and I wondered how in God's name I could have ever become involved in a fool's situation like this. I was glad there were no reflecting windows or glass doors or mirrors in the sheriff's office, because I was sure that the present image of Hackberry Holland—ripped silk shirt, mud-streaked trousers, swollen temple and blood-matted hair, and face white with concussion and hangover—wouldn't help me resolve my torn concept of self.

I walked outside into the sunlight to wait for Rie. The sun and shadow sliced in patterns across the lawn, and a warm breeze from the river carried with it the smell of the fields. I sat on the concrete steps and let the heat bake into my skin. My clothes and body reeked of the jail, and the odor became stronger as I started to perspire. Two women passing on the sidewalk looked at me in disgust. "Good morning. How are you ladies today?" I said, and their eyes snapped straight ahead.

A few minutes later Rie and the others came out the front door. The faces of the Mexicans were lined and bloated with hangover, and the guitar player and college boy looked like definitions of death. Their faces were perfectly white, as though all the blood had been drawn out through a tube. Rie carried her sandals in her hand, and she looked as lovely and alive as a flower turning into the sun.

"Thanks for going the bail," she said.

"I'll mark it off on my expense account as part of my expanded education. Right now I need to pick up my car, unless our deputy friend set fire to it last night."

"Rafael's brother has a truck at the fruit stand. He'll take us back."

"Yeah, I don't think I could walk too far this morning," I said.

"Say, man, you really took on that bastard, didn't you?" the college boy said. His face was so wan that his lips moved as though they were set in colorless wax.

"Afraid not," I said. "It was a one-sided encounter."

We started walking across the lawn towards the open-air market. My head ached with each step.

"No, man, it takes balls to go up against a prick like that," he said.

"Stupidity is probably a better word," I said.

The shade was cool under the trees, and mockingbirds flew through the branches overhead. Across the street a Mexican was wetting down the rows of watermelons in the bins with a hose. Their fat green shapes were beaded with light in the sun. We crossed the street like the ragged remnant of a guerrilla band, and people in passing automobiles twisted their faces around and stuck their heads out of windows at this strange element in the midst of their tranquil Tuesday morning world.

One of the Mexicans and Rie and I got into the

cab of a pickup truck and the others climbed in
back, and we headed into the poor district. The
driver pulled out a half-pint of Four Roses from under the seat and took a drink with one hand on the
steering wheel. His face shook with the taste. Then
he took three more swallows like he was forcing
down hair tonic, and offered the bottle to me.

"Not today," I said.

He screwed the cap on and passed the bottle out
the window of the cab to one of his friends in back.
The bottle went from hand to hand until it was
empty, then the Negro banged on the roof when
we passed the first clapboard beer tavern on the
road. He and the Mexicans piled out and went in
the screen door, pulling nickels, dimes, and quarters
from their bluejeans. Before the truck started up
again I could already hear their laughter from inside.

The driver dropped the rest of us off at the union
hall. My Cadillac was powdered with white dust so
thick that I couldn't see inside the windows.

"Come in and I'll put something on your head,"
Rie said. The truck rattled back down the road towards the tavern.

"Unless I figured that sheriff wrong, he's already
been to the hotel and my suitcase is waiting for me
on the front step."

"Your eye is starting to close."

"I keep a couple of glass spares in my glove compartment."

She put her arm through mine and moved towards the porch.

"All right, no protest," I said.

"I thought he'd killed you."

"I don't believe you're a hard girl after all."

"Your eyelids turned blue. I even cried to make that asshole take you into emergency receiving, and he shot me the finger."

"Don't worry. I'm going to make this fellow's life a little more interesting for him in the next few weeks."

"I didn't think you believed in charging the barricade."

"I don't. There's always ten others like him who'll crawl out of the woodwork to take his place, but you can't fool with the Lone Ranger and Tonto and walk away from it."

We went inside, and I sat in a chair while she washed the lump on my head with soap and water. The tips of her fingers were as light as wind on the bruised skin.

"There's pieces of rock and dirt in the cut. I'll have to get them out with the tweezers," she said. "You should go to the hospital and get a couple of stitches."

"Do you have a quart of milk in your icebox?"

She went into the kitchen and came back with a carton of buttermilk and a pair of tweezers in a glass of alcohol. I drank the carton half empty in one long chugging swallow, and for just a moment the thick cream felt like cool air and health and sunshine transfused into my body, then she started picking out the pieces of rock from the cut with the edge of the tweezers. Each alcohol nick made the skin around my eye flex and pucker.

"Goddamn, what are you doing? I don't need a lobotomy."

"You probably don't need blood poisoning, either." Her eyes were concentrated with each metallic scratch against my skin.

"Look, let me have the tweezers and give me a mirror. I used to be a pretty fair hospital corpsman."

"Don't move your head. I almost have it all out." She bit her lip and squeezed out a splinter of rock from under the cut with her finger. "There."

Then she rubbed a cotton pad soaked with alcohol over the lump.

"Listen, goddamn it, there's other ways to clean a cut. They ought to give first-aid courses in the Third World before you kill somebody with shock."

"Wait a minute," she said, and went into the kitchen again and returned with a piece of ice wrapped in a clean dish towel. She held it against my head, her almond eyes still fixed with a child's concern.

"A cold compress can't do any good after the first two hours," I said.

"What was that Bean Camp stuff about last night?"

"Nothing. I create things in my head when I try to run up Jack Daniels' stock a couple of points."

"Were you in a prison camp during the war?"

"No."

The whiskey edge was starting to wear off, and gray worms and spots of light swam before my eyes when I tried to stand up. She pressed her hand down on my shoulder.

"You ought to pull the fish hooks out. You're all flames inside," she said.

"I feel like I've been dismantled twice in three days, and I'm not up to psychoanalysis right now. It seems that every goddamn time my brain is bleeding someone starts boring into my skull with the brace and bit."

"Okay, man, I'm sorry."

"I've got a brother that can make you grind your teeth down to the nerve with that same type of morning-after insight. There's nothing like it to send me right through the goddamn wall."

"So I won't say anything else," she said.

I felt myself trembling inside, as though all the wheels and gears were starting to shear off against one another at once. My palms were sweating on my knees, and I realized that my real hangover was just beginning.

"Let me have one of your cigarettes," I said.

She laid the ice compress down, lit a cigarette, and put it in my mouth. The smoke was raw in my throat, and a drop of sweat rolled off my lip onto the paper.

"Does it always take you like that?" she said.

"No, only when I'm stupid enough to get my head kicked in by a redneck cop."

I smoked the cigarette and exhaled slowly, while my temple and eye beat with pain, then pushed the sweat back into my hair with one hand.

"Look, you're not a drinker, so you don't know the alcoholic syndrome," I said. "I'm not a shithead all the time."

"Sit down. Your cut is bleeding."

"I'm going down the road. I'll take a couple of those hot beers with me if you don't mind."

My legs were weak, and the blood seemed to drain downward in my body with the effort of standing.

"You can't drive anywhere now."

"Watch."

"You're pulling a dumb scene."

I started towards the counter where the remaining bottles of Jax stood, and a yellow wave of nausea went through me. The sour taste of buttermilk and last night's whiskey came up in my throat, and I felt a great throbbing weight on my forehead. My cigarette was wet down to the ash from the sweat running off my face.

"Goddamn, I really got one this time," I said.

"Come in the back," she said, and put her arm around my waist. My shirt stuck wetly against my skin.

We went down the hallway through a side door into a small bedroom. The shade on the window was torn, and strips of broken sunlight struck across the floor. An old crucifix was nailed against one wall above a Catholic religious calendar with two withered palms stuck under the top edges. I drew in on the dead cigarette and gagged in the back of my throat. You've just about made the d.t.'s this time, I thought. Work on it again and you'll really get there.

My body felt as rigid as a snapped twig. She pressed me down on the edge of the bed with her hands and turned on an electric fan. The current of air was like wind blowing over ice against my face.

"Lie down and I'll put a dressing on your cut," she said.

Something was rolling loose inside me, and my fingers were shaking on my knees.

"Look, you don't need—"

"Lie down, Lone Ranger." Then she leaned over me with her breasts heavy against her blouse, her brown face and wild curly hair a dark silhouette above me, and pressed me back into the pillow.

She rubbed ointment on the cut in a circular motion with her fingers and taped a piece of gauze over it. I could feel the heat of the sun in her skin and hair, and her eyes were filled with a dark shine. I touched the smoothness of her arm with my hand, then the light began to fade beyond the window shade, the fan blew cool over my chest and face, and somewhere out in the hills a train whistle echoed and beat thinly into a brass sky. I heard her close the door softly as on the edge of a dream.

It was afternoon when I awoke, and the wind was blowing hard against the building. The shade flapped back from the window, rattling against the woodwork, and dustdevils spun in the air outside. The boards in the floor quivered from the gusts of wind under the building, and there were grains of sand on my skin. My head was dizzy when I stood up, my face tingling, and I could taste the hot dryness of the air in my mouth. I tripped over the fan and opened the door to the hallway. The sudden draft tore the religious calendar and withered palms from the wall, and the mobile made from beer bottles clattered and twisted in circles on the ceiling in the main room. I leaned against the doorjamb in the numbness of awaking from afternoon sleep. Through the front screen I could see the clouds of dust blowing along the street into the trees. I heard Rie walk out of the kitchen towards me. She held a tall glass of ice water in her hand, and she had put on a pair of white shorts and a navy denim shirt. There were freckles on the tops of her bare feet.

"How do you feel?" she said.

"I'll let you know in a minute." I took the glass of ice water from her hand and drank it down to the bottom. I didn't believe that I had ever been so thirsty. The coldness ached inside my empty stomach.

"You have bad dreams," she said.

"Yeah, I've got a whole wheelbarrow full of them." I walked past her into the kitchen and put my head under the iron pump. I worked the handle, and the water poured over my neck and shoulders and inside my shirt. I wiped my face slick with the palm of my hand. Down the slope the Rio Grande was rippled and dented by the wind. The brown current was turning white around the wreck of the submerged car.

"You can stay here. You don't have to go back today," she said.

"I'd better hit it."

"Wait until the wind storm passes."

"They don't pass this time of year. That's a three-day affair out there." The water dripped off my clothes onto the floor.

"You can't see out of your eye."

"I sight with one eye over my Cadillac hood just like a pistol barrel," I said.

"I'll ride to the hotel with you."

"No, the sheriff will probably be hanging around there somewhere. I think you've had enough innings with a lefthanded pitcher for one day."

The building shook in the wind, and pieces of newspaper blew by the window. Across the river two Mexican children were leading a flat-sided, mange-scarred cow off the mud bank into a shed. Her swollen, red udder swung under her belly.

"I don't want to see you get busted again," Rie said.

"You take care, babe." I put my hands on her shoulders and kissed her on the cheek. For just an instant the nipples of her breasts touched me and I turned to water inside. Her mouth and eyes made my heart race. "I expect I'll be back here eventually and try to do something for that yankee mind of yours."

"Be careful with yourself, Hack."

I walked out into the dust and drove to the hotel. Leaves were shredding from the trees on the court-

house lawn and blowing along the sidewalk. An
empty tomato basket bounced end over end in the
middle of the street, and the wood sign over the
hotel slammed back and forth on its iron hooks.
The fat deputy who had let me out of the cell that
morning sat in the swing on the verandah with his
feet propped against the railing. He looked off casually at the yellow sky when I passed him, his huge
stomach bursting against his shirt buttons.

"Mr. Holland, we'll be needing your room tonight," the desk clerk said inside. His eyes were
focused about three inches to the side of my face,
then they would flick temporarily across the bridge
of my nose and back again to a spot on the far
wall.

"By God, that's right, isn't it?" I said. "The Cat-
tlemen's Association is holding its world convention here this week."

My room had been cleaned, the bed made, the
empty beer bottles carried out, as though I had
never been there, and my suitcase was packed and
closed and sitting just inside the door, ready to be
picked up in one convenient motion. Someone had
even put a Gideon Bible on the dresser top.

I paid my bill at the desk, and the clerk managed
to show me nothing but the crown of his head
while he marked off the ticket and counted out my
change.

"You don't sell cigars in here, do you?" I said.

He fumbled in the middle of his counting, his eyelids blinking nervously, and I thought I had him, but he regained his resolve and kept his eyes nailed to the counter. "No sir, but you can get them right next door," he said, and turned away to the cash register.

I started down the steps to my car, then I heard the swing flop back empty on its chains and the boards of the porch bend under the deputy's massive weight. Shit, what a time not to have a cigar, I thought.

"Mr. Holland, the sheriff wanted me to give you this road map," he said, pulling it out of the back pocket of his khaki trousers. The paper was pressed into an arc from the curve of his buttocks. "He don't want you to get lost nowhere on that highway construction before you get into the next county."

"I guess that would be easy to do unless I had a map. Say, you don't smoke cigars, do you?" I said. "Let me get a Camel from you, then."

His eyes looked at me uncomprehendingly out of his white volleyball face. His greased black hair, combed over the balding pate, had grains of sand in it. He pulled a cigarette out of his shirt pocket with two fingers and handed it to me.

"This is goddamn nice of you and the sheriff, and

I appreciate it." I borrowed his lighter, which had a Confederate flag on the side of it, and lit the cigarette. "Look, I've got two lifetime World Rodeo Association passes that I never use. They're good for box seats at any livestock show or ass-buster in the state. Here, you take them."

I pulled the two thick, cardboard passes from my billfold and stuck them in his shirt pocket.

"Well, thank you, Mr. Holland," he said.

I went next door to the tavern, bought a box of cigars and a six-pack of cold Jax, and headed down the road in the blowing clouds of dust, the corn stalks rattling in the wind, the gold of the citrus exposed among the swelling green trees, and each time I made a curve between two hills at ninety miles an hour I felt the old omnipotence vibrate smoothly out of the engine through the steering column into my hands. The fields of cotton, watermelons, and tomatoes flashed by me, and the late sun splintered in shafts of light through the dust clouds and struck on the tops of the hills in soft areas of pale green and shadow. Then the country began to become more level, the twilight took on all the violent purple and yellow colors of an apocalypse, and I felt the wind driving with me eastward down a narrow blacktop highway that stretched endlessly across empty land towards the gathering darkness on the horizon.

CHAPTER

FIVE

The poplar trees along my front lane were bent in the wind when I got back to the ranch that night. Under the full moon their shadows beat on the white gravel, and the air was full of swirling rose petals from Verisa's gardens. Someone had forgotten to chain the windmill by the barn, and the blades were spinning in a circle of tinny light while the water overflowed from the trough onto the ground. I could see the dark shapes of ruined tomatoes lying in the rows, and some of the cotton had started to strip. Then I saw Sailor Boy, my Tennessee walking horse that I had bought from Spendthrift Farm for six thousand dollars, knocking against the rails in the lot. His nostrils were dilated, his black head shiny with moonlight and fear, and he was running in a broken gait against each of the rick fence corners, rearing his head and kicking dirt and manure in the air. I climbed into the lot with him, worked him back easy against the rails with both my arms outspread, and got a halter over his head. There was a four-inch cut in one flank, and he had broken a shoe and splintered part of a hoof against the barn wall. I led him into a stall, slipped an oats bag over his ears, pulled the rest of the shoe, and dressed the ragged split in his skin. Then I went into the house, my blood roaring.

Verisa was reading a book under a lamp in the living room. She wore her nightgown, and she had two curlers set in the front of her hair. A cigarette was burned down to its filter in the ashtray. She had the nocturnal, isolated composure of a woman who might have lived by herself all her life.

"Question number one: who in the hell left Sailor Boy out in the lot?" I said.

She turned and looked at me, and her face whitened under the lamp.

"What—" I saw her eyes trying to adjust on the swollen side of my head.

"Who left my goddamn horse out in a wind storm?"

"Hack, what in God's name have you done now?"

"I want to know which idiot or combination of idiots left my horse to tear himself up in the lot."

"I don't know. Why don't you stay home and take care of him yourself?"

"The perfect non-think answer. If his gait is thrown off I'm going to set fire to somebody's hair."

"You'd better not be talking about me."

"Read it like you want. It takes a special type of fool to do something that stupid to a fine horse."

"You just stop your shouting at me."

"I'll crack the goddamn ceiling if I want. And as long as we're on it, question number two: who forgot to chain the windmill? Which might strike you as a minor thing to consider between book pages, but right now our water table is almost dry and there are some crops that have a tendency to burn when they're not irrigated."

"I'm getting sick of this," she said.

"I'm not asking you to walk around in the manure with a cattle prod in your hand. I'd just like you to stick your head out the door occasionally and make sure the whole goddamn place hasn't blown away."

"I don't know where your present adventure took you, but you must have damaged some of the brain tissue. I'm going to bed. If you want to shout some more, either close the door or go down the road to your tavern."

"Don't you know what it means to hurt a horse like that?"

"Good night, Hack."

She set her book down with a marker between the pages and walked past me in her best remote fashion. Her blue nightgown swirled around her legs in a whisper of silk, then she closed the door behind her. I had a drink out of the decanter on the bar, while my chest rose and fell with my breathing. Outside, the trees scratched against the house, and the door on the barn loft kept slamming like a tack hammer in the wind.

In the morning I went to the office in Austin and began work on Art's appeal. I was supposed to help Bailey that week on two large insurance suits, but after he had recovered from staring at my bandaged head and the swollen corner of my eye under my sunglasses, I told him that he would have to carry it alone for a few days. He was still angry from the weekend, and now his exasperation with his younger brother almost made his eyes cross. He sat with one thigh over the corner of my desk, his hands folded, straining like a stoic to retain his patience, while each word tripped out like an expression from a peptic ulcer.

"This is a two-hundred-thousand-dollar deal, Hack," he said. "We waited on it for six months."

"So I'll pick it up next week."

"We're going to try to settle next week."

"They're not going to settle. Forget it. We'll be in court a year."

"Give that case to the A.C.L.U. They handle them all the time."

"I just want three goddamn uninterrupted days."

"Even if you win appeal, you won't get him out of prison on bond."

"I might if I can get some work done and be let alone for any random period of time."

"What happened in Pueblo Verde?"

"You won't buy a car accident, will you? All right, a peckerwood cop kicked the hell out of me and I spent a night in a drunk tank. I was also indirectly presented with a map from the sheriff so I could find my way out of the county. In the meantime I managed to get a dozen other people arrested. Lastly, I'm going to write off their bail on my expense account. Now you can worry about the wire services picking up a sweet piece of interesting journalism on a congressional candidate. Does that make your day any better?"

"I don't believe you."

"I have a receipt for the bail if you would like to look at it."

His stomach swelled as he drew in on his dead pipe. It made a sound that hurt something in the inner ear. His vexed, almost desperate eyes focused out the window. Then his control began to slip, the anger and impotence rose in his face, and he ranted for fifteen minutes in clichés about responsibilities, major accounts, a judge who said that he never wanted me in his chambers again, my career in politics (and its profitable effects on our law practice), and my pending trip to Walter Reed Hospital with Senator Dowling.

"Oh, that's right," I said. "We view the Claymore mine and AK-47 cases this weekend. Why don't you come along, Bailey? You missed the Korean show. These guys are a blast."

He slammed the door behind him, and I lit a cigar and looked up at the picture of Old Hack and my father on the wall. In the faded photograph, now yellow around the edges, his black eyes still burned from his face, which had begun to grow soft and childlike in his old age. His eyes turned directly into mine as I moved the swivel chair in either direction. They were like shattered obsidian, filled with fire and the quiet intensity of a leveled rifle. His bobbed hair was as white as his starched shirt, and his stiff black coat looked as though a pistol ball would flatten out against it. Next to him, my father's gentle face and straw skimmer and summer suit made me think of two strangers who had met in the middle of an empty field and had decided to have their picture taken together.

I worked the next three days on the appeal with an energy and freshness that I hadn't felt in years. In fact, I even felt like a criminal lawyer again rather than an expensive manipulator for the R. C. Richardson account. My bottle of Jack Daniels stayed in the desk drawer, and I came to the office at seven in the morning and stayed until dusk. As I said before, the appeal should have been a foregone conclusion, but I began to wonder if any judge in the Austin court would believe that so many absurdities could have actually taken place in one trial. Moreover, each time I went through the transcript I didn't believe it myself. Thursday afternoon, after I'd had the secretary in my office for five hours of dictation and typing, Bailey's patience cracked apart again and he came suddenly through the door, his face stretched tight with anger. (The air conditioner was broken, and we had the windows over the street open. The hot air was like warm water in the room.)

"All right, you can let two hundred thousand dollars go to hell, but I'm still paying half the overhead around here," he said.

"Bailey, look at this goddamn thing, then tell me that I ought to let this guy sit it out in the pen while some kid lawyer from the A.C.L.U. plays pocket pool with himself."

"I don't want to look at it. I have a desk covered with twice my ordinary load of work."

"Then have a drink of water. You look hot."

"Goddamn it, Hack, you're putting me over the edge."

"I just want you to glance at what can happen in a legal court without one voice being raised in protest."

"What did you expect to find down there? Those union people knew the terms when they came in here."

"I think I heard a deputy sheriff say about the same thing while he was pouring his mouth full of chewing tobacco."

And once more Bailey slammed out the door, a furious man who would never understand the real reasons for his anger.

I spent Friday night in an Austin motel, and Saturday morning I met the Senator's private plane at the airport. I stood on the hot concrete by the terminal in my white suit, and watched the plane tilt across the sky and approach the runway, its wings and propellers awash with sunlight. One wing lifted upward momentarily in the wind, then balanced again, and the wheels touched on the asphalt as smoothly as a soft slipper. The heat waves bounced off the fuselage, and the sun turned the front windows into mirrors exploding with light. At the end of the runway the pilot feathered one engine and taxied at an angle towards me, and I saw the Senator open the back door and wave one arm, his face smiling.

I walked to the plane, and the backdraft from the propeller blew the tail of my coat over my shoulders. The Senator was grinning in the roar, and he extended his hand and helped me into the compartment. I pulled the door shut after me, locked the handle down, and the plane began to taxi out on the main runway again. The Senator was dressed in slacks, a Hawaiian sports shirt, and calfskin loafers. There was fresh tan on his face and a few freckles along the hair line of his white, crew-cropped head. In the opposite seat, with a drink resting on his crossed knee, was a man whom I didn't know, although I sensed at the time that I probably would never forget him. He wore a charcoal business suit, silk shirt with cuff links, a gray tie, and his face was pale and expressionless behind his sunglasses. The mouth was small and compressed, as though he never spoke except with a type of quiet finality, and his manicured, half-moon fingernails and confident reserve reminded me of a very successful corporation executive, but there was something about the hue of his skin and the trace of talcum powder on his neck that darkened the image.

"Hack, this is John Williams, an old friend from Los Angeles," the Senator said.

We shook hands, and I felt the coldness in his palm from the highball glass.

"How do you do," he said. Only the mouth moved when he spoke. The face remained as immobile as plastic. He pushed his smoky, metallic hair back on one temple with his fingertips.

The plane gained speed, the engines roaring faster, then it lifted off the runway, and I felt the weightless, empty feeling of dropping unexpectedly in an elevator as the countryside spread out below us and the blocks of neat houses and rows of trees seemed to shrink away into the earth.

John Williams, I thought. The name. Where?

"What happened to your head?" the Senator said. "I hope you haven't run into another tennis player with a bad aim."

"A minor car accident." *You shithead*, I thought.

"Well, John, this man is going to be the youngest congressman from the state in November."

Williams nodded and took a sip from his drink. I tried to see his eyes through his sunglasses. John Williams, goddamn, where did I see it?

"John's not from Texas, but he's a good friend to the party."

"I see," I said.

"I've had him at the ranch for a few days of shooting. I'm trying to convince him that the only place to build industry today is in the Southwest."

"A beautiful state," Williams said. His face was turned to me, but it was impossible to read his meaning or intention.

"Do you mind if I have a drink?" I said.

"I'm sorry, Hack. I usually don't drink this early myself, and I forget that other people don't have my same Baptist instincts." The Senator opened the cabinet door to the bar and folded out a small table from the wall. He picked up three cubes from the ice bucket with the tongs and dropped them into a tall glass and poured in a shot of bourbon.

"I was glad to see you at the airport," he said. "I thought maybe we were too forceful last Sunday in getting you to come along."

"Oh, I keep my promises, Senator."

"We'll only be there a short while. A couple of the state news services will meet us at the hospital, and then we'll have dinner and take off again this evening."

"News services?" I said.

"Yes, the local ones. They usually like to cover this sort of thing for the state television stations."

"I didn't know about that."

"I see you're a bit new to politics," Williams said. There was just a touch of a smile at the corner of his mouth, a faint wrinkle in the plastic skin.

"No, no, Hack's father was a congressman. In fact, a very fine one. It's just that Hack had some private reservations at first about visiting Walter Reed."

"Why's that, Mr. Holland?"

"I suppose it's connected with superstition. You know, bad luck," I said.

"Really?" The skin wrinkled again at the corner of his mouth, and he clinked the ice in his glass. I felt the pulse begin to swell in my neck.

"Probably a silly thing, but I never found much pleasure in visiting a veterans' ward," I said.

Williams' face remained opaque as he looked at me, but I saw one finger tighten on his glass.

"Maybe it's something about the smell of a dressing on a burn. I really couldn't tell you," I said.

He continued to stare at me, and I knew that behind those sunglasses his eyes were burning into mine.

"How about another drink, John?"

"I'm fine."

"I suppose I shouldn't have brought it up. Actually, Hack was wounded in Korea and spent some time in the V.A. after the war."

"Is that right, Mr. Holland?"

"It wasn't of much consequence. A flesh wound. The John Wayne variety," I said.

"It was a little more serious than that," the Senator said.

"I'd like to talk with you about your experiences

sometime," Williams said. His voice was as dry as paper.

"They're not very interesting, but anytime you're passing through DeWitt County on your way between Washington and L.A., we'll sure crack a couple of bottles."

"You'll see John at my ranch. He visits often," the Senator said. "Your glass is empty, Hack."

I wouldn't have believed it, but the Senator was uncomfortable. His acetylene-blue eyes were bright, and his easy laugh had a fine wire of strain in it. He poured another shot in my glass and pressed the stopper hard in the bottle neck with his thumb. And I began to feel that John Williams was a much more formidable person than I had realized.

"If you continue in politics I'm sure we'll see a lot more of each other," Williams said. I could almost taste the bile in his teeth. "It looks like your career is going to be a very good one."

"I expect that's one of those things you never know about."

"I wouldn't say that."

Again, I couldn't tell if there was a second meaning in what he said, or if he used deliberate vagueness to keep his opposition full of unspoken question marks. But I did know that the Senator was still sitting a bit forward in his seat, and his thigh muscles were tensed under the crease of his trousers. Yes, there's a real lesson in this, I thought. Even the predators sometimes have to lie under the reef while the shadows of much larger fish move through the dark waters overhead. I lit my first cigar of the day and squinted at the Senator and Williams through the smoke, and I wondered what umbilical cord connected them.

I didn't say anything else that would test that delicate pattern of membrane behind the Senator's healthy smile, and Williams sensed that the match was over. He set his drink on the table, folded his hands on his knee, and looked out the window like a withdrawn demiurge at the pools of fire in the clouds.

Three hours later I was on my fourth bourbon and water as we began our approach to Dulles Airport.

The air in Washington was humid and hazy with smog. There had been rioting in the Negro district off Pennsylvania Avenue during the week, and from the plane I had seen plumes of smoke blowing across the blocks of red-brick tenement buildings towards the Capitol and the Lincoln Memorial, that island of green and marble and blue water in the center of a colossal slum. Now, standing on the drive among the potted plants in front of the terminal, I could smell just the hint of burned wood in the air, and my eyes watered in the yellow pall that hung over everything in sight.

The Senator's chauffeured Cadillac limousine picked us up, and on the way to Walter Reed I fixed another drink from the portable bar built into the back of the driver's seat. The Senator didn't like it, but he confined his objection to a steady look at the amount of bourbon in my glass. Williams sat silently on the fold-out seat, his back straight and his face turned indifferently to the window; however, I could feel his sense of superiority in the knowledge that I was starting in heavy on the whiskey. That's all right, motherfucker, I thought. Wes Hardin and I will kick your ass any day in the light-year you want to choose.

Two television newsmen from Houston and Fort Worth were waiting for us by the information desk in the main room of the hospital. They were both young, dressed in narrow-cut suits and knitted neckties and button-down collars, and their hair looked as though it were trimmed every day. They had been leaning against the counter with their cameras hanging loosely in their hands, and when they saw the Senator they snapped into motion and came towards us with their leather soles clicking on the marble floor. Their college-boy faces showed the proper deference and energetic respect, and I thought, *ahhh*, there are two young men who will never live within breathing distance of the Fort Worth stockyards.

Three hospital administrators joined us, and we began our tour of the wards holding the Viet Nam wounded. I had a fair edge on from the whiskey, but now I wished that I had made a bigger dent in the bottle. The beds, with high metal rails on the sides, stretched out in long rows, and the afternoon sun slanted across the bodies of the men under the sheets. I had made a cynical remark to Williams about the smell of a dressing on a burn, but that was only part of it. The astringent odor of the antiseptic used to scrub the floors mixed with the reek of the bedpans, the sweaty and itching flesh inside the plaster casts, the urine that sometimes dried in the mattress pads of the paraplegics, and the salve oozing from bandages that covered rows of hard stitches. There was another odor in the air, too, one that might be called imaginary, but I could smell the distant rain forests and the sores that formed on men's bodies from living in wet uniforms and in boots that hardened like iron around the feet. The stench of terror and dried excrement on the buttocks was there, also, and if you wanted to think hard on it you could fill your lungs and catch the sweet-sour gray smell of death.

The Senator shook hands cheerfully from bed to

bed, and each time he found a man from Texas he made several banal remarks while the cameras whirred away. A few of the men were bored or irritated at seeing another politician, but the majority of them grinned with their boyish, old men's faces, propped themselves up on their elbows with cigarettes between their fingers, and listened to the Senator's thanks about the job they were doing. Only one time did he have trouble, and that was with a Negro Marine who'd had an arm amputated at the shoulder. The Negro's eyes were bloodshot, and I saw a bottle of paregoric sticking out from under his pillow.

"Don't thank me for nothing, *man*," he said. "When I get out of here you better hide that pink ass behind a wall."

The cameras stopped whirring, and the Senator smiled and walked to the next bed as though the Negro and his anger were there only as the result of some chance accident not worth considering seriously. Then the cameras started working again, the two newsmen were back to their coverage, and the Marine pulled out his bottle of paregoric and unscrewed the cap by flipping it around with one thumb. His bloodshot eyes continued to stare into the Senator's back.

At the end of each ward the Senator made a speech, and I wondered how many times he had made it in the same wards during World War II and the Korean War. He had probably changed some of the language to suit the particular cause and geographic conquest involved, but the content must have been the same: The people at home support you boys. We're proud of the American fighting man and the sacrifices he's made to defend democracy against Communist aggression. You've taken up the standard that can only be held by the brave, and we're not going to let anyone dishonor that standard. It's been bought at too dear a price. . . .

And on and on.

As I watched him I remembered sitting in a similar ward in 1953 after the last pieces of splintered lead had been removed from my legs, and listening to a state representative make almost the same speech. I didn't remember his name, or even what he looked like, but he and the Senator were much alike, because in the intense emotional moment of their delivery they believed they had fought the same battles as the men lying before them, felt the same aching lung-rushing gasp when they were hit, bled into the same dark soil, and had fallen through the same endless morphine deliriums in a battalion aid station.

But the Senator had one better. After all the

hackneyed patriotic justifications for losing part of one's life, he outdid himself:

"I bet you boys aren't burning your draft cards!"

And they replied in unison, one hundred strong: "NO SIR!"

The Senator went through the doorway with the three hospital administrators, who all the time had been smiling as though they were showing off a nursery of hot-house plants, and one of the newsmen turned his camera on me.

"Get that goddamn thing out of my face," I said.

He didn't hear me over the electric noise of his machine, or he didn't believe what he'd heard, and he kept the lens pointed at the center of my forehead.

"I mean it, pal. I'll break it against the wall."

He lowered his camera slowly with his mouth partly open and stared at me. He didn't know what he had done wrong, and all the reasons for his presence there in the hospital were evaporating before him. I don't know what my face looked like then, with the cut on my temple and my slightly swollen eye, but evidently it was enough to make a graduate of the Texas University School of Journalism wince. He dropped his eyes to the camera and began adjusting the lens as though the light had changed in the last ten seconds.

"I had a car accident this week and I don't want any of the guys at the country club thinking my wife hit me in the head with a shoe," I said. I laughed and touched him on the arm.

He smiled, and I saw that his pasteboard frame of reference was secure again. He walked into the next ward after the Senator, and I thought, I hope that thirty-thousand-dollar house in the Fort Worth suburbs will be worth it all, buddy.

Later, back in the Cadillac, with the sun steaming off the hood, I poured a half glass of straight bourbon and took two deep swallows. The yellow haze outside was worse now, and the air-conditioning vents were dripping with moisture.

"That Negro soldier should be brought to the attention of his commanding officer," Williams said.

"He was a Marine," I said.

"Regardless, there's no excuse for a remark like that," he said.

So you're a propriety man as well, I thought.

"It's nothing," the Senator said. "His attitudes will change back to normal with time. I've seen many others like him."

"I didn't like it," Williams said.

"Maybe he doesn't care to be part of the science of prosthesis," I said. "Provided they can fit something on that stub."

Williams looked at me steadily with his opaque,

pale face. For just a second his fingertips ticked on his thigh. I knew that if I could have looked into his eyes I would have seen flames and grotesque mouths wide with silent screams.

"Do you like that brand of bourbon, Mr. Holland? I'd like to send you a case of it," he said.

"Thanks. I'm a Jack Daniels man myself, and I get it on order straight from Lynchburg."

"You must have a very good relationship with the whiskey manufacturers, then."

I smoked a cigar and finished my drink in silence while we moved through the late traffic towards the downtown district. When I noticed that Williams was irritated by the smoke I made a point of leaving the cigar butt only partly extinguished in the ashtray. Originally, the Senator had planned for the three of us to have dinner together, one of those charcoal steak and white linen and pleasant conversation affairs that the Senator was fond of; but now it was understood between us that Williams should be dropped off at the Hilton, where he kept a permanent suite.

He stepped out of the car on the sidewalk and bent over to shake hands with me through the open door. In the hot air there was a tinge of his perspiration mixed with the scent of talcum and cologne. The shadow of the building made his skin look synthetic and dead. His sunglasses tipped forward a moment, and I caught a flash of color like burned iron.

"Another time, Mr. Holland."

"Yes, sir," I said.

We drove to the airport and I waited for the Senator to begin his subtle dissection. I was even looking forward to it. I felt the whiskey in my head now, and I would have liked an extension of last week's tennis match. But he surprised me completely. His attack came down an entirely different street, and I realized then that he probably disliked Williams even more than I did, although for different reasons.

"You weren't in a car accident last week, Hack. You were put in jail with several members of that Mexican farm union."

I had to wait a moment on that one.

"The sheriff could have charged you with attempted assault on a law officer."

"Your office reaches much farther than I thought, Senator."

"You might also know that I made sure the story wouldn't reach the wire services."

"As a long-time friend of our family you probably also know that I've had other adventures of this sort."

"Another one like it could end your career in Texas."

"I don't think either one of us believes that, Senator."

"I'm not talking about a drunken escapade. If you involve yourself with a radical movement, you'll find yourself on the ticket as an independent. The party won't support you. I don't think your father would enjoy the idea of your associating yourself with people who are trying to destroy our society, either."

He was after the vulnerable parts now.

"It always seemed to me that my father's work with the New Deal was considered pretty radical at the time," I said. "However, I don't have any connection with the United Farm Workers. I was trying to help a friend from the service."

The sun was starting to set among the purple clouds on the horizon, and through the car window I could see airplanes approaching Dulles with their landing lights on.

"I think you should turn over your friend's case to someone else."

"Well, in eight years of practice I haven't lost a criminal case, Senator, and I'm usually a pretty good judge about what clients our firm should handle."

"I hope you are, Hack, and I hope that we don't have this same kind of discussion again."

The chauffeur pulled into the terminal drive, and

I went into the restaurant and had a dozen steak sandwiches made up while the Senator waited for me at the passenger gate. His plane taxied out of the hangar and rolled along the apron of the run-way towards us, and in minutes we were back aboard and roaring towards the end of the field.

We lifted off sharply into the sun, the city spar-kling below us in the twilight, and the interior of the plane was filled with a diffused red glow. My glass of bourbon and ice rattled on the table with the engines' vibration.

"Who is he, anyway?" I said.

"John Williams? He owns the controlling stock in two of the government's largest missile sup-pliers."

CHAPTER

SIX

I spent the next week working on Art's appeal while the July days grew hotter and my broken air conditioner cranked and rattled in the window. The temperature went to one hundred degrees every afternoon, and the sky stayed cloudless and brilliant with sun. The sidewalks and buildings were alive with heat, and sometimes when the air conditioner gave out altogether I'd open the window and the wind would blow into my face like a torch. In the street below, people walked under the hot shade of the awnings away from the sun's glare, their faces squinted against the light and their clothes wet with perspiration. The humidity made your skin feel as though it were crawling with spiders, and when you stepped off a curb into the sun the air suddenly had the taste of an electric scorch.

In the evening, when the day had started to cool,
I would drive out into the surrounding hills with
the windows of the car down. (I had taken a hotel
room in town so I could come to the office early
each morning, and also Verisa was holding two
cocktail parties at the house that week, and I wasn't
up to another round of drinking, and the disaster
that always followed, with empty-headed women.)
In the mauve twilight the oak trees and blackjack
took on a deeper green, and deer broke through
the underbrush and ran frightened across the blacktop road in front of my car, their eyes like frozen
brown glass. The air was sweet with the smell of
the hills and woods, and jackrabbits and cottontails
sat in the short grass with their ears folded back
along their flanks. I remembered as a boy how I
used to flush them out of a thicket and then whistle
shrilly through my teeth and wait for them to stop
and look back at me, their ears turned upward in
an exact V. A slight breeze blew through the willows growing along the river bank, and I could see
the bass and bream breaking the water among the
reeds and lily pads. Fishermen in rowboats with fly-
rods glided silently by the willows, casting popping
bugs into the shadows, then the water would ex-
plode and a large-mouth bass would climb into the
air, shaking the hook in the side of his mouth, and

the sun's last rays would flash off his green-silver sides like tinted gold.

One evening, after a flaming day and a one-hour harangue from Bailey about all my deficiencies, I drove down to the Devil's Backbone, a geological fault where the land folded sharply away and you could see fifty miles of Texas all at once. On the top of the ridge, there was a Mexican beer tavern built entirely of flat stones, and as I looked out over the hills at the baked land, the miniature oak trees in the distance, the darkening light in the valleys, and the broken line of fire on the horizon, I felt the breath go out of me and the ground move under my feet. In the wind I could smell the shallow water holes, the hot odor of the mesquite, the carcass of a lost cow that was being pulled apart by buzzards, the wild poppies and bluebonnets, the snakes and the lizards and the dry sand, the moist deer dung in the thickets of blackjack, and the head-reeling resilience of the land itself. I knew that if I stood there long enough, with the shadows spreading across the hills, I would see the ghosts of Apache and Comanche warriors riding their painted horses in single file, their naked bodies hung with scalps and necklaces of human fingers. Or maybe the others who came later, like Bowie and Crockett and Fannin and Milam, with deerskin clothes and powder horn and musket and the self-destructive fury that led them to war against the entire Mexican army.

The stone tavern was cool inside, and the cigarette-burned floor, the yellow mirror behind the bar, the shuffleboard table, and the jukebox with the changing colored lights inside the plastic casing were right out of the 1940's. Cedar-cutters and Mexican farmhands sat at the wooden tables with frosted schooners of beer in their hands, the bartender set down free plates of tortillas, cheese, and hot peppers, and the long-dead voice of Hank Williams rose from the jukebox. The last cinder of the sun faded outside, bugs beat against the screen door, and a brown moon sat low over the hills. I ordered a plate of tacos and a draft beer and watched two cedar-cutters sliding the metal puck through the powdered wax on the shuffleboard. For some reason the Mexican farmhands kept toasting me with their glasses every time they drank, so I bought a round for three tables, and that was the beginning of a good beer drunk.

The next morning I drove to the state penitentiary with my head still full of beer and jukebox music. The blacktop highway stretched through the rolling hills of red clay and cotton and pine trees, and my tires left long lines in the soft tar surfacing. The smell of the Piney Woods was sharp in the heat, and thin cattle grazed in the fields of burned grass. The rivers were almost dry, the sand-bars like strips of bleached bone, and flocks of buzzards turned in slow circles over the woods. The corn had started to burn on the edges, and in two more weeks, with no rain, the stalks would wither and the ears would lie rotting in the rows.

As I approached the city limits I saw all the familiar warning signs for this world and the next posted along the roadside:

DO NOT PICK UP HITCHHIKERS
STATE PENITENTIARY NEARBY

PREPARE TO MEET THY GOD

SAVE AMERICA AND
IMPEACH EARL WARREN

JESUS DIED FOR YOU
HAVE YOU BEEN SAVED

DON'T WORRY
THEY'RE ONLY NINETY MILES AWAY.

And farther on, in a happier mood,

DON'T FAIL TO SEE THE HOME OF SAM
HOUSTON AND JACK'S SNAKE FARM

I stopped at the main gate of the prison and showed my identification to the guard. He wore a khaki uniform and a lacquered straw hat, and his hands and face were tanned the color of old leather. One jaw was swollen with chewing tobacco, and after he had looked at my Texas Bar Association card he spat a stream of brown juice through the rails of the cattleguard, wiped the stain off the corner of his mouth, and handed me a cardboard visitor's pass with the date punched at the bottom.

"Don't try to drive back out till the gate man goes through your car," he said.

The main complex of buildings was at the end of a yellow gravel road that wound through acres of cotton and string beans. The inmates, in white uniforms, were chopping in the rows, their hoes rising and flashing in the sun, while the guards sat on horseback above them with rifles or shotguns balanced across their saddles. The sun was straight up in the sky, and I could see the dark areas of sweat in the guards' clothes and the flush of heat in the inmates' faces. Except for the motion of the hoes, or a horse slashing his tail against the green flies on his flanks, they all seemed frozen, removed, in the private ritual that exists between jailer and prisoner. Sometimes a trusty, sharpening tools in the shade of the cedar trees at the edge of the field, would carry a water bucket out to the men in the rows, and they would drink from the dipper with the water spilling over their throats and chests, or a guard would dismount and stand in the shade of his horse while the men sat on the ground and smoked for five minutes; but otherwise the static labor of their work day was unrelieved.

The dust clouds from my car blew back across the fields, and occasionally an inmate would raise his head from his concentration on the end of his hoe and look at me, one of the free people who drove with magic on the way to distant places. And as one of the free people I was the enemy, unable to understand even in part what his microcosm was like. From under his beaded forehead his eyes hated me, and at that moment, looking at my air-conditioned car and the acrid cloud of dust that blew into his face, he could have chopped me up with his hoe simply for the way I took the things of the free world for granted—the women, the cold beer, the lazy Saturday mornings, the endless streets I could walk down without ever stopping.

But I did know his world, maybe even better than he did. I knew the sick feeling of hearing a cage door bolted behind you, the fear of returning to solitary confinement and the nightmares it left you with, the caution you used around the violent and the insane, the shame of masturbation and the

temptation towards homosexuality, the terror you
had when a cocked gun was aimed in your face,
the months and years pointed at no conclusion, the
jealousy over a guard's favor, and the constant press
of bodies around you and the fact that your most
base physical functions were always witnessed by
dozens of eyes. I knew how the weapons were
made and where they were hidden: a nail sharpened
on stone and driven through a small block of wood;
a double-edged razor wedged in a toothbrush handle; barbed wire wrapped around the end of a club;
spoons and strips of tin that could open up wrists
and jugular veins; and all of it remained unseen,
taped between the thighs, carried inside a bandage,
tied on a string down a plumbing pipe, or even
pushed into the excrement in the latrine.

The reception building was surrounded by trees
and a green lawn. Three trusties were trimming the
hedges, edging the sidewalks, and weeding the
flower beds. They looked right through me as I
walked past them to the entrance. I didn't know
why, but I always felt a sense of guilt when I was
around prison inmates, as though I should apologize for something. I knew the sequence of absurdities that often put them there, and I knew, also,
that the years of punishment and the debilitating
ethic that went with it had almost nothing to do
with correction; but if I thought too long on any

of that I would have to fold my law degree into a paper airplane and sail it out my office window. I looked directly at the Negro clipping the top of the hedge (he was so black that his white uniform looked like an insult on his skin), and he moved the clippers at a downward angle on the side of the hedge so that his face turned away from me.

In the distance I could see one of the crumbling gray blockhouses left over from the last century, and I wondered if that was the one where John Wesley Hardin spent years chained to the wall of a dark cell. They fed him gruel and water, and whipped him every day with a leather strap to break him, and when he was finally taken out to work in the fields they manacled an iron ball to one ankle, and two guards always stood over him with shotguns. He served his hard time like that, fourteen years in chains with the whip and horse quirt laid across the buttocks.

And I remembered the songs that Leadbelly had sung on the same farm: "The Midnight Special," "There Ain't No More Cane on the Brazos," and "Shorty George," and the lines about the "black Betty," a four-inch-wide razor strop, three feet long, nailed to a wooden handle.

I sat in the scrubbed reception room and waited for the guard to bring Art from the fields. The room was divided by a long, low-topped counter, and the

inmates sat on one side and the visitors on the
other, their heads bent towards one another in a
futile attempt at privacy. There was a sign on the
far wall that read: DO NOT GIVE ANYTHING TO THE
PRISONERS; CIGARETTES CAN BE LEFT WITH THE PER-
SONNEL. At one end of the counter a huge guard,
with rings of fat across his stomach, sat in a wooden
chair that strained under his weight. There was a
dead cigar in his mouth and a filthy spittoon by his
feet. Most of his teeth were gone, and he licked
his tongue across the strings of tobacco on his
gums. His face was like a pie plate, and the washed-
out eyes wouldn't focus in a straight line. Occasionally, he looked at his watch and pointed one
thick finger at an inmate to tell him that his visiting
time was over, then he would suck on the flattened
end of his cigar. I could almost hear the digestive
juices boiling in his stomach.

Art came through a back door with a guard behind him. His black hair was dripping sweat, and
the cobweb scar in the corner of his eye was white
against his tan. His palms were grimed and his forearms filmed with dirt and cotton lint. There were
black rings in the creases of his neck, and his
clothes were rumpled and stained at the knees. He
had lost more weight, and the veins in his hands
stood out like knotted pieces of cord.

"How long we got, boss man?" he said, taking a package of Bugler tobacco from his shirt pocket.

"Fifteen minutes," the guard said.

Art sat down and curled a cigarette paper between his fingers. He didn't speak and his eyes remained downcast until the guard had walked back to the door.

"What do you say, cousin?" he said.

"I think we'll get a new trial."

"Half the guys in here live on new trials. They don't talk about nothing else. They write letters like paper is going out of style."

"The difference is that you're not guilty of anything."

"You know that don't have nothing to do with serving time."

"Listen, as soon as the appeal goes through I'm going to have you out on bond."

"That ain't good-guy jive, is it?"

"I don't bullshit a client, Art."

"All right, you don't. But I'm hanging by my ass in here. This is a rough joint, man."

"What's happened?"

He rolled the cigarette and folded down the wet seam with his thumb, watching the guard at the end of the counter.

"A couple of the hacks are laying it on. They

know I'm with the union, and they're getting off
their rocks while they got me in the field. Three
days ago the hack said I was dogging it in the cotton and they gave me the apple-box treatment.
They take you down to the hole without supper,
and all night you have to stand on an upended
apple crate, even though you piss your pants. If you
fall off, the hole boss gives you a few knots to get
your attention."

He took a book of paper matches from his shirt,
split one longways with his thumbnail, and lit his
cigarette. He breathed the smoke out through the
empty space in his teeth.

"The field boss already told me I'd have to wear
out a hoe handle a week if I wanted to earn good
time from him," he said. "He stays so close on my
ass that horse is shitting and pissing all over me.
They're going to make me build the whole five,
man, and I'll run before I do another month."

"Don't do that."

"I'll run or I'll ice one of those bastards. I'm
through with that pacifist shit. When I was standing on that box with the hole boss looking down
at me from the cage, it hit me what a dumb sonofabitch I've been for the last five years. The anglos
want us to be pacifists, just like they taught us that
blessed are the poor crap in church. Man, we never
knew how blessed we were. They want us to keep

our hands in our pockets while they knock the piss out of us."

"Forget about that running stuff, you hear?"

"It's not something you plan. You start thinking about all that time and your clock gets wound up, and you're ready to go through the wall with your fingernails."

Art's voice had risen, and the guard was looking at us with his crooked eyes. The fat tissue of his mouth was pressed in a small circle around his dead cigar.

"I spent a little time in a prison compound, too," I said.

"Then you know what that patience shit sounds like."

"Give it another couple of weeks and I'll turn every handle I can to have you on the street."

"I tell you, buddy, if I make the street they'll never get me back in again. New trial or not, they better bring the whole goddamn army with them."

"You'll walk out of it clean, and I have a feeling that Cecil Wayne Posey's ass is going to get bar-becued, at least if I have anything to do with it. Also, the deputy at the jail is going to have a few interviews with the F.B.I."

"Say, you cats really pulled a scene, didn't you? I heard them bring you in that night. Something hit the cell floor like a sack of cement, and one of the blacks in the drunk tank told me it was a tall blond guy in ice-cream pants. You didn't believe me when I told you to keep your head down."

"I'm learning. I haven't made a career of getting my head beat in."

"So I have, huh? The greaseball who always gets his ass caught in the watermelon fence."

"I met some of the people you have to deal with. I know it's bad."

"Man, you didn't see nothing. You never got closer to a migrant camp than the highway."

"I had a small taste of the local law enforcement."

"I got two purple hearts in my trunk and you can have both of them." He put out his cigarette, peeled the paper back carefully along the seam, and poured the unused tobacco in his Bugler pack.

"Do I get to be the dart board again?" I said.

"The next time you're in Pueblo Verde get Rie to give you a tour of the farm worker camps. Stick your head in a few of those stinking outdoor toilets, or talk with the kids sitting in doorways with flies swarming over their faces. Have dinner with a few of the families and see how the food sits on your stomach. Get a good breath of the dead rats under the houses and the garbage rotting in the ditches. Check the scene out, man. It really comes alive for you when you breathe it up both nostrils."

"It looks like I have to stay white when I talk with you, doesn't it?"

"You're a good friend, Hack, but you're a straight and your mind is white as Clorox."

He got to me with that one.

"What should I be?" I said. "You want me to apologize because I was born me instead of you?"

"No, man. You still don't see. It's mind style, something you grew up with. Your people go through life like they're looking down a long tunnel and they never see anything on the edges. You roar down the highway a hundred miles an hour and never remember anything later except a motel billboard because everything on the other side of the fence is somebody else's scene. It don't belong to you. It's painted by some screw who lost his brushes and forgot what he was doing."

"I don't like to tell you that you're full of shit."

"Take the tour, buddy."

"I've been on the tour. I grew up around it."

"No point, cousin. You're right in the middle of the pipe."

"Another gringo, right? One of the oppressors. A dickhead with the liberal tattoo."

The guard heard me, and he took the cigar out of his mouth between his fingers and leaned forward, with his stomach folding over his gunbelt.

The chair legs splayed slightly under his buttocks, and his crossed eyes were fixed in the smooth fat of his face.

"Look, Hack, if I make the street we're going on a sweet drunk together. We'll hit every chicano joint in San Antonio. We won't have to pay for nothing, either. We'll slop down the booze and ball with brown-skin chicks till our eyes fall out. Yokohama on a three-day pass. A real wild one."

"You're cooking with butane now," I said.

"I ain't kidding you. I'm going to wash this jailhouse stink off me in the Guadalupe and buy my own beer truck. We'll just tool around the roads drinking and slinging bottles at the highway signs. Then when I get back to Pueblo Verde they're going to learn what real shit smells like."

"You want to go back for some more?"

"The ballgame's just starting. We're going to hit them with a strike in August. I don't know if we can win, but a lot of cotton is going to burn in the rows if we don't."

"Our defense will work like piss in a punchbowl if you have a half dozen new charges against you."

"I can't sweat that."

"You'd goddamn better, unless you want to end up here again with another five to do."

"The only thing we got on our side is us. The cops, the legislature, the farm bureau, the whole fucking bunch—we got to bust them the only way we can, and that's to shut down the harvest until they recognize our union and start to negotiate."

"You can't make a strike work in the fields. There's ten people standing in line for the job you walk off of."

"They're going to win in California. We'll win here, too, as long as they can't scare us or turn us against each other. You see, man, that's what their real bag is all about. We twist the screws because of the shacks they give us and the seventy-dollar rents, and they throw out twenty or thirty families and tell them they got to do it because the union's forcing standards on them they can't meet. But people ain't buying that shit anymore."

The guard looked at his watch and pointed a fat finger at us, then cleared his mouth of tobacco spittle and spat it into the spittoon.

"I left two cartons of cigarettes for you at the desk," I said.

"Yeah, thanks, man. Look, you were straight when you said two weeks, weren't you?" His dark eyes were concentrated into mine, and one hand opened and closed on his forearm.

"I can't set it on the day."

"I know that. I ain't dumb about everything."

"I'll start on the bond as soon as the appeal goes through."

"Okay," he said, and smiled for a moment. "I just don't want to go on the nutmeg and coffee kick and start flogging my rod in the shower like most of the stir freaks in here. Take care, cousin, and look around for that beer truck."

I walked back outside into the hard light, and I was perspiring before I reached my automobile. The trusty gardeners were sweeping the cut grass from the sidewalk, their faces turned downward, and a crew of men from the fields were walking in file along the road, four abreast, their hoes over their shoulders in military fashion, with two mounted guards on each side of them. The sun had moved farther into the west, and the shadows from the cedar trees fell to the edge of the cotton field. The sunburned faces and necks of the men ran with sweat, and the guards had their hats slanted over their eyes against the sun.

I drove back down the dusty road and stopped at the gate while two guards looked through my car and in the trunk. As I rumbled over the cattle-guard and turned onto the highway I felt a strange release from that confined world behind those high walls. The oaks along the road were greener, the sky a more dazzling blue, the hot wind heavier with the smell of the pine woods, the murderous sun less of an enemy. The billboard signs advertising char-coaled steaks and frosted bottles of beer penetrated the eye with their color, and even the weathered farmhouses and barns with metal patent-medicine signs nailed on their sides looked like an agrarian romanticist's finest dream. There's a line of separation between the world of free people and the confined which you never realize exists until you discover yourself on the opposite side. Once there, behind the barbed wire or mesh screens or concrete walls, all objects and natural phenomena have a different color, shape, angle, and association from anything you had ever known previously. And no one who hasn't been there can understand the light-headed opulent feeling of walking back into the free world.

Fifty miles up the road I stopped at a tavern and steak house built on stilts above the edge of a green river. The board walls were gray and peeling, and the open windows were covered with screens to keep out the clouds of mosquitoes in the shadows of the willow trees along the bank. A screened eating porch shaded by a tall cypress tree extended over the water, and I sat at one of the checker-cloth tables and ordered a steak and a pitcher of beer. The bottom of the river was soap rock, a type of smooth gray sandstone that the Indians had used to bathe with, and in the middle, where the current had eroded deeply into the rock over thousands of years, you could see the dark shapes of huge catfish and carp moving in and out of the light and shadow, then the surface would ripple with the wind and they would break apart and dissolve in the sun's refraction. I cut into the steak and soaked up the hot grease with bread, and washed it down with beer. The pitcher and mug were crusted with ice, and the beer was so cold that it made my throat ache. Cowboys and oilfield roughnecks in hardhats were bent over the bar with dozens of empty bottles before them, and the barmaid, in shorts and a sun halter, was opening more bottles as fast as she could pull them from the beer case. Across the river a group of Negroes were cane fishing with worms in the shallows, their black faces shaded with flop straw hats, and the moss in the cypress tree straightened and fell like silk in the wind.

In two more hours I would be back at the ranch, and then Verisa and I would begin to enact our ritual that usually worked itself towards one of three conclusions. The least unpleasant would be a pointless and boring conversation about the office, a new account, a cocktail party at the Junior League, or one of Bailey's trite suggestions for the campaign. Each of us would listen to the other with feigned interest, the head nodding, the eyes flat and withdrawn. Then, after a careful period, I would change clothes and go into the horse lot, or Verisa would remember at that moment that she had

planned to invite people to the ranch from Victoria
for the weekend.

More unpleasant was the possibility that the control wouldn't be there—the Mexican girl had
burned everything on the stove, the gardener had
dug out the wrong plants from the flower bed, the
odor from the gas wells had made the house smell
like a Texas City refinery—and the conversation
would quickly deteriorate into a sullen silence and
a door slammed sharply in another part of the
house.

The last alternative was the worst: nothing would
be said when I came into the house until we were
forced by geographical necessity to be in the same
room together for sixty seconds, and then our
exchange would have the significance and intensity
of two people talking at a bus stop. I'd spend my
time in the library with the door closed, drinking
bourbon and playing my guitar, and finally when I
was in a drunken fog, my fingers thick on the guitar
neck, with the house humming as loud as my own
blood and Old Hack's angry ghost walking the
front porch, the seams would start to strip and Mr.
Hyde's bloody eyes would look into mine, and Verisa would have to lock the bedroom door until the
next morning.

However, Verisa wasn't always like the person
I've described here. When I met her at a country

club dance in San Antonio eight years ago she was
Verisa Hortense Goodman, the only daughter of a
millionaire stock financier, a hard-shell Baptist who
never drank or smoked and kept his hard body trim
with fifty pushups a day until he dropped dead from
a heart attack. That night on the terrace under the
mimosa trees the moon-sheen tangled in her auburn
hair and her white skin glowed in the light from
the Japanese lanterns. Her face was cool and pale,
the small mouth achingly beautiful as she looked
up at me. There were always men around her, and
when she moved across the terrace, her legs like
grace in motion against her tight silver gown, the
men would follow her, eager, smiling, their own
dowdy women left at the drink table. I took her
away from her date that night, and we went on a
wild ride with a magnum bottle of champagne
through the hill country to an open-air German
dance pavilion in San Marcos. I had a Porsche con-
vertible then, and I kept it wide open through the
black-green hills, drifting across the turns, while
she poured the wine in two crystal glasses for us.
Her face was happy with adventure and release, her
voice loud above the roar of the engine and the
wind, and she told me she was sick of country club
men and beaux who hadn't outgrown Kappa Sig,
and I knew then that I had her.

The next four months were all green and gold

days and turquoise evenings, fried chicken picnics on the Guadalupe River, a burning hour under a willow tree in an afternoon shower, tennis and gin rickeys at the club, horseback riding into the hills and swimming in the black coldness of the Comal under the moon. We spent weekends at the bull-fights in Monterey, with breakfasts of eggs fried in hot sauce and chicory coffee and boiled milk, and our mornings were filled with sunshine and mad plans for the rest of the day. We danced in beer gardens, hired a mariachi band at a street party in the San Antonio *barrio*, went to cowboy barbecues, and always kept a bottle of champagne in an ice bucket on the back seat of the Porsche. She never tired, and after another furious night of roaring across the countryside from one wonderful place to the next, she would turn her face up to be kissed, her eyes closed and the white edge of her teeth showing between her lips, and I would feel every-thing in me drain like water poured out of a cup. I'd leave her at her front door, the mockingbirds singing in the gray stillness of first light, and the road back to the ranch would be as lonely and empty as a stretch of moonscape.

We were married in Mexico City and spent the next three weeks fishing for marlin in the Yucatan. I rented a villa on the beach, and at night the waves crested white in the moonlight and broke against the sand and the Gulf wind blew cool with the smell of salt and seaweed through the open windows in our bedroom. In the mornings we raced horses in the surf, and I taught her how to pick up a handkerchief from the sand at a full gallop. Her skin darkened with tan, and in bed I could feel the heat in her body go into mine. While we ate lobsters in a pavilion on the beach after the afternoon's fishing, her eyes would become merry, flashing at me privately, and I would already see her undressing before our closet mirror.

But later, as the months went by at the ranch, I began to see other things in Verisa that I had overlooked previously. She was conscious of class, and underneath her rebellion towards country club romance and the pale men with family credentials who had courted her, she was attached to her father and the strict standard he had followed and expected in other men. He was the son of a small grocery-store owner, and after he became wealthy he learned, with some pain, the importance of having family lineage as well as money, and he never failed to remind Verisa that she belonged to a very special class of people who did not associate with those beneath their station. She had learned the lesson well, although she was probably never aware of it. She simply didn't recognize the world of ordinary people, those who lived on salaries, rode Greyhound buses, or carried drinks from behind a bar; they were there, but they moved about in another dimension, one that existed in the center of hot cities, drab neighborhoods, and loud, workingmen's taverns.

Also, she didn't like drunkenness. Although she considered herself an agnostic, a good deal of her father's devotion to the Baptist church had been left in her (he attributed his financial success to his early redemption at a Dallas revival and the fact that he practiced the teachings of Christ in his business; once he stared me straight in the face and told me that the Jews in the stock market were afraid to deal with a truly Christian man; he also believed that F.D.R. was a Jew). I never liked her father, and I always made a point of serving highballs, filling the room with cigar smoke, and drinking too much when he was at the house. He was glad to have Verisa married into the Holland family, and privately he asked her to name a child after him; so he was always restrained when I poured double shots of whiskey or asked him if he knew a Baptist minister in Dallas who was a grand dragon in the Ku Klux Klan. At first Verisa was indulgent towards my performances with her father, and occasionally, after he had left the house with his face disjointed in concern, she would say something mild, a quiet reproof, in hopes that I would be tolerant of him.

But I couldn't stand his bigotry, his illiterate confidence in the reasons for his success, and his simplistic and sometimes brutal solutions for the world's problems. Also, I resented the influence he'd had on Verisa's mind, that early period when he had infected her with the stupidity of his class. As she grew older I knew she would become more like him, much more sophisticated and intelligent, but nevertheless marked with the rigid social attitudes of the new rich. Worse, as my dislike for him became more open and his weekly visits turned into embarrassing periods of silence in the living room and then finally stopped altogether, I pushed her closer to him and she began to make comparisons between her father and other men who had been *given* everything. Sometime later, after I had come in drunk from a duck-hunting trip, she commented that heavy drinking was a symptom of the weak who couldn't stand up under competition.

I paid my bill at the steak house and took two cans of Jax with me for the drive home. Evidently, I was confused about Verisa's schedule for the week, because one of her afternoon lawn parties was under way when I arrived. The Negro bartender was shaving ice for mint juleps on the screened porch, and blue-haired ladies in sundresses sat around tables on the lawn under the oak trees. *Goddamn, here we go,* I thought. Two men from the state Democratic committee were there, neither of whom I wanted to see, and somebody had ridden Sailor Boy and had left him thirsty in the lot with the saddle still on. I went around the far side of the house and entered the library through the side door, but an insurance executive from Victoria and his wife were there, staring at my gun case with drinks in their hands. They turned their flushed faces at me, smiling. "Hello. Good to see you," I said, and went straight through and into the kitchen. Cappie, an old Negro who lived on the back of my property and sometimes barbecued for us, was chopping green onions and peppers with a cleaver on the drainboard. His gray hair was curled in the thick furrows on the back of his neck.

"Cap, get that goddamn saddle off of Sailor Boy and turn him out."

"There some young ladies been riding him, Mr. Holland."

"Yeah, I know. Nobody thinks he drinks water, either."

"Yes, sir."

I started up the staircase to the bedroom, and then one of the Democratic committee men called

from behind me and I was caught in the center of
it. I drank mint juleps under the oaks with the blue-
haired ladies, listened with interest to their compliments about my wife and ranch, explained
politely to a mindless co-ed that Sailor Boy was a
show horse and shouldn't be ridden into barbed-
wire fences, and laughed good-naturedly with the
two committee men at their Kiwanian jokes. People
came and left, the sun started to set beyond the
line of trees on the horizon, and the bartender
moved among the groups with a tray of cool drinks,
and at dusk Cappie served plates of barbecued links
and chicken and potato salad. My head was drum-
ming with the heat, the whiskey, and the endless
conversation. Verisa stood next to me with her
hand on my arm, accepting invitations to homes
that I would not enter unless I was drugged and
chained. Finally, at nine o'clock, when the party
moved inside out of sheer exhaustion, I took a bottle of bourbon from the bar and drove down the
back road to one of the ponds that I'd had stocked
with bass. One of Cappie's cane poles was leaned
against a willow tree, and I dug some worms out of
the wet dirt by the bank and drank whiskey and
bottom-fished in the dark until I saw the last headlights wind down my front lane to the blacktop.

    During the next ten days I spoke at a free Dem-
ocratic barbecue in Austin (it was crowded with

university students and working people, most of whom stayed at the beer kegs and didn't know or care who was giving the barbecue), addressed two businessmen's luncheons in San Antonio (the American and Texas flags on each side of me, the plastic plants forever green on the linen-covered tables, the rows of intent faces like expressions caught in a waxworks), talked informally at a private club in Houston ("Well, Mr. Holland, regardless of the mistake we made in Viet Nam, don't you think we have an obligation to support the fighting men?" "Granted that colored people have a grievance, do you believe that the answer lies in destruction of property?" "Frankly, what *is* your position on the oil depletion allowance?"), and spent one roaring drunk afternoon in a tavern with two dozen oilfield roughnecks and pipeliners who all promised to vote for me, although almost none of them came from the district.

The appeal came through at the close of the second week since I had seen Art. The judge who had reviewed the trial record, a hard old man with forty years on the bench, wrote in his decision that "the conduct of the local court was repugnant, a throwback to frontier barbarism," and he ordered Art's release from the state penitentiary on appeals bond pending a new trial. I set down the telephone, took a bottle of Jack Daniels and a glass from my desk drawer, and poured a large drink. On my second swallow, with a fresh cigar in my mouth, Bailey walked through the door and hit the broken air conditioner with his fist.

"Why don't you turn the goddamn thing off so the building can stop vibrating a few minutes?" he said. It had been a bad two weeks for Bailey. The heat bothered him much worse than it did me, and we had lost one of our big accounts, which he blamed on me. He believed that he was developing an ulcer, and each morning he drank a half bottle of some chalky white medicine that left him nauseated for two hours.

"Just turn the knob, Bailey, or you can hit it some more."

"I see you're getting launched early this afternoon."

"No, only one drink. Do you know where I can buy a beer truck?"

"What?" A drop of perspiration rolled down from his hairline like a thick, clear vein.

"I tell you what, buddy. Let's lock up the office in about an hour, and I'll take you on a three-day visit to all the Mexican beer joints in San Antonio."

"Put up the whiskey."

"Come on. For one time in forty years of Baptist living, close the office early and tie on a real happy one."

"Did you look at our calendar for this afternoon between drinks?"

"Yeah, R. C. Richardson is about to get burned again, and he needs us to clean up his shit."

"You accepted him as a client. I don't like the sonofabitch in the office."

"You don't understand that old country boy, Bailey. He's not a bad guy, as far as sons of bitches go. Anyway, his ass can burn until Monday. Get a glass and sit down. The only ulcer you have is in the head, and you're going to have a few dozen more there unless you let some cool air into that squeezed mind of yours."

"If you want to get into the bottle and blow half our practice, do it, but shut off that patronizing crap. I've pretty well reached my level of tolerance in the last two weeks."

"Look, I won appeal today on Art Gomez and the judge has set bond, and you have to admit that we haven't sprung many of our clients from the state pen. So take a drink and lower your blood rate, and I'll pick up Richardson's case early Monday morning."

"I can't get it through to you, Hack. You've got cement around your head. The office isn't a tennis club where you play between drinks."

"All right, goddamn, forget it," I said, and picked up the telephone and dialed the number of a bonds-

man we dealt with. I turned my eyes away from
Bailey's vexed face and waited in the hot stillness
for him to leave the room.

The bondsman was named Bobo Dietz. He was
a dark, fat man, who always wore purple shirts and
patent-leather shoes and a gold ring on his little
finger. He had moved to Austin from New Jersey
ten years ago, set up a shabby office next to the
county jail, and in the time since then he had
bought two pawnshops and three grocery stores in
the Negro slum. He considered avarice a natural
part of man's chemistry, and you were a sucker if
you believed otherwise; but he was always efficient
and you could count on him to have bail posted
and the client on the street a half hour after you
set him in motion.

He assured me over the phone, in his hard Cam-
den accent and bad grammar, that the ten-
thousand-dollar bond would be made before five
o'clock and Art would be released by tomorrow
morning. For some reason Bobo liked me, and as
always, when I went bail for a client on my own,
he wouldn't charge me for anything except ex-
penses. Many times I wondered if there was some
strange scar in my personality that attracted people
to me like Bobo Dietz and R. C. Richardson.

I turned off the air conditioner and opened all
the office windows. The stale afternoon heat and

noise from the street rose off the yellow awnings below me. My shirt stuck to my skin, and the odor of gasoline exhaust and hot tar made my eyes water. In the middle of the intersection a big Negro in an undershirt was driving an air-hammer into the concrete. The broken street surfacing shaled back from the bit, and the compressor pumped like a throbbing headache. I sipped another straight drink in the windowsill, sweating in the humidity and the heat of the whiskey, then I decided to give Bailey and his Baptist mentality another try. I took a second glass from the drawer, poured a small shot in the bottom, and walked into his office.

He was dictating to our secretary, his eyes focused into the wall, and I could see in the nervous flick of his fingers on his knee that he expected an angry exchange, profanity (which he hated in front of women), or a quick thrust into one of his sensitive areas (such as his impoverished bachelorhood, the empty weekends in his four-hundred-dollar-a-month apartment). I leaned against the doorjamb, smoking a cigar, with a glass in each hand. He faltered in his dictation, and his eyes moved erratically over the wall.

"Hack, I'll talk to you later."

"No, we have to shut it down today. It's Friday afternoon and R. C. Richardson will appreciate us a lot more Monday morning. Mrs. McFarland, my brother needs to direct me into the cocktail hour today, so you can leave early if you like."

The secretary rested her pencil on her pad, her eyes smiling. Her hair was gray, streaked with iron, and her face was cheerful and bright as she waited for the proper moment either to stop work or resume the dictation.

I set Bailey's drink down before him.

"I'd like to finish if—"

"Sorry, you're unplugged for the day, brother," I said. "Go ahead, Mrs. McFarland. There's a slop chute down the road where I need a warden."

Bailey saw that I had the first edge of a high on, and he let the secretary go with an apology. (He was the only Southerner I ever knew who could have been a character in a Margaret Mitchell novel.)

"That's too goddamn much," he said. "I've had it with this type of irresponsible college-boy shit around the office. When you're not loaded you're coming off a drunk, or you're spending your time on a union agitator's appeal while our biggest account gets picked up by a couple of New York Jews. You've insulted everybody who's tried to help you in the election, you got yourself put in jail because you were too goddamn drunk to know what universe you were in, and you had the balls to file a civil rights complaint against the man who arrested you."

"Bailey—"

"Just shut up a minute. Senator Dowling kept that story off the wire services, but since you felt so outraged that you had to file a complaint with the F.B.I. we should have some real fine stuff in the newspapers before November. In the meantime you haven't been in a courtroom in three months, and I'm goddamned tired of carrying your load. If you want out of the partnership, I'll sign my name to a check and you can fill in the amount."

"I started off to have a drink with you, brother, but since you've brought the conversation down to the blood-letting stage, let's look at a couple of things closely. Number one, the criminal cases we've won in court have been handled by me, and our largest paying accounts, keeping Richardson and his kind out of the pen for stealing millions from the state, have been successful because I know how to bend oil regulation laws around a telephone pole. Number two, you haven't been pumping my candidacy for Congress just because you want to see your brother's sweet ass winking at you from Washington, D.C. I don't like to put it rough to you like that, Bailey, but you don't understand anything unless it comes at you like a freight train between the eyes. You have all these fucking respectable attitudes and you heap them out on everybody else's head and ask them to like you for it. You better learn that you have a real load of shit in that wheelbarrow."

On that note of vicious rapport I received the call from Bobo Dietz. Bailey's face was white, the veins swollen in his neck, his eyes hot as he raised the whiskey to his mouth and I picked up the receiver.

"I don't know what kind of deal this is, Mr. Holland," Dietz said.

"What are you talking about?"

"That man's dead."

"Look, Dietz—"

"I called the warden. He said a couple of boons chopped him up with bush axes yesterday afternoon."

CHAPTER

SEVEN

It took me a half hour to get the warden on the phone. He didn't want to talk with me, but after I threatened to see him in his home that night he read me the guard's report about Art's death and added his own explanations about the unavoidable violence between the Negro and Mexican inmates.

Two Negroes had hidden a paper bag full of Benzedrex inhalers in the tractor shed, and they had been drinking bottles of codeine stolen from the pharmacy and chewing the cotton Benzedrine rings from at least two dozen inhalers when Art went inside the shed to get a lug wrench. A few minutes passed; a mounted guard working a gang in the cotton field heard a single cry, and by the time he rode to the shed and threw open the door the Negroes had disemboweled Art, torn the flesh from his back like whale meat, and severed one arm from his body.

There wasn't much more to the report. Art had probably been killed with the second or third blow. The Negroes were so incoherent they couldn't talk, and the guard had no idea why they had attacked Art instead of a half dozen other men who had been in and out of the shed earlier, although the warden added that "a doped-up nigger isn't a human being no longer." The Negroes had been put in solitary confinement and refused to talk about killing Art, if they even remembered doing it, and Art's body was to be buried in the prison cemetery unless his family was willing to pay for shipment back to Rio Grande City.

I hung up the receiver and sat numbly in the chair with my eyes closed and my fingers trembling on my forehead. So that was it. Just like that. Two crazed men single out another man, for no reason other than the fact that he walked into their bent, angry minds at the wrong time, and then they tear all the thirty-six years of life and soul from his body in seconds. My right hand was still sweating from the heat of the phone receiver and my ears burned with the casual language of the guard's report and the warden's footnotes. I couldn't shut out the vision of the two Negroes dismembering a man who had nothing to do with their lives, their brains boiling in a furnace of satisfaction, just as sometime in the future several other madmen would seat them in a wooden chair fitted with leather straps and buckles and metal hood and place a cotton gag in their mouths and burst every cell in their bodies with thousands of volts of electricity. Bailey poured a drink in a glass and placed it in my hand. I watched the brown light shimmering in the whiskey. My arm felt too weak and lifeless to raise the glass to my mouth.

"I'm sorry, Hack," Bailey said.

I stood up and set the glass on the desk. My movements seemed wooden, disconnected from one another, as though I had just awoke in the center of a vacuum. I could feel the beat of my pulse swelling into my eardrums. For just a moment the room looked unfamiliar, the ordered arrangement of chairs and desk and file cabinets foreign to anything that was me. I began putting on my coat.

"Where are you going?" Bailey said.

"I'm going to try to explain how a—"

"Sit down a minute and finish your drink."

"I said I'm going down to the valley and try to explain how a good man was murdered in a prison where he shouldn't have been in the first place. And then I'll explain how I won appeal on a man twenty-four hours after he was dead."

"Don't let it take you like this, Hack."

"How should we take it, Bailey? Maybe if I go to work fast I can arrange to have his body shipped home before he's buried in a prison cemetery with a wood marker. And if I'm too late to prevent that, I can always work on a court order to have the body exhumed. And while we're doing all that we can consider that a lynch court had this in mind for him when he was first charged."

"Here, drink it, and I'll go with you."

"You wouldn't like it."

"I'll rent a plane and we'll fly down tonight."

I drank from the glass, but the whiskey had no taste. I had started to perspire under my coat, and the shapes and late afternoon shadows in the room were as strange as the distorted lines in a dream. Outside, the air-hammer thudded into the asphalt. I felt the sweat dripping off my hair down the back of my neck. The glass was empty in my hand.

"They wouldn't like you, either," I said.

"Goddamn it, Hack, you can't drive like this."

"They don't buy that work-with-the-system shit. And I don't feel like telling them the system is all right, except for those twenty-four-hour differences that you have to take into allowance. And I don't like to tell them that I was having drinks with the D.A.R. ladies and shaking hands with the paraplegics while Art's clock was one day behind the court's. Give me another one."

He put his arm on my elbow and tried to turn me towards the chair.

"Just get the goddamn bottle, Bailey. Pour yourself a super one while you're at it."

He went to the desk and came back with the bottle of Jack Daniels. He held the stopper in one hand.

"All right, sit down, and I'll call the airport."

"Would you listen to me just for one goddamn time?" I said. "I'm not going down to meet with a Rotarian luncheon, and number two I'm not a fucking lunatic who needs his older brother to strap a control harness on his back."

I took the bottle out of his hand and drank from the neck. I swallowed until the muscles in my throat closed and the whiskey backed up in my mouth.

"There, goddamn. That glues everything a little tighter," I said.

"Hack."

I left him standing in the open door with the bottle in his hand, his lined face covered with pinpoints of moisture.

On the four-lane highway west of town I opened up the Cadillac, lowered the windows, and passed long strings of late afternoon traffic, hitting the shoulders and showering gravel over the asphalt. The red sun burned across the tops of the hills and

lighted the dark edges of the post oaks and blackjack, and the shadows of the cedar-post fences
along the road broke silently against my fenders
like a blinking eye. Although I had driven that same
highway hundreds of times, the sunset gave a different cast and color to the land than anything I
had seen there before. The windmills were motionless in the static air; the cattle in the fields were
covered with scarlet, their heads stationary in the
short grass, and the neat white ranch houses
seemed as devoid of life and movement as an abandoned film set; the irrigation ditches were dry and
cracked with drought, the thickets of mesquite like
burned scratches against the hillsides, and the few
horses in the pastures looked as though they had
been misplaced.

The shadows deepened over the hills, the traffic
thinned, and I kept the accelerator to the floor for
the next fifty miles. The sign boards, the oil rigs,
and the three-dollar Okie motels sped past me in
the twilight, but none of it would click together as
a stable piece of geography that I had lived around
all my life. It was removed, unconnected, and the
whiskey from my flask made it even emptier and
more disjointed. As a Southerner I had been
brought up to believe that through conditioning
and experience you could accept with some mea-
sure of tranquility any of the flaws in the human

situation. But death is one flaw that always lands like a fist in the center of the forehead. No matter how many times you see it, or smell its grey rotting odor, or come close to buying it yourself, each time is always like the first. No amount of earlier experience prepares you for it, and after it happens the world is somehow unfairly diminished and bent out of shape.

It was night and just the horn of the moon shone above the hills when I reached Pueblo Verde. Lights glowed inside farmhouses beyond the dark fields and orchards of citrus trees, and the river was as black as gun metal under the starless sky. Everything was closed on the main street except the hotel and beer tavern, and I turned down the rutted road into the Mexican district, wondering what type of inadequate words I would choose to tell Rie and her friends that Art's death had come about the same way that a stupid fool steps on your foot aboard a crowded bus. I understood why Western Union offices always kept a pamphlet of prepared condolences on their counters. Death is the one occasion when words have as much relevance as a housewife talking across her back fence about a broken washing machine.

My flask was empty. I stopped in the Mexican tavern for a fifth of Jack Daniels and had two drinks from the bottle in the car before I pulled up in front of the union headquarters. Bugs flicked against the screen door and turned in the yellow square of light on the porch. One of the windows had a large, spider-webbed hole in the center, and someone had taped a piece of cardboard over it from the inside. *Okay, doc, let's go*, I thought.

I walked up the dirt path and knocked on the door. The Negro and two Mexicans in cowboy shirts and bluejeans were talking at a table piled with cardboard picket signs and bumper stickers. Only the Negro turned his head towards the door when I knocked; the other two kept talking, their faces calmly intense with whatever they were saying, their hands and fingers gesturing in the air with each sentence.

"Say, hello," I said.

The Negro looked back at the door again, then pushed back his chair and walked towards me with a beer in his hand, his cannonball head shining in the light. He squinted at the screen with his red-rimmed eyes.

"That's my whiskey brother out there, ain't it?" he said. "Come on in, home. You ain't got to knock around here."

He pushed open the door for me and put out his large, callused block of a hand.

"Is Rie here?"

"She's laying down. I'll get her."

"Maybe I should come back tomorrow."

"No, she'll want to see you. Get yourself a beer off the counter."

"Look—"

"No, man. It's all right."

He went into the back of the building, and a few minutes later Rie walked out of the hall into the light. She was barefoot and wearing bluejeans and a flowered shirt, and her curly, sunburned hair was uncombed. I looked once at her face and realized that she already knew about Art's death.

"How you doing, babe?"

"Hello, Hack."

"I started to call first."

The skin around her eyes was pale and there was no color in her mouth. I felt empty standing in front of her.

"Do you want to go for a drive?" I said.

Her eyes blinked a moment without really seeing any of us.

"There's a meeting tonight," she said.

"That's them church people coming tonight," the Negro said. "They don't offer us nothing but prayers. You all go on."

"I know a place to eat across the river," I said. "Come on. I might run into a Carta Blanca sign by myself."

I had peeled off the cellophane wrapper from a

cigar and I couldn't find an ashtray to put it in. It seemed that every word I spoke and every movement I made was somehow inappropriate.

"That's right. Go on out of here," the Negro said. "I'm going to run them church people off, anyway. Every time they come here they start sniffing at my wine breath."

She pushed her hair back with her fingers and slipped on a pair of leather moccasins. She was too strong a girl to have cried much, but her face was wan and drawn and the suntan on it looked as though it didn't belong there.

We walked out into the dark, down the path, and I put my arm around her shoulders. When I touched her and felt the trembling in her back I wanted to pull her into me and press her head against my chest.

"I spent three hours thinking of the wrong words to say," I said.

"You don't need to, Hack."

"Yes, I do. A man's death deserves an explanation, but I don't have it. Every time I saw a guy buy it in Korea I tried to see some rational equation in death, but it had no more reason or meaning than those faded billboard signs out on the highway."

"Art's brother phoned this afternoon and told me how he died. It didn't have anything to do with anybody. There's nothing to say about it."

So I didn't try to say anything else. I turned the Cadillac around in the dust, and we drove back down the corrugated road between the rows of clapboard shacks and dirt yards to the main street. The slip of moon had turned yellow and risen above the hills in the dark sky. The air was hot, motionless, and the oak trees on the square looked as though they had been etched in metal. The deputy who had given me the road map out of town stood under the neon sign in front of the beer tavern, talking with two men in overalls. His khaki shirt was dark around the neck and armpits with perspiration. He took the toothpick out of his mouth and stared hard as the car passed.

"Have they been bothering you?" I said.

"We had three arrests on the picket last week, and two nights ago somebody burned a cross in the front yard. It's strange to walk out on the porch and see something that ugly in the morning light. They'd nailed strips of tires to the wood, and I could still smell the melted rubber."

"Well, by God, we can do something about the Klan. The F.B.I. wants to nail them any way they can."

"The local fed thinks it was high school kids, even though some chicanos in the tavern saw a half dozen men in the back of a pickup with the cross propped against the cab."

"Rie, we have civil rights statutes that can get those men one to ten in Huntsville."

"We don't care about them."

"Listen, those men are dangerous and violent people, and they should be in the penitentiary."

"We've given the farm companies until Monday to sign, and then we shut it down. We have enough people organized now to do it, too."

"Do you know what it's going to be like when the cotton starts burning in the rows and the citrus goes soft because it wasn't picked in the first week? Those farmers are going to lose their ass, and those K.K.K. bastards will have chains and baseball bats next time."

"They won't stop the strike."

"Goddamn, I don't want to see them pouring kerosene on your house, either."

"Let's don't talk about it any more, Hack. I'm really tired."

And then I felt that I had selected almost every bad sentence possible in the three hours of driving from Austin to the Valley. I followed the blacktop south of town and crossed the concrete bridge over the Rio Grande. The low, black water rippled through the trash caught in the pilings, willow trees and scrub brush grew along the sandy banks, and the windows of the adobe huts on the Mexican side glowed with candle light and oil lamps. I stopped at the port of entry, and a tired Mexican immigration official in a rumpled khaki uniform and plastic-brim hat told me not to go farther than fifteen miles into the interior without a tourist's permit. Rie's face had the shine of ivory in the light from the official's small office. If I touched my fingers to her cheek I knew the skin would be as cool and dry as stone. All the pain was way down inside her, and it would stay there without ever burning through her composure. Somewhere she had learned how to be a real soldier, I thought. Either in those insane billy-swinging, head-busting campus riots, or maybe in a Mississippi jail where they put cattle prods to civil rights workers, but somewhere she had earned her membership in a private club.

I drove down the bad tar-surfaced highway between tall rows of cedar and poplar trees. The evening star flickered dimly above the bare hills in the west, and a hot breeze had started to blow across the flatland from the Gulf. Most of the adobe houses by the roadside were in ruins, the mudbricks exposed and crumbling, the roofing timbers hanging inside the doorways like long teeth. I could never drive into old Mexico at night without feeling the presence of Villa and Zapata in those dark hills, or the ghosts of Hood's Texas cavalry who chose exile in a foreign country rather than surrender when the Confederacy fell. Even on my drunken excursions to meet three-dollar Mexican whores, the wild smell of the land and the long stretch of burned hills and all the mystery in them cut through my sexual fantasies. Even now, with Rie beside me, her drawn face painfully beautiful as she held a match unevenly to her cigarette, I still heard the jingle of sabers and the cock of rifles, pointed by the thousands down a hill at some forgotten army.

Ten miles from the port of entry there was a small town of flat, adobe buildings, cobbled streets caked with horse manure, whorehouses, two or three dangerous bars, a rural police station, and a cemetery against the hillside with a stucco wall around it. High up on the hill and formed with whitewashed fieldstones were the words PEPSI-COLA. The adobe houses were as brown as the land, but the doors were painted blue, fingernail-polish red, and turquoise to prevent spirits from crossing the threshold. Most of the people in the town were poor Indians, but the whorehouses and the bars were run by either the police or marginal gangsters from Monterey. Oilfield workers sat in the open-front cantinas with fifteen-year-old girls, the juke-boxes blaring with mariachi horns, and farther up the narrow main street two policemen in dirty uniforms stood in the lighted doorway of the town's largest whorehouse. One of them beckoned to me as I passed, then he saw Rie and turned his attention to the car behind me.

The *cervezería* and cafe was across the small square from the church. The owner had hung lights in the mimosa trees over the outdoor tables, and the shadows flickered in webbed patterns on the flagstones and the white oilcloth table covers. In the middle of the square was a weathered bandbox, with a round, peaked roof, and I could see the altar candles burning in the darkness beyond the open door of the church. We sat under the trees, with the dappled shadows breaking across us, and I ordered dinner and two bottles of Carta Blanca.

"Could I have a tequila?" Rie said.

"The stuff they sell here is like pulque. It's yellow and you can see the threadworms swimming in it."

"I'd like one just the same."

The waiter brought us a quart bottle with a cork in it, two slender shot glasses, and a plate of sliced limes and a salt shaker. I poured into our glasses, and she drank it neat, without touching the limes or the water chaser, her eyes fixed on the darkened square. She winced a little with the bitter taste, and for just a moment there was a flush of color in her cheeks.

"That's not the way to do it," I said.

"Let me have another one."

"You can burn holes the size of a dime in your stomach with that stuff."

"I would like for you to pour me another one."

"All right. Hold the lime in your left hand and put some salt between your thumb and forefinger, then sip it."

I watched her tilt the glass to her lips and drink it down in two swallows. She choked slightly in the back of her throat and sucked on the lime.

"It's better the second time," she said. Her eyes had already gone flat.

"If you like I'll pour some in the ashtray and touch a match to it, and you'll get some idea of the raw alcohol content."

"I don't think it's as bad as you say." She drank out of the Carta Blanca bottle and looked past me into the square.

"I've invested a good deal of time in it," I said.

"It makes you feel quiet inside, doesn't it?"

"Then it pulls open all kinds of doors you usually keep shut."

"Why don't you teach me how to drink it, then?"

I gave the waiter my best American tourist look of irritated impatience, and he nodded in return and went to the kitchen window to hurry the cook.

"Give me another one," she said.

"You're not a drinker, Rie. Don't try to compete with the professionals."

"Here, I've finished the beer and I don't like it. I want you to show me how to drink tequila."

"The best way is to fill your glass and pour it in your automobile tank."

"Hack."

"No, goddamn it."

"Maybe we should go. It's hot, anyway, isn't it?"

"I don't like to go out on abortive missions."

"Yes, you do, even to make one point about your knowledge of drinking."

"Okay, Rie. You nailed me to the wall with that one." I filled her shot glass and lit a cigar.

"Do you enjoy being angry?"

"No, but I'll be goddamned if I'll take on my idiot brother's role with somebody else."

"I believe you enjoy it when the blood starts beating in your head."

"I'm all out of fire tonight, babe. My white flag is tacked to the masthead."

She sipped out of her glass and fixed her flat eyes on my face. I drew in on the cigar and waited for it.

"Was there anything we could have done?"

"No."

"Anything at all so he wouldn't have been in that tool shed."

"It was all done."

"I visited him the day he was transferred to prison. I watched them take him down the court-house sidewalk in handcuffs, then I went back on the picket the same afternoon, just like nothing had changed."

"I turned every lock I could. We were almost home free. It was one of those dumb things that nobody can do anything about."

She raised the glass again, and her almond eyes looked electric in the light from the trees.

"But it had to be black men who killed him. Not a sadist or a racist guard. Two spades who probably lived everything he did."

The waiter placed our dinner before us, holding the plates by the bottom with a folded napkin, and looked quickly at Rie, then at me.

"Dos mas Carta Blanca," I said.

"Si señor," he said, and drew his curiosity back inside himself.

"I don't think I'm hungry now," she said.

"Eat a little bit."

"I don't want it. I'm sorry."

"Be a doll."

"Let's go, Hack."

"I'll have the waiter wrap it in waxpaper."

"Please, let's just go."

I paid the check inside, and the waiter looked offended because we hadn't eaten, until I explained that my wife was ill and told him to keep the rest of the tequila for himself. We drove back down the cobbled street past the loud bars, and a barefoot Indian child in ragged clothes ran along beside my window with his hand outstretched. The two policemen in front of the whorehouse were helping a drunk American in a business suit from his automobile. He leaned against a stone pillar, his face bloated and white with alcohol under the Carta Blanca sign, and gave each of them a bill from his wallet. I shuddered with the recollection of stepping unsteadily out of taxicabs on similar streets and walking through other garish doorways under the slick eyes of uniformed pimps, and I wondered if my face had looked as terrible as the man's under the neon sign.

I accelerated the Cadillac past the last cantinas and turned back onto the dark highway. The moon broke apart in the branches of the tall cedar trees sweeping by me.

"Why did you say we were almost home free?" she said.

Goddamn you, Hack.

"I thought I could have him out with some more time." I kept my eyes on the highway and didn't look at her when I spoke. "It's one of those things you can't tell about. You do everything you can and wait for the court to act."

I could hear her breathing in the dark.

"It could have gone in the other direction," I said.

"Oh goddamn, Hack," she said, and put her face against my chest with her hands clenched around my arm. Her tears wet the front of my shirt, and she held on to me tighter each time she tried to stop crying. I pulled her close into me and rubbed the back of her neck and her curly hair; her forehead felt feverish against my cheek and she trembled inside my arm like a frightened girl. I could smell the sun in her hair and the raw tequila on her breath, and I wanted to pull onto the side of the road and press her inside me.

Her face was as white and smooth as alabaster in the light from the dashboard, and when she had stopped crying and tried to sit up straight I held her close against me and pushed my fingers up through her hair. Her eyes were closed, her breasts stopped rising, and I felt the muscles in her back tense once more and then go loose under my palm. She breathed slowly into my neck, and by the time we reached the border she was asleep.

I rolled across the bridge over the Rio Grande, and an immigration official in a Stetson hat looked once at my Texas Bar Association card and waved

me through. The hot night air was sweet with the
ripe citrus and watermelon, and there was just a
taste of salt in the wind from the Gulf. The moon
had risen high above the hills now, and a strip of
black storm cloud hung off of one yellow horn. I
drove slowly over the ruts and chuckholes through
the Mexican and Negro district and parked along
the broken fence in front of the union headquarters.
The light was still on in the front room, and a man
was silhouetted behind the screen door with a bottle in his hand. I eased my arm from behind Rie's
neck and rested her head against the seat. Her eyelashes were still damp, her cool face caught the
softness of the moon, and when she parted her lips
slightly in her sleep I felt the blood sink in my
heart. I leaned over and kissed her lightly on the
mouth. The screen door slammed, and the Negro
walked out on the porch. I went around to the
other side of the car and picked Rie up carefully in
my arms and carried her up the front path. Her
eyes opened momentarily, then shut again, and she
turned her face into my neck. The Negro held the
door back for me, and I laid her down on the bed
in the back room and switched on the electric fan.
Her hair moved on the pillow in the breeze, and
the alabaster color of her face was even more pale
and cold in the half light. I heard the Negro opening two bottles of beer in the front room, and I

closed the door behind me and went back through the hallway.

"Sometimes people got to get high and boil it out," the Negro said. He put a bottle of Jax in my hand.

"I'll get some vitamin B and aspirin out of my car. Give it to her if she wakes up before you go to bed."

"I been on that spodiodi route a long time, man. You ain't got to tell me how to fight it."

"I guess we went to the same school."

"There you go," he said. "Look, I'm glad you taken her out tonight. Some dudes come by and wanted to give us some shit. For a minute I thought they was really going to get it on."

"What happened?"

"A couple of carloads of young studs come down the street throwing firecrakers at the houses. Then they parked out front, drinking wine and rolling them cherry bombs up on the porch. I figured they'd get tired of it after a while, but three of them come up to the door and said they wanted to skin out a nigger. Yeah, they said they ain't hung a nigger up on a skinning hook in a long time. They was blowing wine in my face, and I could smell lynch all over them, just like piss on fire. One of them started to pull open the door, and then a dude in the car blew the horn and hollered out, 'Don't

waste it on a jig. Let's find them hippy freaks.' Two
of them cut, but this stud with the door in his hand
wanted a pair of black balls. If the chicanos hadn't
started coming out of their houses, the shit would
have gone right through the fan, and I'd be up for
icing a white kid. Because I tell you, whiskey
brother, I give up on the days of letting white people shove a two-by-four up my ass until the splin-
ters are coming out of my mouth."

I drank from the beer and looked at the Negro's
face. For the first time since I had met him I saw
the hard glass quality in his eyes, the flicker of humiliation in them, the thin raised scar, now as colorless as plastic, on his lower lip. His gleaming
head was covered with drops of perspiration, and
the lumps of cartilage behind his ears pulsed as
though he were chewing angrily on something
down inside himself.

"What the hell are you doing here, anyway?" I
said.

"I got a bad habit, man. I picked it up in the
army digging latrines all over Europe for sweet pink
assholes. I figure a yard of white shit went into the
ground for every shovelful of dirt I turned. When
I got out I decided I paid my dues to Mr. Charlie's
bathroom and I ain't applying at the back door no
more for my mop and pail. You know what I mean,
man?"

He licked his tongue over his bottom lip, and the scar glistened like a piece of glass. For the second time that day I felt I had nothing to say. Outside, the cicadas were singing in the stillness. I finished my beer and left him at the table, lighting one of my cigars.

I didn't believe that I would be welcome again at the rooming house, so I drove thirty miles to the next town on the river and checked into a motel. I lay on the bed in the air-conditioned darkness with my arm over my eyes, and each time that I almost made it into sleep, broken images and voices would click together in my mind like the edges of a splintered windowpane, and I would be awake again with the veins drawing tight against my scalp. The highway rolled towards me out of the twilight, then the bush axes were raised high in the air once more, glinting redly in the gloom of the toolhouse, and a Chinese private leaned his face down to the sewer grate and spat a long stream of yellow saliva on my head. I sat on the edge of the bed in my underwear and drank half the bottle of Jack Daniels before I fell asleep in the deep whiskey quiet of my own breathing.

The next morning I dressed in a pair of khakis, my old cowboy boots, and a denim shirt (all of which I carried in a suitcase that always stayed in the trunk of the Cadillac), had my hangover breakfast of a steak with a fried egg on top and a slow cup of coffee and a cigar, then started down the road for Pueblo Verde. The sun was white on the horizon, and the washed-out blue sky hurt your eyes to look at it. The green of the citrus orchards, the fields of corn and cotton, and the sear hilltops floated in the humidity and heat. Watermelons lay fat in the rows, shimmering with light, and the cucumber vines were heavy with their own weight. Even with sunglasses on I had to squint against the glare. Hawks circled over the fields, and on some of the cedar fence posts farmers had nailed dead crows, salted and withered in the sun, to keep the live ones out of the corn. In the middle of an empty pasture, far from the roadside, a sun-faded billboard warned that THE COMING IS SOON, LISTEN TO BROTHER HAROLD'S NEW FAITH REVIVAL ON STATION XERF.

Outside Pueblo Verde I pulled into a clapboard country store shaded by a huge live oak. There was an old metal patent-medicine sign nailed to one wall, three pickup trucks parked on the gravel in front, and on the wood porch was a rusted Coca-Cola cooler with bottle caps spilling out of the opener box. The inside of the store was dark and cool and smelled of cheese and summer sausage and cracklings in quart jars. I bought a wicker picnic basket, a tablecloth, two bottles of California bur-

gundy, some peppered German sausage, white
cheese, a loaf of French bread, and six bottles of
Jax pushed down in a bag of crushed ice. A small
barefoot Negro boy, with bluejeans torn at the
knees, helped me carry the sacks to the car. Then
I turned back onto the highway into the white brilliance of the sun above the Rio Grande.

The high sidewalks in town were crowded with
people, and the beer taverns and pool halls were
filled with cowboys and cedar-cutters who had
come into town to drink every piece of change in
their bluejeans. I was always struck by the way that
all small Texas towns looked alike on Saturday
morning, whether you were in the Panhandle or the
Piney Woods. The same battered cars and farm
trucks were parked at an angle to the sidewalks; the
same sun-browned old men spat their tobacco juice
on the hot concrete; the young boys in crewcuts
and Sears Roebuck straw hats with health and
blond youth all over their faces stood on the street
corners; and the girls with their hair in curlers and
bandannas sat in the same cafes, drinking R.C. Cola
and giggling about what Billy Bob or that crazy Lee
Harper did at the drive-in movie last night.

I drove down the dusty street of the Mexican
district with the lisping voice of a local hillbilly
singer blaring from my radio:

I warned him once or twice
To stop playing cards and shooting dice
He's in the jailhouse now.

Rie was sitting at the table in the front room of the union headquarters with a cup of coffee in her hand. She was barefoot and wore a pair of white shorts and a rumpled denim shirt, and her face was pale with hangover. I went through the screen door without knocking.

"Get in the car, woman. I'm going to do something for that yankee mind of yours today," I said.

"What?" She looked at me with her hair in her eyes.

"Dinner on the ground and devil in the bush, by God. Come on."

"Hack, what are you talking about?" Her words were slow and carefully controlled, and I knew she really had one.

"I'm going to introduce you to my boyhood. Goddamn it, girl, get up and stop fooling around."

"I don't think I can do anything today."

"Yes, you can. Never stay inside with a hangover. Charge out into the sunlight and do things you never did before."

"How much did I drink?"

"You just did it with bad things in your mind."

"I'm sorry about last night. I must have seemed like a real dumb chick."

"You could never be that."

She smiled and pushed the hair out of her eyes.

"I'm sorry, anyway," she said.

"Right now there's a green river about seventy miles from here, and under a big gray limestone rock there's an eight-pound bass with one of my flies hanging in his lip, and unless you get your ass up I'm going down the road by myself."

"You're a real piece of pie, Hack."

"No, I ain't. I'm shit and nails and all kinds of bad news. You ought to know that by this time. If you need any references you can contact my brother. I left him yesterday with his ulcer bulging out of his throat."

She put her fingers to her forehead and laughed, and that wonderful merry flash of light came back into her eyes.

"I'll be out in a minute. There's some chickory coffee and cornbread on the stove," she said.

"Well, goddamn, for a yankee girl you may be all right after all," I said, and watched the smooth curve of her hips against her shorts as she walked into the back of the house.

We drove north through the hills and flat farmland of string bean and corn fields and cow pasture to a wide, green, slow-moving river lined with wil-

low, redbud, and juniper trees, where I had fly-
fished as a boy with my father. The river was low
from the drought, and the surface was covered with
seeds from the juniper trees, but there were still
eddies and deep holes behind the boulders in the
current, and I knew that I could take all the crappie,
bream, and bass that I could put on a stringer. The
mudbanks were covered with the sharp, wet tracks
of deer and raccoons, and mockingbirds and bluejays flew angrily through the hot shade of the trees.
The sunlight reflected off the water, and farther
down, where the river turned by a grove of cypress
trees, the sandbars gleamed hard and white in the
middle of the current. Dragonflies flicked over the
reeds and lily pads near the bank, and the bream
were feeding in the shade of the willows, denting
the water in quiet circles, like raindrops, when they
rose to take an insect.

I took my three-piece Fenwick flyrod in its felt
cover and the small box of number-eighteen dry
flies from the trunk, and we walked through the
trees and dead leaves and twigs to the river. Comanche and Apache warriors used to camp here on
the banks to cut and shave arrow shafts from the
juniper wood, and for a moment my eyes became
twenty years younger as I looked for the place
where they had probably built their wickiups and
hung their venison in the trees over smoking fires.

I knew that if I looked long enough I could find their old camp: the fire line a foot or so below the soil, the flint chippings from a work mound, the bone awls and shards of pottery. Since I was a boy I always felt that the land breathed with the presence of those dead men who had struggled on it long before we were born, and sometimes as a boy, particularly in the late evening, I almost felt that they were still living out their lives around me, firing their arrows from under the necks of war ponies at pioneer cabins that had long since decayed into loam. Once when I was plowing a field that we had always used for pasture, I felt something hard and brittle snap against the share and grind into pieces over the moldboard. I felt it right through the vibration of the tractor, and before I had shut off the engine and turned around in the metal seat I already knew that I had scraped across a warrior's grave. The shattered skull and bits of white vertebra were scattered in the furrow, and all of his rose quartz arrowpoints gleamed among his ribs like drops of blood.

We sat under a cypress tree close to the water, and Rie opened the beer and made sandwiches of sausage and cheese while I tied a new tapered leader with one-pound test tippet. I waded out into the warm water and false-cast under the overhang of the trees, pulling out the line from the reel easily

with my left hand, and shot the small brown hackle
fly into a riffle on the far side of a boulder. The
Fenwick was a beautiful rod. It was as light as air
in my palm, and it was tapered and balanced so
perfectly in its design that I could set the hook hard
with one flick of the fingers. The fly drifted through
the riffle twice without a strike, but on the third
cast a large-mouth bass rose from the bottom of
the pool, like a green air bubble floating slowly
upwards, and broke the surface in an explosion of
light. He took the fly in the corner of his lip, shaking his head violently, his dorsal fin and tail boiling
the water, then he dove deep again towards the
heavy current. I kept the rod high over my head
with my right arm outstretched and let the line run
tightly between my fingers. He sat on it once, deep,
pointed downstream, and the tip of the rod bent
downward until I knew that he was about to break
the leader and I had to give him more line. I waded
with him in the current, working him at an angle
towards the bank, then he rose once more, the
hook now protruding close to his eye, and hit the
water sideways. He tried to turn his head back into
the current, but he was weakening fast, and I started
pulling in the line slowly with my left hand. He
waved his tail in the shallows, clouding the water
with sand, and each time I lifted the rod to bring
his mouth to the surface he sat on it again and bent

the tip in a quivering arch. I let him spend his last strength against the spring of the rod, then I worked my hand down the leader and caught him carefully under the stomach. He was heavy and cold in my hand, and I slipped the hook out of his mouth, watching the eye, and placed him back in the water. He remained still for a moment, his gills pulsing, then he moved slowly off through the shallows and dropped into the green darkness of the current.

I leaned the rod against the cypress trunk and drank a bottle of Jax with a sausage and cheese sandwich. The Spanish moss overhead looked like wisps of cobweb against the sun, and I could smell the dank, cool odor of the rotted stumps and worm-eaten logs back in the woods. Rie had waded on the edge of the river while I fished, and her bare, suntanned legs were coated with sand. She sat with her arms behind her, looking at the sandbars and stretch of willows on the far side of the river, and I had to force myself from dropping my eyes to her breasts.

"How did you find such a wonderful place?" she said.

"My father used to take me here when I was a boy. In the spring we'd fish the riffle from that rose-bud tree down to where the river turns in the shade.

Then we'd dig for an old Indian camp. I found my first bannerstone in the bottom of that wash."

I sat down beside her on the tablecloth and drank from the beer. A shaft of sunlight struck inside the amber bottle.

"It must be fine to have a father like that," she said.

"Yeah, he was a good man."

"Was he a lawyer?"

"He taught southern history at the University of Texas, then he was in Congress two terms during Roosevelt's administration. He took me deer hunting once on John Nance Garner's ranch in Uvalde, but I was too small then to believe that the Vice President of the United States could chew on cigars and spit tobacco juice. My father had to convince me that Mr. Jack really did work in an important capacity for the government."

"Gee, what a great story," she said.

"I shook hands with Roosevelt once at Warm Springs, too. I wanted to look at the metal braces on his legs, but his eyes were so intense and interested, even in a boy's conversation, that you couldn't glance away from them. I was full of all kinds of pride and sunshine when I realized that my father was a personal friend of this man. I watched them drink whiskey on the verandah together, and for the first time I knew my father had another life that I'd never imagined before."

I drank the foam out of the bottle and looked at the summer haze on the river. It was a wonderful place. The juniper seeds on the water turned in swirls past the sandbars, and stray sea gulls that had wandered far inland dipped and hovered over a dead gar on the mudbank.

"Go on," she said. Her face was happy and so lovely in the broken shade that I had to swallow when I looked at her.

"I don't like people who show home movies," I said.

"I do, especially cowboy lawyers that dig up old arrowheads."

"I told you I'm shit and nails, didn't I? The Lone Ranger with a hangover."

"You just think you're a bad man."

"There are probably several hundred people who will disagree with you."

"You're not even a good cynic."

"You're taking away all my credentials."

"Go on. Please."

"The old man knew Woody Guthrie, too. He stayed at the house once during the war, and every evening I'd sit with him on the front steps while he played that beat-up old Stella guitar and his har-monica. He always wore a crushed felt hat, and when he spoke his words had a cadence like talking blues. He could never talk very long, at least while he had a guitar in his hands, without starting another song. He played with three steel banjo picks on his fingers, and he had the harmonica wired to a brace around his neck. He played Negro and workingmen's beer-joint blues so mean and fine that I didn't want him to ever leave. When we drove him to Galveston to catch a merchant ship my father asked him what the migrant farm workers thought of the movie *Grapes of Wrath*, and he said, 'Most of the people I know ain't going to pay a quarter to see no more grapes, and I don't expect they need any more of this here wrath, either.' "

"Wow, did your father know anybody else?"

"Those were the best ones. And I'm all out of stories, babe."

"Your father must have been an unusual man."

"Yes, he was." I bit the tip off a cigar and looked at the haze on the water and the line of willows beyond, and for just a moment, in the stillness and heat of the summer morning, in the time that the flame of my match burned upward in one sulfurous curl, I saw my father lying half out of the chair in the library, the circular explosion of gunpowder on the front of his cream-colored coat, with his mouth locked open as though he had one final statement to make. The pistol had flown from his dead hand with the weight of its own recoil, and his arm had caught behind him at a twisted angle in the chair. His eyes were receded and staring, and his gray hair hung down on his forehead like a child's. As I stood in the doorway, unable to move towards him, with the shot still loud in my ears and Bailey running down the stairs behind me, I thought: *It was his heart. He had to do it. He couldn't let it kill him first.*

"Hey, come in, world," Rie said.

"The old man had rheumatic fever when he was a kid. All of the things he loved to do put his heart right in a vise."

She touched the back of my hand with her fingers and looked quietly into my face. Her strands of sunburned hair were gold in the broken light through the cypress tree.

"All right, goddamn, how about opening another beer?" I said.

"You're a special kind of guy, Hack."

"How did we get on this crap, anyway? Come on, girl. Get the beer open."

"Okay, kemosabe." Her eyes went flat, and she reached inside the sack of crushed ice.

"I mean, you're hurting my badass identity."

She worked the opener on the bottle cap without answering.

"Say, Rie. Come on."

"You kick doors shut real hard," she said.

"Look, I behave like a sonofabitch so often that sometimes I don't think about who I'm talking to."

"You don't like anyone to get inside you, and maybe that's cool, but you ought to hang out a sign for dumb chicks."

"I'm sorry."

"It's a swell day and you're still a piece of pie."

I leaned over her and kissed her on the mouth. I felt her heavy breasts against me, and I slipped my arms under her back and kissed her forehead and her closed eyes and put my face in her hair. She breathed against my cheek and ran her hands under my shirt.

"Oh, Hack," she said, and moved her whole body into me.

My blood raced and I could feel my heart clicking inside me. Each time I kissed her my head swam, my breath became short, and I felt myself dropping through her into the earth.

She put one leg in mine and held me closer and ran her fingernails up my neck through my hair. When she moved her body against me the dark green of the trees and the summer haze on the river seemed to spin in circles around me.

"I felt you kiss me last night. I didn't want you to stop," she said. "All night I wanted to feel you around me."

"My southern ethic wouldn't let me take advantage of a bombed girl."

"You have so many crazy things in your head, Lone Ranger." She moved her lips over my cheek and bit me on the neck, and then I couldn't stop it.

I put my hand under her shirt and felt her breasts. They swelled out each time she breathed and I could feel her heart beating under my palm. I unzippered her white shorts and touched her thighs and her flat stomach.

"I'm sorry for the woods. I should take you up the road, but you really got down inside me, babe," I said.

She smiled and kissed me, and her almond eyes took on all the wonderful color and mysterious light that a woman's eyes can have when they make you weak with just a glance.

That evening we drove back through the hills and the baked fields of string beans and corn, and stopped at a roadside restaurant and beer tavern north of Rio Grande City for Mexican food. On the broken horizon the sun was orange behind clouds that looked as though they had been burned purple. The sky seemed so vast and empty in its darkening light that my head became dizzy in looking at it. (Sometimes, at moments like this, I felt a south Texas sunset was so hard I could strike a match against it.)

We finished dinner and drank bottles of Carta Blanca while two drunk cowboys played the jukebox and arm-wrestled with each other at the bar. We had chickory coffee, and I brought in my flask of Jack Daniels from the car and poured a shot into our cups. On the jukebox Lester Flatt and Earl Scruggs rolled out a Blue Ridge song, in their mournful southern accents, of ancient American loves and distant mountain trains:

> I can hear the whistle blowing
> High and lonely as can be
> Each year is like some rolling freight train
> Cold as starlight upon the rails.

I don't know if it was the whiskey (I eventually drained the whole flask into my cup), the events and emotional fatigue of the past two days, or my need to confess my guilt of fifteen years ago, or a combination of the three, but anyway I began to talk about Korea and then I told her all of it.

CHAPTER

EIGHT

My legs were on fire as we marched the five miles along a frozen dirt road from the freight train to a temporary prison compound. The sky was lead gray, and the dark winter brown of the earth showed in patches through the ice and snow that covered the fields and hills. The few peasant farmhouses, made from mudbricks mixed with straw, were deserted, and at odd intervals across the fields there were old craters left from a stray bombing. Our Chinese guards, in their quilted uniforms and Mongolian hats, walked along beside us with their burpguns slung on straps at port arms, one gloved finger curled inside the trigger guard, hating us not only because we were Occidentals and the enemy but also for the cold and misery in their own bodies. When a man fell or couldn't keep pace with

the line or find someone to help him walk he was
pushed crying (or sometimes white and speechless
in his terror) into the ditch and shot. The Chinese
were thorough. Two and sometimes three guards
would fire their burpguns into one shivering, helpless man.

By all chances I should have bought it somewhere along that five miles of frozen road. My
pants legs were stiff with dried blood, and each step
sent the flame in my wounds racing up my body
and made my groin go weak with pain. I had never
known that pain could be as prolonged and intense
and unrelieved. I saw the guards kill six men and I
heard them kill others behind me, and I knew that
I was going to fall over soon and I would die just
as the rest had, with my arms across my face and
my knees drawn up to my chest in an embryonic
position. But a Marine major from Billings, Mon-
tana, a huge man with lumberjack arms, caught me
around the waist and held me up, even when I felt
my knees collapse entirely and the horizon tilted
quickly as in a feverish dream. His right ear was
split and crusted with black blood, and his eyes
were bright with control of his own pain, but it
never showed in his voice and his arm stayed
locked hard around my waist.

"Stay up, doc. We're going to need all of our
corpsmen," he said. "Just throw one foot after an-

other. Don't use your knees. You hear me, son? These bastards won't march us much farther."

And for the next four miles we went down the road like two Siamese twins out of step with each other. That night the guards put us in a wooden schoolhouse surrounded by concertina wire, and in his sleep the major cried out once and tore open his mutilated ear with his fingernails.

Several months later I heard that he died of dysentery in the Bean Camp.

I was in three camps while I was a P.O.W. Whenever the complexion of the war changed or a new offensive was begun by one side or the other, the Chinese moved us in cattle cars or Russian trucks or on foot to a new camp where there was no chance of our being liberated, since we were an important bargaining chip at the peace talks. I spent two months at the Bean Camp, a compound of wretched wooden shacks used by the Japanese to hold British prisoners during World War II, and for reasons unknown to me, since I had no military knowledge worth anything to the North Koreans or the Chinese, I was singled out with twelve others, including two deranged Greeks, for transfer to Pak's Palace outside of Pyongyang. Major Pak conducted his interrogations in an abandoned brick factory, and each morning two guards led me across the brick yard covered with fine red dust to a small,

dirty room that was bare except for two straight-
backed chairs and the major's desk. A rope with a
cinched loop in one end hung from a rafter, and
when everything else failed the major would tie the
hands of a prisoner behind him and have him
drawn into the air by the arms and beaten with
bamboo canes. It was called Pak's Swing, and the
screams that came from that room were not like
human sounds.

Major Pak's personality was subject to abrupt
changes. Sometimes his eyes burned like those of
a religious fanatic or an idealistic zealot who reveled in the pain of his enemies. His tailored uniform
was always immaculate, as though he were born to
the professional military, but the wrong answer
from a prisoner would make his face convulse with
hatred and his screaming would become incoherent. Then moments later his eyes would water, his
constricted throat would relax, and his voice would
take on the tone of a tormented man who was
forced to do things to people who couldn't understand the necessity of his job or the historical righteousness of his cause. The two Greeks suffered
most from him, because he was sure that their insane, pathetic behavior was an act. Each night they
were returned to our building streaked with blood
and moaning in words that we couldn't understand.

The major also had fixations. He threatened to tear out my fingernails with pliers unless I told him where the 101st Airborne planned to drop into North Korea. I infuriated him when I answered that I was a Navy corpsman and that I had spent only six days on the line before capture. He believed that all Americans lied instinctively and looked down upon him as an Oriental of inferior intelligence. He struck me in the head with the pliers and cut my scalp, and as I leaned over with the blood trickling across my eye I waited for him to order the guards to draw me up on the rope. However, he threw a glass of water in my face and pulled my head up by the hair.

"Americans are weak. You can't accept pain for yourselves. You only expect others to bear it," he said.

Then I realized that it really didn't matter to him whether or not I knew anything about the 101st Airborne. He hated me because I was everything which he identified with the young American archetype portrayed in *The Saturday Evening Post:* I was tall, blond, good looking, unscarred by hunger or struggle or revolutions whose ideology was just rice. So Major Pak's interest in me was personal rather than of a military nature, and he soon tired of interrogating me in favor of a British commando

who had been caught behind their lines, and I was
sent back to the Bean Camp in a captured U.S.
truck loaded with Australian prisoners.

But my recall deals primarily with Camp Five in
No Name Valley, where I spent the greater portion
of the war until I was exchanged at Freedom Village
in 1953. Also, it was here that I learned that men
can live with guilt and a loathsome image of themselves which previously they didn't believe themselves capable of enduring.

The Yalu River was north of our camp, and in
the winter the ice expanded against the banks and
rang in the cold silence at night, and sometimes we
would hear it break up and crash in great yellow
chunks at a turn in the current. The wind blew all
the time, sweeping out of the bare hills across the
river in China, and when there was no fuel in our
shack we slept on the floor in a group, breathing
the stench of our bodies under the blankets, the
nauseating odor of fish heads on our breath, and
the excretions of men with dysentery who couldn't
control themselves in their sleep.

We were always cold during the winter. Even
when we had fuel to burn in our small iron stove
the heat would not radiate more than a few feet,
and the wind drove through the cracks in the
boards and would drop the temperature enough to
freeze our jerrycan of water unless we kept it close

to the fire. During the day the sun was a pale yellow orb in the sky, and the light was never strong enough through the gray winter haze to cast a hard shadow on the ground. Three men were taken out with a guard once a week to forage for wood, but the landscape was largely bare and the sticks and roots that hadn't already been picked up were now covered by ice and snow. We had one pair of mismatched knitted mittens in our shack, and when the wood detail went out one man would take the mittens and be responsible for gathering the largest share of fuel, as our fingers would often be left cut and swollen or discolored at the tips from frostbite after a day of ripping frozen sticks out of the snow.

There were oil stoves in the camp, but these went to the progressives, those who had signed peace petitions, confessions to participating in germ warfare, or absurdly worded statements denouncing Wall Street capitalists. The progressives were kept in two oblong buildings on the far side of the compound, separated from the rest of us by a barbed-wire fence and a wooden gate that stayed locked with a chain. Many of them were informers, or "snitches," and they would have been killed had they been forced to live with the rest of the prisoner population. In the morning they exercised in the yard behind the wire fence, their faces averted so they wouldn't have to look at the rest of us.

They received the same diet as we did, bean cakes, millet, and boiled corn, but much more of it, and occasionally they were given some greens and hardboiled eggs, and they didn't have to worry about beriberi and diarrhea that left your entrails and rectum burning day and night. I should have hated them for the weight on their bodies and the flush of health in their faces, the Red Cross packages they were given by the guards, but I was always too sick, cold, or afraid to care what they did on their side of the fence. Like most of the others I didn't believe that we would ever be liberated or exchanged. New prisoners told us that the Chinese had poured into South Korea, the ROK's had thrown down their weapons and run, and our forces were being pushed into the sea. So even the most optimistic and strong knew that freedom was probably years away, and our death rate in the camp averaged a dozen men a day.

Some died quietly in their sleep under their blankets, and in the morning we found them white and stiff, the skin hard as marble, and we dragged them outside the shack like pieces of stone and left them for the burial squad. Others died delirious with agony, their eyes feverish and rolling white in their heads, their inflamed entrails bulging out the colon like inflated rubber. There was nothing to do for them—no medicine, no priest, not even the option of killing out of mercy.

There were fifteen enlisted men in my shack (the Chinese kept the officers, NCO's, and enlisted men separated from one another so there would be no system of military order or authority among us). We spent our days in boredom or listening to ridiculous lectures by Colonel Ding and a "group monitor," one of the progressives whom Ding always brought with him. Ding was a small, thin man, with a harelip and a face that was as lifeless as wax. There were spaces between his front teeth, and when he ranted about imperialism and the American bombing of Pyongyang his disfigured mouth gave his face the appearance of a lunatic's. He was fond of telling us that he had attended the University of California for a year in the thirties, and also that he had been with Mao on the Great March. Many times he would digress from his tirades on the evils of the Western world and slip into a history of his own career, which seemed to give him a special pleasure. Sometimes he would ask where each of us was from, and then show the knowledge that he had of that area, although he often referred to such places as "San Antonio, Missouri." The group monitor was usually even more pathetic. He would stand behind the colonel, embarrassed, his gloved hands never able to find a pocket more than a few moments, and sometimes he would light a cigarette nervously, then pinch it out and put it back in the pack when our eyes looked into his. After the colonel had finished, the monitor would read to us from his journal, his self-deluding confession of guilt, and tell us that American troops were waging a war against innocent people and that we were as much victims of the defense industrialists as the people whom we killed. But his face always stayed buried in the notebook, as though he couldn't read his own handwriting, or he stared above our heads at the distant hills. Many times his words faltered and he would look help-lessly at the colonel, who would only nod for him to go on. I suppose that I felt more pity towards the progressives than anger. They were cared for and would live, and eventually they would have to face some of us after the peace came.

However, our classes weren't merely an exercise in Marxist buffoonery. The Chinese knew a great deal about the effect of compromise on the indi-vidual. The progressives did not end up on the other side of the wire fence simply because they knew that the rations were better there. It was a gradual process, much like the irreversible stages of seduction portrayed in a stag movie. Most of us knew that it was a matter of time before we died

of hunger or any of the diseases that accompanied
it, and if we volunteered for Ding's classes, although it was never stated, we knew that the guards
would put extra bean cakes in our shack's food
bucket at night. And once we were in the classes
all we had to do was sign a non-political peace
petition, asking in the most general terms for an
end to the war (supposedly these were sent to the
United Nations), and our millet would include fish
heads, which we could boil into broth with roots
and give to those who had the worst cases of dysentery. Then if we wanted an occasional hardboiled
egg or a package of tobacco for the shack, we could
say a couple of sentences against war into a tape
recorder without identifying ourselves. Many
nights we sat close to the small stove in silence, the
honey bucket reeking in the corner, and thought
about the next stage in the progression. Sometimes
we would discuss the morality of signing a peace
petition or whether or not it was all right to do it
if you misspelled your name or gave your serial
number incorrectly, since someone would surely
know that you didn't mean it after all and you had
beaten the Chinese at their own game, and I
thought of Chaucerian monks debating the virtue
of their fornication.

"Fuck it. I'm going to sign what the bastard
wants," one man would say. "Nobody believes that

shit, anyway. It probably don't even go out of
camp. Ding gets his rocks off and we get some
more chow. It's just a piece of paper. He probably
wipes his ass with it."

We wrote journals for Colonel Ding, confessing
imaginary sins and describing the poverty of our
lives in America (many times this was done as much
to relieve our boredom as it was to earn extra rations). He particularly liked descriptions of slums
and sweatshops. Often we would collaborate on
one journal and invent accounts of social injustice
that would make Charles Dickens pale. Orphans
were beaten with whips by Catholic nuns, virtuous
young girls were forced into prostitution and infected with venereal disease by fat bankers, southern policemen fired their pistols from car windows
into Negro homes, a dismal pall of despair and political oppression hung over the tenement buildings
of the working classes while Zionists with faces like
sleek pigs filled their bank accounts with the profits
of war. We all had committed every type of sin,
from sodomy and incest to fornication with sheep.
In the candle light at night we reveled in our in-
iquity and wrote detailed histories of ax murders,
arson, screwing a dead woman, and male rape in
the shower at the Y.M.C.A. No group of men had
ever been guilty of greater crimes, and the more

depraved the confession the more generous Ding became towards his captives.

We all grew to know each other in the intimate and physical way that men do when in confinement. There was no secret shame or weakness that one of us could conceal from the others for very long. We shared our love affairs, our nights of depravity in Japanese brothels, our memories of a beating by a bully on the elementary school ground, our failures with wives and company bosses. We knew each other's smell, latrine habits, particular nightmares, or when one man was masturbating under the blanket. Through hunger and fear our virtues and inadequacies burned just below the skin. When one man in the shack died and was replaced by a new prisoner, we knew him within a week as well as we had the lifeless piece of stone we had dragged out into the compound for the burial detail.

We were of every background and mental complexion; the helpless who already had the smell of their dying in their clothes; the strong ones, the gladiators, with iron in their bodies, who knew they could live through anything and boiled their fish heads into broth for the sick; the brave and the terrified, the cowards and the Shylocks, the hoarders, the dealers, the religious, and those whose self-sacrifice made them glow, in the hush of their deaths, with the aura of early martyrs. There was Joe Bob Winfield from Baton Rouge, a redneck hill-billy and an ex-convict at nineteen, with leg-iron scars on his ankles and a story about every type of crime and prison caper; Bertie Fast, the house mouse, our one roaring homosexual, who was raped his first week in camp and liked it so much that he went professional; a Sears Roebuck shoe salesman from Salt Lake who wrote endless letters to his wife and children which Ding threw in the garbage can; O. J. Benson from Okema, Oklahoma, a bootlegger who used to run whiskey from Joplin in a book-mobile before the war; a reactivated World War II paratrooper, the oldest man in the shack, who had spent two years in a German concentration camp; Cigarette Williams, the other Navy corpsman, from Mount Olive, Alabama, a six-foot-five country singer who hanged himself during the night be-cause his feet were so frostbitten he couldn't put boots on them; the Australian miner who called Ding a bloody yellow nigger and was strung up all day on a rafter by his hands; and the wild Turk who knew no English, a man on fire, a killer with insane eyes and a bricklayer's trowel hidden in his tick mattress.

There were many others who came and died or were transferred for interrogation, but only two of them from my shack are important in this brief account of my Korean experience. Pfc. Francis Ramos from San Angelo had Indian-black hair, wide-set intense eyes, hard bones in his face, and hands and wrists that could break boards in half. He used to drive a beer truck before he was drafted, and the muscles in his shoulders and chest were as taut and hard as concrete from years of loading and stacking metal beer kegs. There were white scars on his knuckles where they had been mashed on a warehouse ramp, and another thick, raised scar that he had received in a whorehouse brawl ran back in a crooked line through his hair. He had an obsession with escape. He had spent six months in a city stockade once for nonsupport, and he was released only after the jailer became convinced that he was mad, and solitary confinement and beatings with rolled newspapers would not make him less of a threat to the guards and the rest of the prison population. He had been Golden Gloves middleweight champion of Texas in high school, and sometimes when I looked at his huge fists and the swollen veins in his wrists I had nightmarish images of what he must have done to his opponents in the ring.

He couldn't sleep at night. After Sergeant Tien Kwong handed us our food bucket and locked the chain on the shack door, Ramos's eyes flicked wildly across the walls and ceilings, his breathing

became deeper, and then he would set about doing
dozens of unnecessary things with the frenetic energy of a man on the edge of hysteria. He put fuel
into the stove when we were trying to conserve
every twig, boiled water to make soup when we had
no fish heads, shook out his blankets and folded
them so he could unfold them again, restrung his
bootlaces, tried to teach the wild Turk English, and
eventually sat alone in the darkness after the rest
of us had gone to sleep. He would be so tired the
next day that sometimes his head would fall on his
chest during one of Ding's lectures, which meant
one night in the hole under the sewer grate.

Then there was Airman First Class Lester Dixon,
captured when the Chinese overran Seoul, a teen-
age hoodlum from Chicago, one of the dealers, a
ten percenter, a poolroom hustler and reefer salesman on the South Side, slick, a kid with a venal
mind and an eye for the profit to be made from
free enterprise, blue movies, dope, and fifteen-year-
old Negro prostitutes. He had tattoos of skulls and
snakes' heads on his arms, and his hair had grown
out long enough to comb back in ducktails. His
colorless face was like the edge of a hatchet. He
thought of charity as naïveté, bravery as stupidity,
and honesty with others, even in a prisoner of war
compound, a fool's venture.

He shared nothing. He stood first in line for his

bean cakes and millet, and ate alone from his tin plate in one corner while the rest of us put small bits of our food into the soup pot on the stove for the Australian who was dying of beriberi. He was never ashamed of not sharing, or at least he didn't show it; he ate with his face in his plate, his chopsticks scraping against the metal, as though his whole being were concentrated into one scrap of bean cake that he might miss.

It was a cold, windswept gray morning with hailstones on the ground, and Dixon had just left the shack with the wood detail.

"I think he's a snitch," Ramos said. "I seen him eating some vitamin pills in the dark last night."

We were hunched around the iron stove, bent forward towards the heat. Our breaths steamed out like ice in the silence.

"Are you sure?" I said.

"He took three of them out of his pocket and swallowed them dry."

"I don't know about no vitamin pills," Joe Bob, our ex-convict, said, "but I got something in my pecker that goes off when I get near a snitch, and that boy gives me a real bone."

"If you're right, what are we going to do with him?" another man said.

"For openers, you better start shutting up about running," Joe Bob said. His sandy red hair stuck out from under his stocking cap, and he chewed on the flattened end of a matchstick in one corner of his mouth.

"We ice him," Ramos said.

"Hey, cut that shit, man," Joe Bob said. "Ding'll waste the whole shack."

"No, he ain't," Ramos said. "I'll tell Kwong that Dixon's been spitting blood and ask him for some eggs, and then we wait a few days and smother him."

"I tell you, buddy, they ain't that stupid," Joe Bob said.

"We got to take him out one way or another," O. J., the bootlegger from Okema, said. "If Ding's greasing him, he's got to burn somebody."

"Yeah, you don't fuck around with guys like this."

"There's other ways to get a snitch out of the shack," Joe Bob said. "We can turn the Turk loose on him, and he'll ask Ding to transfer over with the pros."

"You're not sure about him, anyway," I said. "He could have gotten those pills off of somebody else in the yard."

"You know that's a lot of crap, too, Holland. He smelled like a snitch when he first come in here," Ramos said.

"He's a pimp and a wheeler, and that's all he's

been his whole life. That doesn't mean he's working for Ding," I said.

"I'll do it in the middle of the night," Ramos said. "There won't be no sound, and he'll look just like every other guy we drug out in the yard."

"I ain't telling you what to do," Joe Bob said, "but you got some pretty amateur shit in your head for this kind of scene. Ding might be a harelip dickhead, but he ain't dumb and he's going to fry our balls in a skillet before you get done with this caper."

"The sonofabitch has to go. What else are we going to do with him?" O. J. said.

"If you got to ice him, use your head a minute and do it out in the yard," Joe Bob said. "Catch him in a bunch during exercise time and bust him open with the Turk's trowel. You'll probably get shot, anyway, but maybe the rest of us won't get knocked off with you."

"If you don't want in it, just stay out of my face," Ramos said.

"Like I said, I ain't trying to grow any hairs in your asshole. You just don't know what you're doing. Like this escape caper. I chain-ganged in the roughest joint in the South, and I started to run once myself, but you got to be out of your goddamn mind to try and crack a place like this. You got two fences to cut through, there's a hundred yards of bare ground between both of them, and them gooks up on the platform ain't going to be reading fortune cookies while you're hauling for Dixie. You better get your head rewired before Ding lays you out in the yard like he done to that Greek that took off from the wood detail."

"If I get nailed I'll buy it running on the other side of that wire," Ramos said. "I ain't going to stay here and shit my insides out till somebody rolls me into the yard like a tumblebug. There's a colored sergeant with a compass and some pliers for the fence, and he figures if we can make it to the sea we can steal a boat and get out far enough for one of our choppers to pick us up."

"Goddamn, if that ain't a real pistol, Ramos. I once knew a guy that climbed into the back of a garbage truck with chains on, buried himself in the trash, and rode down the highway with the hacks looking all over for him. Except he almost got fried when they unloaded the truck in the county incinerator. But you got him beat, buddy. Running across North Korea with a nigra. Now that's cool. You guys ought to stand out like shit in an ice cream factory."

Ramos didn't say anything more. He glared at the gray ash in the grate awhile, then paced around the shack, beating his arms in the cold. He didn't have the intelligence or prison experience to argue with Joe Bob, but we knew that he planned to kill Dixon, regardless of what anyone said.

And it wasn't long before Dixon knew it, too. He came in from the wood detail late that afternoon, his face red and chafed with windburn, and dropped a load of sticks and roots by the stove. There was snow in his hair, and his quilted pants were wet up to the knees. In the silence we heard Kwong lock the chain on the door. Dixon pulled off his mittens with his teeth and stuck his hands under his armpits.

"Somebody else is going on that bastard next time," he said. "That whole goddamn field's picked clean. I broke two fingernails digging down to the ground."

No one answered.

"Shit, look at them."

We turned our faces away or found things to do that would remove us from the eventual meeting of eyes between Ramos and Dixon. But instead it was O. J. and Bertie Fast, the drag queen, who tore open the wrapper and let Dixon look for just a moment inside the box.

"What is this crap, anyway?" Dixon said. "Maybe I didn't wipe my ass clean this morning or something. Don't I smell sweet enough to you, house mouse?"

"I didn't say anything," Bertie said, his voice weak and his eyes searching for a spot on the far wall.

"House mouse, you better not hold out on me."

"Fuck off, man," O. J. said. He was sticking twigs into the fire grate, and his jawbones were flat against the skin.

"What's the deal, then?" Dixon said. "You want me to kick in part of my chow for the soup? Okay. No sweat. Is everybody cool now?"

"Where did you get vitamin pills?" O. J. said.

"Vitamins? You must have a wild crab loose in your brain." But he was surprised, and there was a flicker of fear in his face.

"Yeah. Like those little red ones Ding gives to the pros," O. J. said.

"You better see a wig mechanic when you get out of here. You got real problems."

"You're holding a hot turd with both hands, buddy," Joe Bob said. "This ain't the time for none of that smartass yankee jive."

"You guys have been flogging your meat too much or something. I mean what kind of joint is this, anyway? I spend the whole day digging in the ice with Kwong jabbing me in the ass, and I come back and you guys got me nailed for a pro."

"How did you get the pills?" I said.

Everyone was looking at him now. The snow in his hair had melted, and his face was damp with

water and perspiration. He held his two bruised
fingers in one hand and glanced at the locked
door.

"I traded them off a spade in the yard for some
cigarettes. All right, so I didn't share them. Big deal.
You going to tear my balls out because I want to
stay alive?"

"Which spade?" O. J. said.

"I don't know. He's with the NCO's."

"There ain't but one over there," Ramos said.

"Maybe he's an enlisted man. What difference
does it make? All those boons look alike."

"Get it straight, cousin. That turd is melting in
your hand," Joe Bob said.

"You guys already want to fry me. It don't make
any difference what I say. You've been pissed ever
since I come in here because I wouldn't put in my
chow for guys that were already dead. All of you
got a purple heart nailed right up in the middle of
your forehead because you keep some poor sonofabitch alive a few extra days so he can shit more
blood and chew his tongue raw. If I buy it I hope
there ain't a bunch like you around."

"Okay, you got the pills off a colored sergeant,"
Ramos said. He sat cross-legged on his blanket
close to the stove, rubbing his dirt-caked bare feet
with his hand. "That's all we wanted to know. Next
time you share anything you get in the yard."

Dixon stared into Ramos's face, and then realized that he was looking at his executioner.

"Not me, buddy," he said. "You're not going to stick my head down in the mattress. None of you pricks are. You find some other cat to hang a frame on. How about Bertie here? He don't keep his ass soft and fat on bean cakes."

"Quit shouting. There ain't anybody going to bother you," Ramos said. "Just don't try to bullshit us next time."

"No, you're going to ice me. You been wanting to do it a long time, you spick, and now you got these other bastards to go in with you. Hey, Kwong!" He began beating against the wooden door with his fists and kicking his feet into the boards. The chain and padlock reverberated with the blows.

"You get down here. You hear me? I want to see Ding!"

O. J. and Ramos started for him at the same time, but Joe Bob jumped up in front of both of them and stiff-armed them with all his weight in the chest.

"The shit already hit the fan. Just ride it out and stay cool," he said.

We heard Kwong running through the frozen snow outside. Dixon's face was white with fear, and he brought his knees into the door as though they could splinter wood and snap metal chain after his feet and fists had failed. Kwong turned the lock and threw open the door, with his burpgun slung on a leather strap around his neck and the barrel pointed like an angry god into the middle of us. His squat, thick body was framed against the gray light and the snow-covered shacks behind him, and his peasant face was concentrated in both anger and anticipation of challenge. He grabbed Dixon by his coat and threw him into the snow, then flicked off the safety on his gun.

"Crazy," Joe Bob said, pointing to his head. "He had the shits all week. *Shea tu*. Blood coming out his hole."

We were all frozen in front of the burpgun, each of us breathing deep in our chests, our hearts clicking like dollar watches. I couldn't look at the gun. Dixon got to his knees in the snow and started crying.

"He needs medicine," Joe Bob said, and held his head back and pointed his thumb into his mouth. "Shits all the time. Got shit in his brain."

"You fucked," Kwong said, and kicked the door shut with his foot, then locked the chain.

He must have hit Dixon with the stock of his burpgun, because we could hear the wood knock into bone, then the two of them crunched off in the snow towards Ding's billet on the other side of the wire.

The next morning at dawn Kwong was back with two other guards. They opened the door and motioned us against the far wall of the shack with their guns before they stepped inside. The fire in the stove had died out during the night, and the room temperature must have been close to zero. We stood in our socks, shivering under the blankets we held around our shoulders, and tried to look back steadily at Kwong while his eyes passed from face to face. He already knew the ones who had been chosen for the first interrogation, but he enjoyed watching us hang from fishhooks. Then he motioned his burpgun at five of us: O. J., Bertie Fast, Joe Bob, the Turk, and me. We sat down in the middle of the floor and laced on our boots, then marched in single file across the yard with the guards on each side of us. The pale sun had just risen coldly over the hills, and as I looked at our dim shadows on the snow I felt that my last morning was now in progress, and that I should have bought it back there in the Shooting Gallery and whoever shuffles the cards had just discovered his mistake and was about to set things straight.

The wounds in my legs had never healed and had become infected, and when I slowed my pace in the snow Kwong jabbed the barrel of his gun into my scalp. I felt the skin split and I fell forward on my hands and knees. Kwong kicked me in the kidney and pulled me erect by my hair.

"You walk, cocksuck," he said.

I put my arm over Joe Bob's shoulder, my side in flames, and limped along with the others to the yellow brick building that Ding used for his headquarters. Bertie Fast's eyes were wide with terror, and I could see the pulse jumping in his neck. He looked like a child in his oversized quilted uniform and all the blood had drained out of his soft, feminine face. Even Joe Bob, with scars from the black Betty on his butt, was afraid, although he held it down inside himself like a piece of sharp metal. But the wild Turk showed no fear at all, or possibly he didn't even know what was taking place. His hot black eyes stared out of his white, twisted face, and I wondered if he had the trowel hidden somewhere inside his clothes. His tangled black hair had grown over his shoulders, and he breathed great clouds of vapor, as though he had a fever, through his rotted teeth. He stood immobile with the rest of us while Kwong knocked on the door, and I thought that beyond those hot black eyes there was a furnace instead of a brain.

Ding sat behind his desk in his starched, high-collar uniform with a tea service in front of him.

Dixon stood in one corner by the oil stove, his face
heavy with lack of sleep, and there was a large,
swollen knot above his right eyebrow. His eyes
fixed on Ding's desk when we entered the room,
and drops of sweat slid down his forehead in the
red glow of the stove.

Ding finished his tea, flicked a finger for a guard
to remove the tray, and lit a Russian cigarette. He
leaned forward on his elbows, puffing with his harelip, his eyes concentrated like BB's into the smoke,
and I knew that we were all going to enact a long
and painful ritual that would compensate Ding in
part for his lack of a field command.

"I know there's a plan for an escape," he said,
quietly. "It's a very foolish plan that will bring you
hardship. There has never been an escape from a
Chinese People's detention center, and you're hundreds of miles from the American lines. Now, this
can be very easy for you, and it will also help the
men who would be shot in trying to escape. Give
me their names and you can return to your building, and nothing will be done to the men involved."

We stood in silence, and the snow melted off
our clothes in the warmth of the room. I looked at
Dixon, and for a moment I wished that Ramos had
killed him as soon as he had come back from the
wood detail. The cut in my scalp was swelling and

drawing tight, and my legs felt unsteady from fear and the pain in my calves.

"You're not in a cowboy movie," Ding said. "None of you are heroes. You're simply stupid. I don't want to punish you. I don't want to see the other men shot. There's no reason for it. This war will be over someday and all of you can return to your families. It's insane for you men to die in trying to escape."

Our eyes were flat, our faces expressionless, and the room was so quiet that I could hear Kwong shifting the weight of his burpgun on its strap.

"Do you want me to punish all of the men in your building?" Ding said. "Do you want to see the sick Australian punished because of a stupid minority? All of you grow up on silly movies about Americans smiling at death. You think the Chinese are busboys in restaurants and laundrymen for your dirty clothes. You believe your white skin and Western intelligence reduces us to fools in pigtails groveling for your tips."

"We don't know about no escape, Colonel," Joe Bob said. "Nobody can crack this joint. Dixon give you a lot of shit last night."

"You do think we're stupid, don't you?"

"No, sir, we don't. I done time before, Colonel, and I don't want to get burned because some jerk wants to run. Believe me, there ain't no break planned."

"What do you have to say, airman?" Ding said, and turned towards Dixon.

Dixon's face blanched and he swallowed in his throat. He hadn't thought it was going to be this tough. His eyes looked up at us quickly and then fixed on the desk again. His words were heavy with phlegm.

"It's like I told you, Colonel. They been planning it a long time."

"How long?"

"I heard them whispering about it in the corner the other night after they blew out the candle."

"Which ones?" Ding drew in on the cigarette and looked at Dixon flatly through the smoke. He was really tightening the rack now, and he enjoyed tormenting Dixon as much as he did us.

"All of them, I guess. It was dark."

"You haven't told me very much to earn all those extra gifts."

Dixon's face flushed and drops of sweat began dripping from his hair.

"You should move away from the stove," Ding said. "It's bad for you to become overheated."

"Colonel, we ain't trying to con you," O. J. said. "We got on Dixon because he wouldn't share nothing and he was eating vitamin pills, and he thought we was going to knock him around. He went off his nut and started beating on the door and screaming for Kwong. There wasn't no more to it."

"Would you like to say something, private?"

"No, sir," Bertie said. I had to turn and look at him. His voice was high with fear, but I didn't believe the resolve that was there, also.

"Do you want to suffer with these other men?"

"They told you the truth, Colonel. There ain't any break."

"You haven't spoken. Would you like a turn?" Ding said to me, and at that moment I hated him more than any other human being on earth, not merely for his cruelty but also for the mental degradation that he could continue indefinitely with his physical power over us.

"There's nothing to say, sir. Dixon lied." I wouldn't let my eyes focus on his face, but he sensed my hatred towards him, anyway, and he smiled with that crooked harelip.

"So the corpsman believes me stupid, too. What are we going to do with you American fighting men? That's how you're called at home, isn't it? What would you suggest if you had my position? Intelligent Western men like you must have suggestions. You're a Texan, aren't you, corpsman? You must have learned many lines from cowboy movies."

"They gave it to you straight, Colonel."

"He was one of them last night," Dixon said. "They were going to smother me in my sleep."

(At the time I would have never guessed that the terrified man in the corner, sweating in the heat of the stove, would one day have his picture on the front page of newspapers all over the world as one of the twenty-two American turncoats who chose to remain in Red China after the peace was signed. However, the photograph would show him with full, clean-shaved cheeks, his cap pointed neatly over one eye, a red-blooded enlistee fresh out of the Chicago poolrooms.)

"Then maybe we should begin with you, corps-man," Ding said, and motioned Kwong with his hand.

The sergeant slammed me down in the wooden chair in front of the desk. Ding lit another cigarette and dropped the burnt match into a butt can. The room was now close with the smell of our bodies and the cigarette smoke. I could almost feel the cruel energy and expectation in Kwong's body behind me.

"Do you want this to be prolonged, or do you want to talk in an intelligent manner?"

I stared into nothing, my shoulders hunched and my hands limp in my lap. I could hear the Turk breathing through his teeth in the silence. Kwong slapped me full across the face with his callused hand. My eyes watered and I could feel the blood burning in the skin.

"Do you think you're in a movie now, corpsman?" Ding said. "Are the Flying Tigers going to drop out of the sky and kill all the little yellow men around you?"

I stared through my wet eyes at the wall. The lines in the room looked warped, glittering with moisture, and the oil stove burned brightly red in one corner of my vision. Ding nodded to the sergeant, an indifferent and casual movement of maybe an inch, and Kwong brought my head down with both hands into his knee and smashed my nose. The blood burst across my face, my head exploded with light, and I was sure the bone had been knocked back into the brain. I was bent double in the chair, the blood pouring out through my hands, and each time I tried to clear my throat I gagged on a clot of phlegm and started the dry heaves.

"He don't know nothing, Colonel," Joe Bob said. "Sometimes the guys bullshit about escape, but he don't even do that. He knows they're bullshitting and he always walks away from it. He don't have no names to give you."

"Would you like to give me some names?"

"It ain't nothing but guys setting around shitting each other about a break, Colonel. Anybody in a

joint does the same thing, or you start beating your
rod with sandpaper after a while. Dixon's a goddamn fish and he couldn't cut it, so he sold you a
lot of jive."

"Your corpsman hasn't been hurt at all. The sergeant can do many other things to him."

"I know that, sir," Joe Bob said. "It just won't do
no good. He can't tell you nothing."

"Then I think you should take his chair," Ding
said.

My hands were covered with blood and saliva,
and I was still choking on my breath, but I wanted
to go over Ding's desk and get my thumbs into his
throat. However, I never got the chance to learn if
I was that brave or desperate with pain and hatred,
because the Turk suddenly stopped breathing a moment, his white face filling with dark areas of rage,
and his hot, black eyes glared insanely. Then he
shouted once, a bull's roar that came out of some
awful thing inside him, and he started for Ding with
his huge hands raised in fists over his head.

Kwong stepped quickly in front of him and
swung the stock of his burpgun upward into the
Turk's mouth. I could hear his teeth break against
the wood. He reeled backward on the floor, his lips
cut open in blue gashes, then Kwong raised his foot
back, poised himself, and kicked him in the stom-

ach. The Turk's breath rushed out in a long, rattling gasp, he drew his knees up to his chin, and his face went perfectly white. His mouth worked silently, the veins rigid in his throat, and his eyes were glazed with pain like a dumb, strangling animal's.

Ding was on his feet, shouting in Chinese at Kwong. His waxlike face was enraged, and he kept stabbing one finger in the air at some point outside the building.

"He's crazy, Colonel," Joe Bob said. "A stir freak. He probably don't even know where he is."

"You wouldn't behave intelligently," Ding yelled. "You stand there with your confident faces and think you're dealing with comical peasants. You're stupid men that have to be treated as such."

Kwong pulled me out of the chair by my collar and pushed me towards the door, then he began kicking the Turk in the spine. The Turk's breath came in spasms, and when he tried to suck air down into his lungs the blood bubbled on his lips.

"Pick him up and carry him!"

Joe Bob and O. J. lifted him between them by the arms. His dirty, black hair hung over his face, and his chest heaved up and down.

"Look, Colonel, we ain't to blame for what some nut does," Joe Bob said. "He ain't much better than that with us. We got to watch him all the time."

Ding spoke again in Chinese to Kwong and the other two guards, and they leveled their burpguns at us and motioned towards the door.

"They're going to kill us," O. J. said.

"Colonel, it ain't fair," Joe Bob said. "We never give you no trouble out of our shack."

"I told you it could have been very easy for you."

"There wasn't nothing to tell you," O. J. said. "Do we got to lose our lives because we give it to you straight?"

"Fuck it," Joe Bob said. "They're going to waste us, anyway."

Kwong hit him in the ear with his fist and pushed us outside. It had started to sleet, and the ice crunched like stones under our feet. The sun was a hazy puff of vapor above the cold hills, and then we saw a lone F-86 bank out of the snow clouds and begin its turn before it reached the Yalu River. It dipped its wings once, as all our planes did when they passed over the camp, and then soared away into a small speck on the southern horizon. We stopped at the work shack, and each of us was given a G.I. entrenching tool. The Turk dropped his in the snow, and Kwong picked it up and punched it hard into his chest.

"You hold, cocksuck," he said.

Kwong chained the door shut, and we marched across the compound, past the silent faces of the progressives who watched us from their exercise yard, past the few men who had stopped scrubbing out the lice from their clothes under the iron pump, past our own shack and the men inside who were pressed up against the cracks in the wall, and finally into the no-man's-land between the two fences that surrounded the camp.

"Here. You dig hole," Kwong said.

"Oh, my God," Bertie said.

"You dig to put in shit." He kicked five evenly spaced places in the snow, and then raised his burp-gun level with one hand.

We folded our entrenching tools down like hoes and started chopping through the ice into the frozen ground. The bridge of my nose was throbbing and the blood had congealed in my nostrils. I had to breathe through my teeth, and the air cut into my chest like metal each time I took a swing. The Turk knelt in a melted depression around him, thudding his shovel into the ground, while large crimson drops dripped from his mouth into the snow. I raised my eyes and saw the compound filling with men. The guards were unlocking all the shacks while Ding delivered a harangue through a megaphone. He had his back to us and I couldn't understand the electronic echo of his words, but I knew the compound was receiving a lesson in the need for cooperation between prisoner and captor.

Hundreds of faces stared at us through the wire, the steam from their breaths rising into the air, and I began to pray that in some way their concentrated wills could prevent Kwong from dumping that pan of bullets into our bodies.

He walked back and forth in front of us, his eyes bright, his hand rubbing the top of the ventilated barrel. His face was as tight and flat as a shingle, and when one man slowed in his digging he jabbed the gun hard into his neck. Some of the prisoners said Kwong had been a train brakeman in North Korea before the war and that all of his family had been killed in the first American bombings. So he enjoyed his work with Americans. And now he was at his best, in his broken English, with the loading lever on the magazine pulled all the way back.

"Deep. No smell later," he said.

We were down two feet, the mud and broken ice piled around us. I was sweating inside my clothes, and strange sounds lifted in chorus and disappeared in my mind. The wind polished the snow smooth in front of me, rolling small crystals across Kwong's boots. His leather laces were tied in knots across the metal eyes. The sleet had stopped, and the shadow of my body and the extended shovel moved about as a separate, broken self on the pile of dirt and ice that grew larger on the edge of my hole.

"I ain't going to buy it like this," O. J. said. "I ain't going to do the work for these bastards."

"You dig deep," Kwong said.

"You dig it."

"Pick up shovel," Kwong said.

"Fuck you, slope." O. J. breathed rapidly, and the moisture from his nose froze on his lip.

"All stand, then."

"Mother of God, he's going to do it," Bertie said.

The sun broke from behind a cloud, the first hard yellow light I had seen since I had come to the camp. My eyes blinked against the glaring whiteness of the compound and the hills. The ice on the barbed wire glittered in the light, and the hundreds of prisoners watching us beyond the fence stared upward at the sky in unison, their wan faces covered with sunshine. The stiff outlines of the buildings in the compound leaped at me and receded, and then Kwong turned his burpgun sideways so that the first burst and recoil would carry the spray of bullets across all five of us.

"You stand!"

We got to our feet slowly, our clothes steaming in the reflected warmth of the sun, and stood motionless in front of our graves. My body shook and I wanted to urinate, and my eyes couldn't look directly at the muzzle of his burpgun. I choked in my throat on a clot of blood and gagged on my hand. Joe Bob's face was drawn tight against the bone, and Bertie was shaking uncontrollably. O. J.'s arms were stiff by his sides, his hands balled into fists, and there were spots of color on the back of his neck. The Turk's heavy shoulders were bent, his ragged mouth hung open, and the blood and phlegm on his chin dripped on the front of his coat.

"You want talk Ding now?" Kwong said, and smiled at us.

No one spoke. The line of men behind the fence was silent, immobile, some of their heads turned away.

"Who first?"

"Do it, you goddamn bastard!" O. J. shouted. Then his eyes watered and he stared at his feet.

"You first, then, cocksuck." Kwong raised the burpgun to his shoulder and aimed into O. J.'s face, his eyes bright over the barrel, a spot of saliva in the corner of his mouth. He waited seconds while O. J.'s breath trembled in his throat, then suddenly he swung the gun on its strap and began firing from the waist into the Turk. The first burst caught him in the stomach and chest, and he was knocked backward by the impact into the grave with his arms and legs outspread. The quilted padding in his coat exploded with holes, and one bullet struck him in the chin and blew out the back of his head. His

black eyes were dead and frozen with surprise before he hit the ground, and a piece of broken tooth
stuck to his lower lip. Kwong stepped to the edge
of the grave and emptied his gun, blowing the face
and groin apart while the brass shells ejected into
the snow. When the chamber locked open he
pulled the pan off, inserted a fresh one in its place,
and slid back the loading lever with his thumb. The
other two guards began to kick snow and dirt from
the edge of the grave on top of the Turk's body.

"You next, corpsman. But you kneel."

The wire fence and the empty faces behind it,
the wooden shacks, the yellow brick building
where it had all begun, Kwong's squat body and
the hills and the brilliance of the snow in the sunlight began to spin around me as though my vision
couldn't hold one object in place. My knees went
weak and I felt excrement running down my buttocks. The wind spun clouds of powdered snow
into the light.

Kwong shoved me backwards into the hole, then
leaned over me and pushed the gun barrel into my
face. His nostrils were wide and clotted with mucus
in the cold.

"You suck. We give you boiled egg," he said.

I clinched my hands and put my arms over my
face. There were crystals of snow, like pieces of
glass, in my eyes, and he brought his boot heel

down into my stomach and forced the barrel against my teeth. My bowels gave loose entirely, a warm rush across my genitals and thighs, and my heart twisted violently in my chest.

"Good-bye, prick. You no stink so bad later," and he pulled the trigger.

The chamber snapped empty, a metallic clack that sent all the air rushing out of my lungs.

Kwong and the other two guards were laughing, their faces split in hideous grins under their fur caps. Their bodies seemed to shimmer in the brilliant light. Kwong pushed his boot softly into my groin, pinching downward with the toe.

"I put new clip in and we do again. Each time you guess."

He spoke to one of the other guards, who handed him a second clip, then he pulled the empty one loose from his burpgun and held them both behind his back.

"Which hand you like, corpsman?"

"You fucking chink. Get it done!" Joe Bob said.

The guard who had given Kwong the clip struck him back and forth across the face with his open hand. Joe Bob's arms hung at his sides while his head twisted and his skin rang and discolored with each slap.

"I pick for you, then," Kwong said, and he

dropped one pan into the snow and snapped the second one into the magazine.

He stood above me, his gun balanced on its strap against his waist, and we went through it again, except this time I curled into a ball like a child, my hands over my face, a sickening odor rising from my clothes, and when the firing pin hit the empty chamber I vomited a thick yellow residue of millet and fish heads out of my stomach.

Then I heard Ding speak in Chinese through the megaphone on the far side of the fence. Kwong's boots stepped backward, and I saw the shadow of his burpgun swinging loose from his body. But I couldn't move. My heart thundered against my chest, my body was drained of any further physical resistance, and I kept my face pressed into the wetness of my coat sleeves.

"You lucky. All go to hole now. Another time we have class."

I heard Joe Bob, Bertie, and O. J. crunch past me, but I still couldn't lift my head. The other two guards picked me up from the grave by my coat and threw me headlong into the snow. The crystals of ice burned on my face and in my eyes. I got to my feet slowly and stood in a bent position, the compound and the hills shrinking away in the distance and then leaping towards me out of the sunlight. I tried to stand erect, and an electric pain burst through the small of my back and rushed upward into my head. Excrement dripped down my calves into the snow. I looked over at the half-covered body of the Turk in his shallow grave. One glaring eye was exposed through the snow, and his curled fingers extended upward as though he wanted to touch his toes. In seconds it seemed that the others were already far ahead of me, crunching silently between the guards towards the far end of the compound. Kwong pushed me forward between the shoulder blades with his hand, and I stumbled along in the slick, wet tracks of the others, tripping on my bootlaces, to the square of barbed wire and row of holes and sewer grates where Ding put the reactionaries.

One of the guards opened the gate and used an ice hook to pull the grates off four holes. Three occupied holes were still covered with tarpaulins from the night before, the creased canvas heavy and stiff with new snow. Ding pushed me forward with his burpgun at port arms into the first hole and kicked a G.I. helmet in on top of me, then slid the grate back in place. He squatted down and leaned his face in silhouette over me.

"You can play with prick when you get cold tonight," he said.

The hole was eight feet deep and four feet wide,

and the mud walls were covered with a dirty film of ice. The inside of the steel helmet was encrusted and foul from the other men who had used it, and the sour smell of urine had soaked into the floor. I heard the grates dropped heavily into place on the other three holes, then the guards moved away in the snow and chained the wire gate shut.

I spent the next six weeks there, although I lost any concept of time after the first three days. We were each given two blankets, and at night the guards marched a progressive into the wire square, and he emptied out our helmets and handed down our food pans before they covered the grates with the tarpaulins. We had to sleep in a sitting position or with our feet propped up against the wall, and there was always a hard pain in my spine, and sometimes at night I dreamed that I was in a chair car on a train and if I could just stretch my legs out in the right direction the pain would go away. Then I would wake with the blankets twisted around me, the small of my back burning, and I would stand in the darkness until my knees went weak.

During the day we would talk to each other by speaking upward through the iron slits, then our necks would become tired or there wouldn't be anything else to say, and each of us would fall back into his silent fantasies on the floor of the hole.

The wounds in my legs had festered and small pieces of lead rose with the pus to the surface of the skin, and many times I slipped off into feverish, distorted scenes that lasted until I heard the ice hook strike the grate at nightfall. Sometimes my eyes stayed fixed on the pattern of iron over my head and the distant, checkered clouds, as though I were staring upward out of a tunnel, and then I would be fifteen years old again in a winter cornfield, the sun bright on the withered stalks, with the single-shot twelve-gauge against my shoulder and a cottontail racing across the dry rows. I aimed just in front of his head and squeezed off the trigger, and when the gun roared in my ears I knew that I had hit him clean, without destroying any of the meat, and that night Cap would deep-fry him in egg batter and flour for supper. Then I would be back in the Shooting Gallery, and I'd feel the heavy weight of the stretcher in both palms while the potato mashers exploded in our wire and the BAR man searched frantically in the bottom of the ditch for another clip. The wounded Marine on the stretcher stared up at me, his eyes full of terror, as I stumbled forward with his weight over the empty ammunition boxes, then the burpguns raked the ditch and knocked men like piles of rags into the walls, and I dropped him and ran. But in one heart-rushing second I saw the expression of helplessness

and betrayal in his eyes, and in my feverish dream
I wanted to go back and close his eyes with my
fingers and tell him that we were all going to buy
it, they had already overrun us, and there was nowhere I could have taken him.

Each day I saw the Shooting Gallery again,
sometimes in an entirely different way from previously, and the faces of the men in the ditch became
confused; their screams when they were hit and
their death cries often sounded like a distant band
out of tune with itself, and I tried to go back to
the winter cornfield and the smell of oak wood
burning in the smokehouse and the rabbit racing
towards the blackjack thicket. I knew that if I just
held that field in the center of my mind, or the
smokehouse with a shallow depression in the
ground under one wall where my father used to
push in the oak logs, I could keep everything intact
and in its proper place and I wouldn't let Ding or
Kwong make me admit that I was guilty of a
wounded Marine's death.

Then on a bright, sun-spangled day I would look
up through the slits at the drifting clouds and
briefly realize, with a sick feeling in my chest, that
they didn't care about the Marine, they only
wanted me to inform on Ramos and the Negro sergeant, and eventually I might begin to cry in my
sleep, as Bertie sometimes did, and one morning ask

Kwong to take me into Ding's office. I heard the
voices of other men from our shack farther down
the row of holes, and Joe Bob whispered hoarsely
up through his grate one day that the World War
II paratrooper had been machine-gunned and buried next to the Turk. The temperature began to go
above freezing in the midafternoon, the melted
snow ticked into the bottom of the hole, and the
reek from the helmet and my own body often made
me sick when I tried to eat my bean cakes. My hair
and beard were matted with mud and the thick residue of fish heads that I licked from the bottom of
my food pan, and my yellow fingernails had grown
out like a dead person's. My ribs felt like strips of
wood to my touch, and although I had masturbated
my first week in the hole, creating geisha girls under me, with their toy, pale faces and sloe eyes, I
couldn't hold the image of a woman in my mind
more than a few seconds. Then on a wet morning,
with the fog lying close against the ground, I heard
the ice hook click against the sewer grates and the
hushed voices of O. J. and Bertie as the guards
helped them out of their holes.

A day later I was still hoping that they would
return. It was too easy now to bang on the grate
with my food pan and shout for Kwong to pull me
out. Whatever I told Ding now wouldn't have any
effect on Ramos and the sergeant, I thought, and

it was insane to die for men who possibly were
already dead themselves. As the fog rolled over me
and drifted through the iron slits I went through
all the ethical arguments about surrender, and I discovered that there were dozens of ways to justify
any human act, even dishonor. I thought of my
grandfather, who had fought the most dangerous
man in Texas, and I wondered what he would do
if he were here now instead of me. I saw the flashes
of Wes Hardin's revolver, and his murderous,
drunken eyes, and my grandfather standing in the
open barn door with the Winchester in his hands.
Then Hardin wheeled his horse and charged, his
fingers tangled in the mane, the shotgun banging
against the saddle, and Old Hack leaped forward
and swung his rifle barrel down with both hands
into the side of Hardin's head. But his wars had
been fought in a different time, between equally
armed men, under hot skies and in dusty Texas
streets, and death or victory came in a matter of
seconds. He hadn't lived in an age when lunatics
locked men in filthy holes and turned them into
self-hating creatures that were sickened with their
own smell.

So that night, at feeding time, I knew that Old
Hack would understand when I held up my hand
silently to the progressive and he pulled me over
the edge of the hole on my stomach.

I was the eighth man to inform. The Australian died in the hole, and it took another week for Ding to break the three remaining men from our shack. Then on a dripping, gray morning we all stood at the wire and watched Ramos and the Negro sergeant executed and their bodies thrown into an open latrine.

NINE

It was dark as Rie and I drove through the sloping hills towards the Valley. Her face was soft in the glow of the dashboard, and she rubbed one hand on my shoulder.

"You've kept all that inside you for fifteen years?" she said quietly.

"There aren't a lot of other places to put it."

"You weren't to blame for their deaths. The others had already informed."

"That's the strange thing about a certain type of guilt. When you try to confess it and draw the whips across your own back, there's always someone there to tell you that you're really not guilty of anything. Dixon came back from China a year after the war, and I testified against him at his court-martial. But I didn't care what happened to

him anymore. I only wanted to confess before some
type of authority and be exposed publicly for cow-
ardice. Each time that I tried to tell them I had
informed, I was told to answer the questions directly and they disregarded anything else I had to
say. After they gave Dixon five years, officers shook
my hand and wished me luck in law school."

"What happened to the others?"

"Bertie died of beriberi before the truce. O. J.
married an Indian girl and was swelling like a bal-
loon with beer fat, and Joe Bob bought a pool hall
in Baton Rouge. Four others from the shack testified
against Dixon, and the afternoon that he got his
five years we all got drunk together, but we found
that we didn't have many good things to talk
about."

She slipped her arm across my chest and kissed
me behind the ear, and I felt her wet eyelashes
against my skin. I wanted her again, more strongly
than I had ever wanted a woman in my life, and I
pressed the accelerator down and the rolling highway raced towards me in the headlights. We
dropped down into the Valley, and I saw the Rio
Grande under the moon and the candlelit windows
of the adobe houses on the far side. She pressed
her breasts close to me, rubbing her curly hair
against my cheek, and I turned onto the main highway towards my motel.

I woke early the next morning and leaned over her and kissed her lightly on the mouth. Her sun-burned hair was spread on the pillow, and without opening her eyes she put her arms around my neck and pulled me down on top of her. Her body was warm with sleep, and she widened her thighs and ran her hands down my back and moved her lips across my cheek. She breathed softly in my ear, touching the lobe with her tongue, and each time she pressed her stomach into me I felt my skin burn. Then my eyes were closed and I felt my body go weak, the heat gathering like a flame in my loins, and I tried to rise on my elbows and hold it back, but she held her breasts tight against my chest and put her legs in mine and ran her fingers up my neck into my hair.

"Do it now, Hack, and then we'll do it again and again and again."

She stretched out her legs and flattened her stomach, and then the flame grew more intense and went out of me in a long heart-beating rush.

It had been years since I had slept with a woman whom I really loved, and the experience now was as strange and wonderful as the first time I had made love to a girl in high school. The times of need with Verisa, which she and I had both grown to accept, with our feigned affection in the dark, and the indifference towards one another when it was over, seemed like a sophisticated imitation of a Tijuana film that we had seen so many times we were no longer embarrassed by it.

Rie lay against me with her arm across my chest and her face close to my cheek, and I felt her large breasts and the heat in her thighs, and she told me about the strange world of revolution and political rage that she came from: her father, the University of Madrid professor, who was marked for execution by the Guardia Civil during the Civil War and walked barefoot across the mountains into France before the border was closed; her Irish mother, a member of the I.W.W., who worked years for the release of the Scottsboro Boys during the 1930's, went to jail during World War II in protest against the treatment of the Nisei Japanese, and was black-listed as a schoolteacher in California during the McCarthy era. Rie joined CORE and the Mississippi Freedom Project when she was nineteen and rode across the country to McComb in an old school bus with a boiling radiator and freedom signs painted in white letters on the sides. They were going to integrate lunch counters, bus depots, and water fountains and sit in front of segregated hotels with their arms locked in a chain and sing "We Shall Not Be Moved." Instead, their bus was burned, they were knocked off lunch-counter stools and beaten senseless by clean-cut high school kids, dragged by their hair along sidewalks and thrown into police vans, shocked with cattle prods, spat on by housewives, hit with nightsticks, and crowded into filthy drunk tanks, and some of them ended up on Parchman Farm.

"Most of the people on our bus were middle-class kids who believed southern cops were a creation out of a Paul Muni movie," she said. "We were taught how to roll up in a ball with our hands over our heads when they started swinging the clubs, but nobody really thought they would do it. It was just something to talk about on the bus, and everyone was sure that if it really got tight Mr. Clean would appear from somewhere with the Constitution in his hand. After it was all over I was able to accept the cops and what they did and the housewives who were having trouble with their period, but there was one scene I couldn't get out of my head for a long time. The first day in McComb we tried to integrate the lunch counter in Penny's, and a thug hit the black guy next to me in the head with a sugar shaker and split his skin. The black guy tried to look straight ahead and hold his head up level, and a blonde chick of about seventeen took the cap off a salt shaker and poured it into the cut."

I felt her breast rise under my hand, and I pulled her close against me and pressed her face into my neck and kissed her hair. The smooth curve of her back felt like the graceful line of a statue, and when she looked up from the pillow to be kissed again her almond eyes and the slight separation of her lips made my head swim and then the fire began to build inside me again.

Later, we had breakfast in a wood-frame cafe filled with farm and ranch families that had come into town for church, then we drove down the highway under the early sun towards Pueblo Verde. There was still dew on the pastures, and the light breaking across the hills cast a purple haze over the sage and short grass. The air was heavy with the smell of morning and the oak thickets and the churned mud around the windmill troughs, and when the breeze changed direction I could smell the horses and cattle in the fields and the burning hickory in a smokehouse. A few clouds were drifting in from the Gulf, and great areas of shadow passed briefly over the cattle and moved across the crest of the hills. For just a moment I thought I could taste rain in the air, and then the sky was clear again and the blacktop highway began to gather pools of light.

There was a union strike meeting and barbecue planned at the Catholic church in the Mexican district that afternoon, and Rie was supposed to provide transportation for the families in the migrant worker camps who didn't have automobiles. Many of them had been brought in on buses from New Jersey, South Carolina, and Florida, and their crew leaders, who contracted the harvest, would do nothing to help the union, and sometimes they refused to take migrants to the next job if they were seen talking with strike organizers. So we waited on the front porch of the union headquarters for a dozen battered cars and pickup trucks to arrive, and then we rolled in a long rattling caravan down a dusty county road to the first of three labor camps.

The land was flat here, without trees, and the weeds in the ditches along the road were covered with dust. The camp was surrounded with a barbed-wire fence, and crude hand-lettered signs were nailed to the cedar posts: NO TRESPASSING, BEWARE OF DOG, TRAILERS FOR COLORED, UNAUTHORIZED PEOPLE STAY OUT. The buildings were made of wood and covered on the sides with red tar paper. The windows didn't have glass or screens, and the wooden shutters were propped open with boards. The corrugated tin roofs reflected brightly in the sun, and I could hear the hum of flies around the community toilets. The yards were bare of grass, and boxes of garbage stood along the dirt lane that ran through the camp. At intervals between every third cabin there was an iron water spigot where the women washed out diapers and cleaned their dishes, but Rie said the handles were often removed

by the camp owner because the children left the
water running. The showers were located in a gray
concrete enclosure without doors or a roof in the
center of the camp, and when you passed close to
it you could smell the wet reek of the walls and the
mold and the sour stench of stagnant water in the
bottom of the stalls.

Men and women with towels over their shoulders
and toothbrushes went inside together, barefoot
brown children in frayed and wash-faded clothes
played in the dirt yards, and emaciated dogs with
bent spines and mange on their bodies slunk about
in the lane. Four dilapidated school buses with broken windows and license plates from several states
on them were parked by a tin trailer with an air-
conditioning unit in the window and OFFICE
painted above the door. Rie walked up on the
porch of a cabin and knocked while I leaned against
the automobile and smoked a cigar. Mexican men
walking towards the shower building looked at me
and the Cadillac, and I dropped my eyes to the
ground and concentrated on the end of my cigar.
I felt the same way that I had when I drove into
the penitentiary to see Art. I had intruded into a
place where even a courteous nod from me and the
world I represented was a form of patronization.

Several children stood ten feet from me and
stared at my face and the interior of the car. Their

black hair was full of nicks and uneven scissors cuts, and their knees and elbows were covered with dirt. A small girl carried a kitten on her shoulder, and one little boy in cut-off overalls had a broken cap pistol in his hand. I smiled at them, but their faces showed no expression in return. I reached inside and turned on the radio, and the insane, blaring voice of some Baptist preacher roared out of the dashboard.

"Do you kids go to school?" I said. Now that's cool, Holland. Come up with another good one like that.

They looked at me with their silent, black eyes.

"We're going to a barbecue this afternoon. Why don't you ask your folks if you can come along?"

The little girl set the kitten down in the dust and pushed at him with her bare foot. The others continued to stare at the strange man who had just dropped from the stratosphere right on his head. I switched off the radio, closed the car door, stuck my hands in the back pockets of my khakis, and looked off into any direction where I wouldn't have to answer those questioning brown faces. Behind me I heard Rie talking with a woman on the front porch of the cabin, and then a man in a dirty T-shirt, with a swollen stomach, as though he had a hernia, stepped out of the tin trailer and walked towards us.

His bluejeans were bursting just below his navel, his crew-cut head was beaded with sunlight in the center, and his fly was only partly zipped. His shoulders were too small for his head, and the bluejeans sagged in the rear. There was a line of sunburn and dandruff where he wore a hat, and his gray eyes went from me to the Cadillac and back again. I took the cigar out of my mouth and nodded at him.

"How do, sir," he said.

"Pretty fine. How are you today?"

"It's a right nice day, all right." He ran one hand over his fat hip and looked at a spot over my shoulder. "I keep the office here, and I'm supposed to take anybody around the camp that wants to see the workers. Sometimes people can't find who they're looking for, and I got all the cabin numbers up in my trailer."

"Thank you. We're just giving some people a lift to the church."

He pulled a dead cigar butt from his pocket and put it in his mouth. He lowered his crew-cut head and scraped his foot in the dust and rolled the frayed end of the cigar wetly between his lips.

"You see, the soda-pop people that own this land don't like just anybody coming on it. It don't matter to me, but sometimes them union agitators come down here and try to fire up the Mexicans and ni-

gras and shut down the harvest, and I'm supposed
to see that nobody like that gets a free run around
here. Now, like that Mexican woman up there on
the porch. Her husband run off two weeks ago and
she's got five kids in there. She can't afford to miss
a day's work because some union man won't let her
get into the field."

We talked politely, on and on, while Rie loaded
the Cadillac full of children and two huge Negro
women. Well, we have a barbecue planned at the
church today. I don't think that would bother the
soda-pop people. Why don't you have a fresh cigar?
Like I don't have nothing against any religion or
group of people, but there's a priest down there
that's preaching communism or something at the
Mexicans, and it's going to come to a lot of broken
heads and people without no paychecks. I can tell
you that for a fact, by God. It ain't any skin off my
ass, I got that trailer and a salary whether they work
or not, but I don't like to see them lose their jobs
and get kicked out of their cabins because they listen to people that steals their money in union dues
while the citrus burns on the vine. Now, that ain't
right. I have a little Jack Daniels in a flask. Would
you like a ditch and another cigar before we leave?
. . . No, sir, I'm working right now, but tonight
when you come back, drop up to the trailer and I'll
buy you a shot with a couple of cold ones behind

it. . . . Thank you. I'm looking forward to it. . . . Yes, sir. You come back, hear?

I drove back out the barbed-wire gate and headed down the road past the rows of identical cabins with their shimmering tin roofs. The dust rolled away behind me.

"You ought to do public relations for us, you con man," Rie said, and smiled at me over the heads of the children sitting between us.

The Catholic church was made of white stucco and surrounded by oak and chinaberry trees. Pickup trucks and junker cars were parked in the side yard, and Negro, Mexican, and a few white families sat on folding metal chairs with paper plates of barbecued chicken in their laps. Their clothes were sun-faded and starched by hand, and many of the women wore flower-patterned dresses that were sewn from feed sacks. A priest in shirt sleeves was turning chickens on the barbecue grill while the Negro from the union headquarters pulled bottles of beer out of a garbage can filled with cracked ice. I parked the car in the shade of a post oak, and the children raced off across the lawn and started throwing chinaberries at each other. In minutes their washed overalls and checkered shirts were stained with the white, sticky milk from the berries.

"Come on. I want you to meet this wild priest," Rie said.

"I never got along with the clergy."

"Wait till you catch this guy. He's no ordinary priest."

"Let's pass."

"Hack, your prejudices are burning through your face."

"It's my Baptist background. You can never tell when the antichrist from Rome is going to sail his submarine across the Atlantic and dock in DeWitt County."

"Good God," she said.

"You never went to church in a large tent with a sawdust floor."

"With a box of snakes at the front of the aisle."

"There you go," I said.

"Wow. What an out-of-sight place to come from." She took my hand and walked with me across the lawn towards the barbecue pit.

Two Mexican men sat on a table behind the priest and the Negro, playing mariachi guitars with steel picks on their fingers. They looked like brothers with their flat, Indian faces and straw hats slanted over their eyes. The steel picks glinted in the sun as their fingers rolled across the strings.

"What do you say, whiskey brother?" the Negro said. His eyes were red with either a hangover or the beginnings of a new drunk, and his breath was heavy with alcohol and snuff. He popped the cap

off of a sweating bottle of Lone Star and handed it
to me. The foam slipped down the side over my
hand.

"I guess I have a couple of shots in the car if the
smoke gets too much for you," I said. Then it struck
me, as I looked at his cannonball head and remembered the humiliation I had seen in his face the
other night, that I had never learned his name.

"I'm cool today, brother," he said. "Saturday's for
drinking, and Sunday you catch all kinds of sunshine with these church people."

The priest looked like a longshoreman. His thick
arms were covered with black hair, and he had a
broad Irish face with a nose like Babe Ruth and a
wide neck and powerful shoulders under his white
shirt. His black eyes were quick, and when Rie introduced us I had the feeling that he had done
many other things before he had become a priest.

"You handled Art's appeal, didn't you?" he said.

"Yes, I did." I took a cigar from my pocket and
peeled off the wrapper.

"His family appreciated it a great deal. The rest
of us did, too."

"I knew him in the service," I said.

"He told me. I saw him before he was sent to
prison."

I chewed off the tip of my cigar and looked away
at the line of battered cars and trucks gleaming in

the sunlight. Overhead, two bluejays were fighting in the chinaberry tree. Every clergyman has to be so goddamn frank, I thought.

"Have you been here very long, Father?"

"Three months, but I'm being transferred to Salt Lake in September."

"He's the church's favorite Ping-Pong ball," Rie said, and laughed. "He's had five parishes in six years. Kicked out of New Orleans, Compton, California, the Pima reservation in Arizona, and now he's going to turn the Mormons on. I bet those guys will be a real riot."

"You're not improving my image, Rie."

"Listen. This was the guy that took black children through those lines of screaming women and thugs when the elementary schools were integrated in New Orleans. He dumped a cop on his ass in the school doorway and said mass in a Negro church the same day in Plaquemines Parish while the Klan burned crosses on the front lawn."

"Rie's given to hyperbole sometimes, Mr. Holland."

"No, I'm afraid she's pretty exact most of the time, Father," I said.

"Well, at least it wasn't that dramatic. A little pushing and shoving and a few truck drivers sitting on the curb with more Irish in them than they deserve."

He filled two paper plates with chicken, rice
dressing, and garlic bread, and handed them to us.
There were small scars around his knuckles, and his
wrists and forearms were as thick and hard as cord-
wood. He smelled of hickory smoke from the fire,
and his balding head glistened with perspiration in
the broken shade. Rie was right—he wasn't an ordinary man. I remembered the television newsreels
about the priest and exparatrooper chaplain who
had led terrified Negro children from the buses
through the spittle and curses in front of an elementary school in New Orleans in 1961. I also re-
called the one short film clip that showed him
backing down four large men who had poured beer
on the children as they walked up the school steps.

We sat in the shade and ate from our paper
plates and drank bottles of Lone Star while the guitar players picked and sang their songs about infi-
delity, their love for peasant girls in hot Mexican
villages, and Villa's raid on a train loaded with *federales* and machine guns mounted on flatcars. The
children had established forts behind two lines of
folding chairs, and chinaberries flew back and forth
and pinged against the metal, and because it was
somebody's birthday the Negro climbed up an oak
tree, grabbing the trunk with his knees, and hung
a *piñata* stuffed with candy from a piece of cloth
clothesline. Then he formed all the children into a

line, in stair-step fashion, with a foaming beer in his hand, and gave the first child a sawed-off broom handle to swing against the cardboard-crepe-paper horse turning dizzily in the dappled light. The children flailed the *piñata*, and twists of candy showered out over their heads. I borrowed a guitar from one of the musicians and ran my fingers over the strings. The sound hole was inlaid with an Indian design, and there were deep scratches on the face from the steel picks that the owner used.

"Go ahead and boil them cabbages down," Rie said.

I couldn't be profane in front of the priest.

"I never play too well sober. Wrong mental atmosphere for hillbilly guitar pickers," I said.

"Will you go ahead?" she said. Her eyes took on that wonderful brightness they had when she was extremely happy.

I tuned the guitar into D and ran a Jimmie Rodgers progression all the way down the neck, then bridged into an old Woody Guthrie and Cisco Houston song while the Negro opened more bottles of Lone Star and the children rolled over one another in the grass after the candy.

> *Ezekiel saw that wheel a-whirling*
> *Way up in the middle of the air*
> *Tell you what a bootlegger he will do*

Sell you liquor and mix it with brew
Way in the middle of the air.

Later, the men on the strike committee pulled
two long tables and several benches together in
the sun. They sat in the glaring heat, sweat dripping from inside their straw hats over their faces,
their browned forearms on the hot wood, as
though the sunlight were no different from the
shade a few feet away. The warm beer bottles in
their hands were bursting with amber light, and
their faces were all of one calm and intent expression while Rie spoke to them in Spanish. Her
voice was even and flat while she looked quietly
back and forth at the two rows of men, and although my Tex-Mex was good enough so that I
could understand most of what she said, I realized
she was speaking in a frame of reference that had
always belonged in the wretched Mexican hovels
on the other side of my property line. As I leaned
against an oak trunk, watching them through my
sunglasses and sipping a beer, I thought about Art's
description of the anglo roaring down the highway
in his Cadillac towards the next Holiday Inn, un-
aware of anything beyond the billboards that
flashed by him like a kaleidoscopic vision. So have
another beer on that one, Holland, I thought. And
polish your goddamn Spanish.

It was late afternoon and hot when the barbecue ended. A dry wind was blowing from the Gulf, and dust devils spun out of the dirt road and whirled away in the fields. We loaded the children and the two Negro women into the car and drove back to the migrant camp. The tarpaper shacks seemed to glow with the heat, and my friend the camp manager was sprinkling the dirt lane in front of his trailer with a garden hose. His clothes were even filthier than they had been that morning, and his face had a red, whiskey flush. He turned off the water and walked over to the car. The fat in his pot stomach bulged against his T-shirt, and his odor was so strong that I opened the door partway to keep him a few feet from me.

"There was a deputy sheriff down here this afternoon, and he says you're working with them union people."

"Must be somebody else." I watched Rie on the front porch of one of the cabins.

"He knowed this car, and he described you exactly. Even them cigars."

"What else did he have to say?"

"He says he's going to lock your ass in jail. And I'll tell you something else, buddy. You come down here and give me a lot of shit about taking them people to a church barbecue. I don't like nobody lying to me when they come on the property, and

I got a ball bat up there in the trailer to handle anybody that tries to make my job harder than it is."

I bit into the soft wetness of my cigar and closed the door carefully. I felt the anger draw tight across my chest, the blood swelling in my temples, and I looked straight ahead at the sunlight beating down on his silver trailer. I coughed on my cigar smoke and picked a piece of tobacco off my lip.

"Well, sir, we should be gone in a few minutes," I said.

"You better get your luck off that porch and haul it down the road a lot faster than that."

I opened the door again, hard, so that it hit him sharply in the knees and stomach, and looked into his face.

"You're about two remarks ahead of the game right now, podner," I said. "Say anything more and you're going to have problems that you never thought about. Also, if you have any plans about using that baseball bat, you'd better find an apple box to stand on first."

His red face was caught between angry insult and fear, and the sweat glistened in his brows over his lead-gray eyes.

"You're trespassing, and I'm putting in a call to the sheriff's office," he said, and walked away in the dust towards his trailer.

Rie got back in the car, and I closed the windows, turned on the air conditioner as high as it would go, and we rolled out the front gate and headed down the county road towards town. There were buzzards drifting high in the sky on the wind stream, and the sun burned white as a chemical flame. The rocks and alkali dust on the road roared away under the Cadillac.

"Say, take it easy, Lone Ranger," Rie said.

"I've been easy all my life. One of these days I'm going to blow all my Kool-Aid and rearrange a guy like that for a long time."

She put her hand on my arm. "That's not your kind of scene, Hack."

"I'm up to my eyes with rednecks that come on with baseball bats."

"Hey, man, you're not acting like a good con man at all. What did he say?"

"Nothing. He's defending the soda-pop people."

"He clicked a couple of bad tumblers over in your brain about something."

"I burn out a tube once in a while with the chewing-tobacco account. Forget it."

"I heard him say something about getting your luck off the porch. Was that it?"

"Look, Rie, I was raised by a strange southern man who believed that any kind of anger was a violation of some aristocratic principle. So I turn the burner down every time it starts to flare, and sometimes I get left with a broken handle in my hand."

"What did he mean?"

The air conditioner was dripping moisture.

"A guy like that doesn't mean anything," I said. "The words just spill out of a junk box in his head."

"Talk straight, Hack."

"It's a racial remark."

"Is it important to you?"

I felt my heart quicken, because we both knew now why he had gotten inside me.

"All right, I lived around that shit all my life, and maybe I'm not as far removed from it as I thought. If I was a cool city attorney with *liberal* tattooed on my forehead I would have yawned and rolled up the window on him. But I never could deal with people abstractly, and he stuck his finger in the wrong place."

The perspiration on my face felt cold in the jet of air from the dashboard. I looked straight ahead at the white road and waited for her to speak. Instead, she slipped close to me and kissed me behind the ear.

"You great goddamn woman," I said, and hit the road shoulder in a spray of rocks when I pulled her to me.

"Let's go back to the house," she said, and put

her hand under my shirt and rubbed her fingers along my belt line.

"What about those college kids and the Negro?"

"I already asked them to do something else this afternoon."

She looked up at me with her bright, happy eyes, and I wondered when I would stop discovering things about her.

I bought a bottle of Cold Duck in town, and we drove down the corrugated road through the Mexican district to the union headquarters. The beer tavern was roaring with noise, and fat women sat on the front porches of their paint-blistered houses, fanning themselves in the heat. Rie walked up the path in front of me, lifting her shirt off her breasts with her fingertips. The rusted Dr. Pepper thermometer nailed to the porch post read 106 degrees, and the sky was so hot and blue that a cloud would have looked like an ugly scratch on it. Rie opened the screen door and a yellow envelope fell down from the jamb at her feet.

"Hey, buddy, somebody found you," she said.

I set the heavy bottle of Cold Duck on the porch railing and tore open the telegram with my finger. Flies hummed in the shade of the building.

WHERE THE HELL ARE YOU ANYWAY. HAD TO CANCEL SPEECH LAST NITE IN

SAN ANTONIO. SENATOR HAS CALLED
THREE TIMES. VERISA QUITE WORRIED.
HACK DO YOU WANT IN OR OUT.
BAILEY.

Rie looked at me quietly with her back against
the screen.

"It's just my goddamn brother with his peptic ulcer," I said.

"What is it?"

"I was supposed to make a speech to the Lions
or Rotary or one of those good-guy bunches last
night."

"Is that all of it?" Her quiet eyes watched my
face.

"Bailey thinks an offense against the business
community has the historical importance of World
War III." I folded the telegram and put it in my
shirt pocket. "He's probably swallowing pills by the
bottle right now. Do you have a telephone?"

"There's one down in the beer joint."

"I'll be back in a few minutes. Put the wine in the
ice box."

"All right, Hack."

"I mean, I don't want the poor bastard to rupture
his ulcer on a Sunday."

"Go on. I'll be here."

I walked down the road in the hot light to the

tavern. Inside, the bar was crowded with Mexican
field hands and cedar-cutters, dancers bumped
against the plastic jukebox, and billiard balls clattered across the torn, green covering of an old pool
table. Cigarette smoke drifted in clouds against the
ceiling. I called the house collect from the pay
phone on the wall, bending into the receiver away
from the noise, then I heard Bailey's voice on the
other end of the line.

"Where are you?" he said.

"In a bowling alley. What's it sound like?"

"I mean where?"

"In Pueblo Verde, where you sent your telegram.
What the hell are you doing at the house, anyway?"

"Verisa's pretty upset. You'd better get back
home."

"What is this shit, Bailey? You knew why I had
to leave Friday."

"The Senator wasn't very pleasant with her when
he called here, and maybe all of us are just a little
tired of you not showing up when you're supposed
to. They waited the banquet an hour for you before
they called our answering service, and I had to
drive to San Antonio at ten o'clock and offer an
apology for you."

"Look, you arranged that crap without asking me
first, and you knew when I left Austin that I
wouldn't be back this weekend. So you hang that

bag of shit on the right pair of horns, buddy. And if the Senator wants to be unpleasant with someone, I'll give you this number or the one at the motel."

"Why do you want to behave like this, Hack? You've got all the easy things right in your hand."

A pair of drunk dancers knocked against me, and then waved their hands at me, smiling, as they danced back onto the floor in the roar of noise.

"I just want a goddamn weekend free of migraine headaches and Kiwanians and telegrams," I said. "I'll be back at the office in a couple of days. In the meantime you can schedule yourself for the next round of speeches with the civic club account."

But he was already off the phone.

"Hack?" Verisa said.

"Yeah." I closed my eyes against her voice.

"I'm not going to say much to you. I warned you in Houston what I'd do if you blew this for us. I've got enough to go into court and win almost all of it. I'll take the house, the land, and the controlling share of the wells, and you can start over again with your alcoholic law practice."

I took a breath and waited a moment on that one.

"I should have called you, but I didn't have time," I said, evenly. "I thought Bailey would tell you why I had to leave."

"Oh, my God."

I started to answer, and instead looked out at the dancers on the floor.

"Why should he have to tell me anything?" she said. "You seem to have a strange idea that Bailey should take care of all your unpleasant marital obligations. He was embarrassed enough apologizing for you last night."

"Well, I'm a little worn out with people selling me by the pound and then telling me how embarrassed they are for me. And it also strikes me that nobody was ever concerned if I was called out of town by a paying client. Maybe some people wouldn't get their ovaries so dilated if I was on another case besides a Mexican farm worker's."

I heard her breath in the phone, and then, "You bastard."

I hung up the receiver softly and walked back outside into the sunlight. The road was blinding in the heat, and the noise from the jukebox and Verisa's voice were still loud in my head. I lit a cigar, sweating, and imagined the stunted rage she was now in. Poor old Bailey, I thought. He would stay at the house the rest of the evening, talking quietly to her while her eyes burned at the wall, and then he would begin to consider all the side streets they could use for my election in November, regardless of what I did in the meantime. He would drink cups of caffeine-free coffee with his ulcer pills, flicking over the alternatives in his mind, and soon he would forget that Verisa was in the room. Or maybe the Senator would phone again, and both of their faces would focus anxiously, their eyes reflecting into one another across the kitchen table, while Bailey's voice measured out his assurances about my sincerity in the campaign and my deep regret that I wasn't able to be with the Kiwanians (or whatever) last night. Then they would both wonder if we would ever get to that marble and green island of power where you carried a small, stamped gold key in your watch pocket.

Rie was sitting on the front steps with her back against the porch railing and one leg drawn up before her. She had changed into a pair of faded Navy ducks, with the laces on the back, and a rose-flowered silk shirt, and in the shade she looked as cool and beautiful as a piece of dark sculpture. There was an unopened can of Lone Star and a tall, cone glass by her foot. My shirt stuck wetly to my shoulders, and my sunglasses were filmed with perspiration.

"You look like Tom Joad beating his way out of the Dust Bowl," she said. "You'd better have one of these."

I sat down beside her and opened the can of

beer. The tin was cold against my hand, and the foam rushed up in the glass and streamed over the lip. I took my glasses off and wiped the perspiration and dust out of my eyes, but I avoided looking at her face. There was a broken anthill by the edge of the path, with a deep boot print in one side, and thousands of ants were moving over one another in a hot swarm.

"Was everything cool back there?" she said.

"Yeah." I drank out of the beer—and squinted my eyes into the bright light. "I'm going to give Bailey a frontal lobotomy team for Christmas. Or a can of alum to drink. He has a remarkable talent for calling up everything bad in a person within seconds."

I heard her take her cigarettes out of her shirt pocket and rip back the cover.

"He's not a bad guy. He's just so goddamn obtuse sometimes."

"Hack, I'm not pressing you."

"Then who the hell is?"

"I don't care what you belong to outside of here."

I looked at her quiet, beautiful face in the shade.

"I love to be a part of your Saturday morning fishing world and your crazy Indian graves," she said. "I'd never ask you about anything back there in Austin."

I took the cigarette from her hand and drew in on the smoke. The trees in the dirt yards along the street were still and green in the heat.

"I put the wine on a block of ice," she said.

"Maybe we had better drink that, then," I said. "What do you think, good-looking?"

She smiled at me with her eyes full of light again, and we walked into the back of the house and opened the tall, dark bottle of Cold Duck. I chipped off a bowl full of ice from the block in the top of the cooler and set it in front of the fan in the bedroom so the wind stream would blow cool across the bed. The sun burned yellow against the window shade, and across the river in Mexico a calf stuck in the mudflat was bawling for its mother. Rie undressed in the half light and put her arms around my shoulders, and I pressed my face into her neck and felt her smooth stomach and breasts curve against me.

That evening we drove over to the Gulf in the fading, lilac twilight, and just before the highway turned out of the citrus fields onto the coast we could smell the salt in the air and the dead seaweed at the edge of the surf. The water was slate-green, and the white caps crashed against the sand and boiled in deep pools, and then sucked out again with the undertow. Brown pelicans and sea gulls, like fat white cigars, dipped out of the sky over the

water, picking small fish from the crest of the waves
with their beaks, and in the distance we could see
the gas flares and strings of lights on offshore oil
rigs and quarter boats. The red sun was as big as a
planet on the horizon, and the light broke across
the water in long bands of scarlet. The stretch of
brown beach and the palm trees were covered with
a dark, crimson glow, and then the sun moved
deeper into the Gulf, with a strip of black cloud
across its flaming edge, and the moon began to rise
behind us over the land.

I bought another bottle of Cold Duck and some
chicken sandwiches in a restaurant, and a Mexican
family camped on the beach sold us two salt-water
cane poles with treble hooks and a carton of live
shrimp. The sand was still warm from the sun, and
we sat behind a dune out of the wind and ate the
sandwiches and drank half the bottle of wine, then
I baited the three-pronged hooks with the shrimp,
slipped the lead sinkers close to the bottom of the
line, and we waded into the surf to fish the bottom
for channel cat and flounder. The tide began to
come in, and the waves broke across the rotted
wooden pilings in the jetties, and when the wind
shifted across the water we could smell the dead
shellfish and baked scales and salt in the pilings.
Rie held her cane pole under her arm, with both
hands raised in front of her, while the waves

swelled against her breasts. The water was splintered with moonlight, and the salt spray in her hair looked like drops of crystal. Then the tip of her pole arched into the water and went all the way to the bottom.

"What do I do now, Lone Ranger?" she shouted.

"Keep his head up or he'll break it."

She leaned backwards and strained with both hands, and a cloud of sand rose in the swell at the end of her pole. Then the line pulled out at an angle, quivering, and the pole went down again. She looked at me helplessly, her face shining with water and moonlight.

"Walk him into the shore," I said.

A large wave crested in front of her and broke across her shoulders.

"Hack, you bastard."

"You have to learn these things to overcome your yankee childhood," I said.

She tried to slip the pole back under her arm and raise it again, but the fish had turned into the waves and was pulling hard for the bottom. I waded over to her and picked up the line with both hands at the water and walked backwards with it towards the beach. The line tightened around my knuckles and cut into the skin, and when I reached the shallows I could see the long blue outline of the channel cat shaking his head against the three hooks caught in his mouth. I dragged him up on the sand and placed my fingers carefully around his spiked ventral fins and made one cut with my pocket knife through his gill and across the spine. He flipped quietly in the sand and then lay still.

"God, the things you Southerners do for kicks," she said.

But I could see the excitement in her face at having caught a large and beautiful blue-black fish under the moon in waves up to her shoulders.

"It's against Texas law to keep this kind," I said. "Maybe we'd better flip him back in."

She stepped down on the top of my bare foot and pinched my arm with her fingernails. I held her close to me and kissed her wet hair and dried her face against my shirt. I could taste the salt on her skin and smell the Gulf wind in her hair, and she put her arms inside my shirt and ran her hands over my back.

We gave the channel cat, the poles, and the remaining shrimp to the Mexican family, and built a fire on the sand out of dried wood and dead palm fronds. The wind caught the flames and sent sparks twisting into the sky, and the fronds, coated with sand, and the polished twists of wood snapped in the fire and burst apart in a yellow blaze. We drank the rest of the wine and sat inside the heat with our clothes steaming. On the southern horizon

dark storm clouds were building over the water.
The moon was high, and I could see the clouds
rolling in a heavy wind off the Mexican coast, and
a few large whitecaps were hitting the pilings
around the oil derricks. The air had become cooler,
and there was a wet smell of electricity in the air.
I lit a cigar, stuck the cork in the wine bottle, and
threw it end over end into the surf.

"We really get it on tomorrow, don't we, babe?"
I said.

She ticked the top of my hand with her finger
and looked into the fire.

The wind was blowing in gusts the next morning
when we arrived at the cannery and loading platform where the union was setting up its main
picket. The sun was brown in the swirling clouds
of dust from the fields, and I could still smell the
wet electric odor of a storm. Dozens of junker cars
and pickup trucks with crude wood shelters on the
back were parked along the railway tracks, and Negro and Mexican field workers had formed a long
line in front of the platform where the harvest
trucks would unload. Their picket signs flopped and
bent in the wind, and the sand blew in their faces,
while a man in slacks and a tie walked back and
forth above them, waving his arms, and told them
to get off the company's property. His tie was
blown over his shoulder and his glasses were filmed

with grit, and after he was ignored by everyone on the picket he went into his office and came back with a camera and began taking pictures. Two Texas Rangers in sunglasses and Stetson hats leaned against a state car, watching with their tanned, expressionless faces. Their uniforms were ironed as stiff as tin. The priest, in Roman collar, stood in the back of a stake truck, with his sleeves rolled over his thick arms, handing out picket signs to the people who had just arrived, and I saw one of the Rangers raise his finger, aim at the priest, and say something to his partner.

"I didn't think this was your kind of scene, whiskey brother."

It was the Negro from the union headquarters, and he was still drunk. His slick face was covered with dust, and he had a wad of snuff under his lip.

"What the hell is your name, anyway?" I said.

"What's a name, man?" He took a bottle of port wine from his back pocket and unscrewed the cap. "Sam, Tom, You. People give me a lot of them. But I like Mojo Hand the best. That's a name with shine. It feels good in your mouth just like all these sweet grapes."

"Put the wine away till later," Rie said.

"Those dicks ain't going to bother me. They know a nigger can't change nothing around here. They want to strum some white heads." He drank

from the bottle and coughed on the tobacco juice
in his mouth.

"They'll use anything they can for the newspapers," Rie said.

"You know it don't make any difference what we
do out here today. It's going to read the same way
tomorrow morning. Ain't that right, whiskey
brother? They could bust up Jesus with them billy
clubs and the people would find out how He started
a riot."

"Let's hang a good one on later," I said.

"Where you been, man? There ain't going to be
no later. These dudes have just been practicing so
far."

"Everything is cool now, isn't it?" I said.

He pulled on the bottle again and laughed, spilling the wine over his lip. "Out of sight. But you're
right. You got to keep thinking cool, cousin. You
got to keep a little shine in your name."

"We don't want a bust this early," Rie said. "Stay
in the car until the rest of our people get here."

But he wasn't looking at us any longer. His red
eyes stared over my shoulder in the direction of
the county road, and I turned around and saw the
two black and white sheriff's cars, followed by three
carloads of townspeople, rolling towards us in the
dust. The whip aerials sprang back and forth on
their springs, and muscular, shirt-sleeved arms hung

out the windows of the other cars, beating against the door sides. The wind flattened the clouds of dust across the road, and a moment later two Texas Ranger cars closed the distance with the rest of the caravan.

"It ain't cool no more, whiskey brother," the Negro said.

The line of cars pulled into the gravel bedding along the railway track, and the Rangers and deputy sheriffs walked casually towards the two Rangers in sunglasses who were leaning against their automobile and looking at the priest. The other men stayed behind and formed in a group by a boxcar, their hands in their back pockets, their faces tight, spitting tobacco juice into the rocks, and glaring at the Mexicans and the Negroes. They had crewcuts and faces put together out of shingles, and they wore T-shirts or bluejean jackets with the sleeves cut off at the armpits. There were tattoos of Confederate flags and Easter crosses, Mother and the United States Marine Corps, inscriptions to Billy Sue and Norma Jean, and even the young ones had pot stomachs. They looked like everyone who was ever kicked out of a rural Texas high school.

Then I saw my friend from the sheriff's office. He walked from behind the freight car with a filter-tipped cigar between his teeth, his khaki trousers tucked inside his half-top boots, and his wide leather cartridge belt pulled tight across his flat stomach. He spoke quietly to the men in T-shirts and denim jackets, smiling, his hands on his hips, and then he and the others turned their faces towards me at one time. His green, yellow-flecked eyes were filled with an intense delight, and his lips pressed down softly on the cigar tip.

"Let's get into the picket before it starts," Rie said.

I walked with her to the back of the stake truck, where the priest was still handing down signs. The wind whipped the dust in our faces, and swollen rain clouds were rolling over the horizon. The air was becoming cooler, and I heard the first dull rip of thunder in the distance. The priest wiped his face on his shirt sleeve and grinned at us.

"How are you, Mr. Holland? We can use a good man from the establishment," he said.

"I know a two-word reply to that, Father," I said.

"I believe I've heard it."

"Mojo's drunk. Try to get him into the truck," Rie said.

"He's not fond of listening to church people," the priest said.

"There's some badass types back by the freight car, and he's been in a winehead mood since some kids tried to get it on with him the other night," she said.

"I'll watch him," he said.

"Watch that bunch of assholes, too. One of the dicks was winding them up."

The priest looked over at one of the Rangers who was talking into the microphone of his mobile radio.

"Get into the line. They're going to start moving in a few minutes," he said.

Rie picked up two cardboard signs tacked on laths and handed me one of them. A single, large drop of rain splattered on the black eagle over the word HUELGA.

"Come on," she said.

"Can I get a cigar lit first, for God's sake?" I said.

"We don't want anybody arrested outside the picket, Hack."

"All right, goddamn. Just a minute."

For some reason I hadn't yet accepted the fact that I would be walking on a picket line that Monday morning, or any morning, for that matter. The sign bent backwards in my hands against the wind, flopping loudly, and my knees felt disjointed as I followed her into the slow line of Mexicans and Negroes in their faded work clothes, battered straw hats, and dresses splitting at the hips. Drops of rain made puckered dimples in the dust, and the wind blew cool inside my shirt, but I was perspiring under my arms, and my face was burning as though I

had just done something obscene in public. I saw
the eyes of the sheriff's deputies, the Rangers, and
the poolroom account watching me, and my head
became light and my cigar tasted bitter and dry in
my mouth. I felt as though I had walked naked in
front of a comic audience. A fat Negro woman behind me held her child, in cut-off overalls, with one
hand and her picket sign in the other. She wore a
pair of rippled stockings over the varicose veins in
her legs.

"You don't worry about these children. They ain't
going to bother them," she said.

I looked away from her brown eyes at the man
in slacks and tie on the platform. He was still taking
pictures, and his face was quivering at the outrage
he had seen that day against the principle of private
property. Storm clouds covered the sun, and the
fields were suddenly darkened and the shadows
leaped across the cannery, the freight cars, and the
county road. The men in T-shirts and denim jackets
were now pulling the caps on hot cans of beer and
spilling the foam down their necks and chests.

"How you doing?" Rie said.

"I think my respect for the demonstrator just
went up a couple of points."

"Look, if those bastards move in on us, you have
to take it. Okay?"

"That doesn't sound cool."

"No shit, Hack. They're waiting for reasons to split heads."

"All right, but when do we finish this caper?"

"We've only been on the picket ten minutes, babe."

Then I saw a television news car pull into the gravel bedding by the railway track. Two young men got out with cameras attached to half-moon braces that fitted against the shoulder. They walked over to the group of law officers by the squad cars, their faces full of confident foreknowledge about their story, and for the first time it struck me that I had never seen a newsman begin a story any differently; without thinking, they went first to the official source before they considered the people on the other end of the equation.

One of them walked towards the picket and did a sweeping, random shot with his camera, the brace pulled tight against his shoulder. Then he lowered the camera and looked at me steadily, his face as bland and unembarrassed as a dough pan. I threw my cigar away and looked back at him with my meanest, southpaw ninth-inning expression. He walked back to his friend and began talking, and the two of them stared in my direction.

"I believe a couple of kids just earned a pay raise," I said.

"I bet you're handsome on film," Rie said.

"Well, here they come. You want to do my P.R. work?"

One of them already had his camera whirring before they were close enough to speak. They had forgotten the cops and the long line of migrant workers; they were both concentrated on the little piece of entrail they might carry back to the station.

"Are you widening your district, Mr. Holland?" His voice was good-natured, and he smiled at me in his best college fraternity fashion.

"No, no," I said, in my best humorous fashion.

Isn't this a delightful game we're about to play, I thought.

"Do you think your support of the union will affect your election?" He held the microphone towards me, but his eyes were looking at Rie.

"I couldn't tell you that, buddy."

"The farm corporations consider this an illegal strike. Do you have a comment on that?"

"I don't know how it can be illegal to ask for a higher wage."

"Does the union plan a strike in your area?" He was cocking the rifle now, but his face looked as sincerely inquisitive as a reverent schoolboy's.

"Not that I know of."

"Does that mean the conditions of the migrant farm workers are better in your area?"

"No, it doesn't," I said. "But I tell you what,

buddy. I need a cigar real bad right now, and it's hell lighting up in this wind with one hand. So how about holding this sign for a minute, and I can get one of these awful things lit and we can talk all day. That's right, just take it in your hand and fold your fingers around the stick."

His face went blank, the lath straining in his palm, and his eyes flicked at his partner and the cops by the railway track. I used three matches to light my cigar while he blinked against the raindrops and shifted his feet in the dust.

"I appreciate that," I said. "Say, did you interview any of those fellows over by the freight car? I bet that bunch of boys would give you some deathless lines."

"We just do a job, Mr. Holland."

"I bet you'll get there with it, too," I said.

"Would you like to say something else, sir?" His face was mean now, the eyes dirty.

"You've got a whole reel of good stuff there, pal."

He turned away from me and put the microphone in front of Rie. The sky was almost completely dark, except for the thin line of yellow light on the distant hills. His partner moved around behind him so the lens would catch me in the same shot with Rie.

"Do you think the families in the farm camps will suffer because of the strike?"

"Why don't you fuck off, man?" Rie said.

Then one of the men by the freight car threw
an empty beer can at the picket line. It missed a
Negro woman's head and clattered across the loading platform. The two newsmen backed away from
us with their cameras turning. A moment later three
more carloads of townspeople arrived and swelled
into the group by the freight car, and then one man
stepped out from them and started walking towards
us, and the rest followed. He wore a tin construction hat back on his shaved head, steel-toed work
boots, and denim clothes that were splattered with
drilling mud from an oil rig. His eyes had a wet,
yellow cast to them, and his front teeth were brown
with chewing tobacco. His scrotum bulged in his
bluejeans between his heavy thighs, and he
stretched out his huge arms, his hands in fists, as
though he were just awakening from sleep, and spat
a stream of tobacco juice in the dirt.

"Hey, buddy," he said to me. "Do you eat Mexican pussy?"

I looked straight ahead, my face burning.

"You better get that chili off your mouth, then,"
he said.

"Leave that man alone, J.R. You know a lawyer
don't have to eat pussy," another said.

"This one does. You get your nose right in it,
don't you?"

The looming outline of the cannery and the

rusted freight cars in silhouette against the light
rain seemed to shrink and expand before my eyes.
My knuckles whitened on the sign lath, and my
breath caught in my throat.

"He might beat you to death with that cardboard, J.R."

"Do you get to try some of these nigger girls?"
the oil-field worker said.

My eyes watered and I felt myself leaping towards him before I had even moved or changed my
line of vision, but several men behind him shouted
and laughed at one time in a phlegmy roar, and he
turned his wide back to me. Mojo had been sitting
in the cab of the stake truck with his wine bottle
until it was empty, and then had decided to join
the picket. His shirt was unbuttoned to the waist,
his socks were pulled down over his heels, and he
walked towards the line as though his knees were
connected with broken hinges. There was a patch
of snuff on the corner of his lip, and the drops of
rain slid over his cannonball head like streaks of
black ivory. An unopened can of beer flew out of
the crowd and hit him above the eye. He reeled
backwards, still standing, and pressed his hand like
a fielder's glove against his head, the blood dripping
down from his dark palm. His uncovered eye was
wide and rolling with pain and shock.

"Goddamn," I said.

"Don't, Hack," Rie said.

"They hurt him bad."

"Stay in the line," she said.

Mojo bent forward and let the blood run down his forearm onto the ground, then he started walking towards us again as though he were holding a cracked flowerpot delicately in place. A man in khaki clothes with a green cloth cap on and a Lima watch fob in his pocket stepped into his path and kicked his feet out from under him. Mojo struck the ground headlong, and his face was covered with strings of dust and blood.

"This is too goddamn much, Rie," I said.

"Don't get out of the line. They'll kill him if you do," she said.

He pushed himself up from the ground and stood erect, the ragged cut on his head already swelling like a baseball. The wind blew his shirt straight out from his body, and his chest heaved and his nostrils dilated when he breathed.

"You can bust me 'cause I'm winehead now, but you ain't going to beat all these people," he said. "They too many for you, and they're going to stand all over this place when you all are long gone."

The oil-field worker moved towards him, his buttocks flexing inside his bluejeans, but two deputy sheriffs walked up behind Mojo and led him away by each arm towards their automobile. Before they put handcuffs on him, they stripped off his shirt and wrapped it in a twisted knot around his head.

The car rolled off down the road, with Mojo in back behind the wire screen, his blood-soaked shirt like a dark smear against the closed glass.

The priest was next, and they had a special dislike for him as a Catholic clergyman. The man in the khaki clothes shook up a hot beer and sprayed it on him, and the oil-field worker put his hot breath in the priest's face and insulted him with every whorehouse statement he could make. Several women had joined the crowd, and they rasped at him with their contorted faces, their eyes shrunken inward at some terrible anger, and then one spat on him. She was small and stunted, her thin arms were puckered and wrinkled at the armpits, and her electric hair was scraped back in a tangle over the thinning places in her head, but she gathered all the energy and juice in her wasted body and spat it in an ugly string over his chest.

He blinked his eyes against the spittle and obscenities, but he kept his face straight ahead, his big hands folded around the sign lath, and never broke his step in the line. His composure enraged the women to the point that they were shouting at him incoherently, their heads bent forward like snakes, the veins in their throats bursting against the skin. Then the deputy sheriff who had arrested me walked to the back of the crowd, put his hand on the oil-field worker's shoulder, and motioned in my direction. Across the railway track I saw two large police vans with cage doors on the back turn off the county road into the cannery gate, and then the crowd came towards me.

Their faces were tight with anger, the lips dry, the eyes hot and receded in the head, as though their own rage had dried out all the fluids in their bodies. In the gloom and swirling patterns of rain their skin looked white and stretched over the bone. Lightning struck against the hills, and the wind was beginning to strip the cotton in the fields.

"We ain't got a lot of time for you, lawyer. So you know what I'm going to do?" the oil-field worker said, and put a half plug of tobacco in his mouth. He pushed it into his jaw with his tongue and chewed it into pulp, then cleaned the juice off his lip with his finger. "I ain't going to touch you with my hand. I'm just going to show you how we treat dip shit around here. Now, when you get tired of it, all you got to do is tear that sign up and walk to your car. There won't nobody hurt you."

"I'll tell you something, motherfucker," I said. "You spit on me and I'll take your head off."

The man in the khaki clothes with the green cap reached out with his fist, off balance, as though he were leaping at a departing train, and struck me in a downward swing across the nose. His ring peeled back the skin, and I felt the blood swell to the surface. I stared at them all stupidly, with the sign in my hands, while my eyes filmed and burned. The oil worker was grinning at me.

"You want to cut bait, dip shit?" he said.

The woman who had spat on the priest flicked a lighted cigarette at my face, then I was hit again, this time across the side of the head with something round and wooden. I felt it clack into the bone, and I tumbled sideways, the ocean roaring in my ears, and struck the ground on one knee and an elbow. My ear and the side of my head were on fire, and I looked up through the unshaved legs and denims stained with grease and cow manure and saw a thin, muscular boy of about nineteen with a freight-door pin in his hand. Somebody pulled my shirt loose from my trousers and poured beer down my spine. I felt a cigar burn into my neck, and a woman slapped wildly at my head with a shoe. I tried to raise my arms in front of me, but someone stepped on my hand and the man in khakis tripped in the crowd and fell across my back. I heard Rie's voice shouting outside the circle of people around me, then the deputy sheriff pulled my head up by the shirt collar and started to raise me to my feet, but before he did he flicked out his knee, in a quick, deft motion, and caught me in the eye. Half my vision exploded in dark red and purple circles, and I pressed my hand into the socket as though I had a piece of sandpaper under the lid. But in the swimming distortion I could still see his khaki trousers stuffed inside his low-topped boots, and his cartridge belt and holster welded against his flat stomach and narrow hips. I rose on one knee and put all my strength into a left-handed swing from the ground and hit him in the stomach an inch above the belt. I felt the muscles collapse under my fist, just like you kick open a door unexpectedly. He bent double, his face white and his mouth open in a wide O, and his breath clicked dryly in his throat. His eyes were drowning, and when he fell forward on his knees in the mud, a line of spittle on his cheek, the crowd stepped backwards in silence as though someone had thrown an unacceptable icon at their feet.

Then the Rangers, the city police, and the sheriff's department went to work. They arrested everybody in sight. They handcuffed my arms behind me while the television cameras whirred, gave artifical respiration to the deputy and strapped an oxygen mask to his face, pushed scores of people into the vans with nightsticks until there was no more room, commandeered the stake truck, and arrested the man with the camera on the loading platform by mistake. Two deputies led me by each arm to the van, squeezing tightly into my torn shirt, their faces like hard wax, and the television newsmen were still hard at work with their lenses zooming across my manacled hands and swollen face. The rain was coming down harder now, and the gravel road was covered with wet boles of cotton and leaves stripped from the citrus orchards. The wind was rattling the tin roof on top of the cannery, and the ditches by the road were slick and brown on the sides with the run-off from the fields. I was the last man put in the second van. The deputies took the handcuffs off me, pushed me inside against the crowd of Mexicans and Negroes, and locked the wire-cage doors. The engine started, and we bounced across the railway track and turned through the cannery gate onto the county road.

The men in the van balanced themselves against the walls and each other and rolled cigarettes, or poured Bull Durham tobacco from the pouch between their lip and gums. Somewhere in back a child was crying. I leaned against the cage door and watched the road shift in direction behind the van, while the wind shook the barbed wire on the fences and bent the weeds flat along the irrigation ditches, and then I heard Rie's voice way back in the crush of people. She pressed her way out between several Mexican men, who raised their arms in the air in order to let her pass, and her face and eyes made my heart drop. She put her arm in mine and touched her fingers lightly against the swollen place on my head, then pulled my arm close against her breast and kissed me on the cheek.

"I was very proud of you, Hack," she said.

"I'm afraid I screwed up your picket. That was an assault and battery caper I pulled off back there."

She hugged my arm tighter against her breast, and the rain poured down on the fields and began to flatten the long, plowed rows even with the rest of the land, and in the distance I could see the citrus trees whipping and shredding in the dark wind.

CHAPTER

TEN

The streets in town were half-filled with water when the vans arrived at the courthouse. Beer cans and trash floated along next to the curb, and the lawn was strewn with broken branches and leaves from the oaks. The deputies, now wearing slickers and plastic covers on their hats, formed us into a long line, two abreast, while the rain beat in our faces, and marched us into the courthouse. The booking room was small, and it took them three hours to fingerprint everyone and sort out the shoe-laces, belts, pocket change, and wallets into brown envelopes. Most of the charges were for trespassing or failure to keep fifty feet apart on a picket line, but after the deputy had rolled my fingers on the ink pad the sheriff filled out my charge sheet per-sonally and he wrote for five minutes. I dripped water onto the floor and looked at his steel-rimmed glasses and the red knots and bumps on his face. His fingers were pinched white on the pencil, and towards the bottom of the page he pressed down so hard that he punctured the paper.

Then he picked up a cigarette from the desk and lit it.

"You want to hear them?" he said.

"I bet you have a whole bunch," I said.

"Assault and battery on a law officer, obstructing an officer in the line of duty, resisting arrest, inciting to riot, and I'm holding a couple of charges open. You ain't going to get this shifted to no federal court, either. You're going to be tried right here in this county, and maybe you'll find out a lawyer's shit stinks like everybody else's."

"I have a phone call coming."

"It's out of order."

"It rang five minutes ago."

"Take him downstairs," he said to the trusty.

I was locked in the drunk tank at the end of the stone corridor in the basement. The room was crowded with men, wringing out their clothes on the concrete floor. Their dark bodies shone in the dim light. There were two toilets crusted with filth, without seats, in the corner, and the drunks who had been arrested during the weekend still reeked of sour beer and muscatel. Through the bars I could see the screened cage where I had talked with Art, and the row of cells with the food slits in the iron doors. The stone walls glistened with moisture, and the smoke from hand-rolled cigarettes gathered in a thick haze on the ceiling. An old man in jockey undershorts, with shriveled skin like lined putty, walked to the toilet and began retching.

Rie had been put with the other women into a second holding room on the other side of the wall. Someone had drilled a small hole in the mortar between the stones, and a Mexican man had his face pressed tightly against the wall, talking to his wife, while a line of other men waited their turn behind him. I wanted to talk with Rie badly, but the line grew longer, and often in the confusion of names and voices the two right people could never get on the opposite sides of the hole at the same time. Twice during the afternoon a deputy, dripping water from his slicker, brought in another prisoner, and each time the door clanged open a tough, bare-chested kid, who was waiting to do a six-year jolt in Huntsville, shouted out from the back of the room, "Fresh meat!" At five o'clock the trusty wheeled in the food cart with our tin plates of spaghetti, string beans, bread and cups of Kool-Aid, and after the group of men had thinned away from the wall I tried to talk through the hole to a Mexican woman on the other side, but she couldn't understand English or my bad Spanish, and I gave up.

That night I dragged my tick mattress against the door and lay with my face turned towards the bars to breathe as much air as I could out of the corridor and avoid the odor of the open toilets and the sweet, heavy smell of perspiration. I had one damp cigar left, and I smoked it on my side and looked at the row of gray, iron doors set in the rock. Mojo was in lockdown behind one of them, and once I thought I saw the flash of his black face through a food slit. I had never been more tired. I was used up physically the way you are after you've thrown every pitch you have in a ten-inning game. There was a raised water blister on my neck from the cigar burn, and a swollen ridge across the side of my head, like a strip of bone, where the boy had caught me with the freight pin. I fell asleep with the dead cigar in my hand, and I slept through until morning without having one dream or even a half-conscious, nocturnal awareness of where I was, as though I had been lowered through the stone into some dark underground river.

I heard the trusty click of the food cart against the bars and the throw of the big lock on the door. The fried bologna, grits and coffee steamed from the stainless-steel containers, and the men were rising from their tick mattresses, hawking, spitting, and relieving themselves in the toilets, or washing their spoons under the water tap before they formed into line. I had to move my mattress for the trusty to push the cart inside, and when I stood up I realized that I felt as rested and solid as a man in his prime. But it took me a moment to believe the man I saw walking down the stone corridor with the sheriff by his side. He wore yellow, waxed cowboy boots, a dark, striped western suit, with a watchchain hooked on his handtooled belt, a bolo tie, a cowboy shirt with snap buttons on the pockets, and a short-brim Stetson hat on the back of his head. He didn't have an undershirt on, and I could see the hair on his swollen stomach above his belt buckle, and his round face was as powdered and smooth as a baby's. There wasn't another man in Texas who dressed like that. It was R. C. Richardson, all right.

"Hack, have you lost your goddamn mind? What the hell are you doing in here?" he said, in his flat, east Texas, Piney Woods accent.

"R.C., you old sonofabitch," I said.

"I was down here buying leases, and I come back to the motel last night and turned on the television, and I couldn't believe it. What you trying to do to yourself, boy?"

"Get a bondsman, R.C."

"I already done that. I got his ass out of bed at midnight, but he wouldn't come till this morning. Do you know the bail they set on you? Ten thousand dollars. I swear to God if you ain't a pistol, Hack."

"I tell you, Mr. Richardson," the sheriff said, "if you go this man's bond, you're also going to be responsible for him, because I don't want to see him again."

"Well, I guarantee you he won't be no trouble," R.C. said. "We might shoot on across the border this afternoon and try the chili, then go on back to DeWitt."

"R.C., are you going to turn the key on me or just drip water on the floor?" I said.

"Hold on, son. That man will be here in a minute," he said. "I told him I'd put a boot up his ass if he wasn't here five minutes after I walked through that door."

"Bail the rest of them out, too," I said.

"You know that brother of yours is right. The whiskey's getting up in your brain."

"R.C., how many years have I kept you out of prison?"

"Goddamn, how much money do you think I carry around with me?"

"Enough to buy this county and a couple of others."

"Hack, I can't do that. There must be fifty people in there."

"There's more in the next room," I said.

"And they'll be spread all over Mexico when they're supposed to be in court."

"Will you stop screwing around and just do it?"

"If you ain't a pistol, the craziest goddamn man I ever met. All right, but I'm going to send your brother a bill for a change, and it's going to bust his eyeballs."

"Good, and give me a cigar while you're at it."

The bondsman arrived, and R.C. wrote out a check on the stone wall for the whole amount. The bondsman, a small man with greed and suspicion stamped in his face, thought he was either drunk or insane. He held the check between his fingers with the ink still drying and looked at R.C. incredulously.

"Call the First National Bank in Dallas collect and use my name," R.C. said, "or I'll find me another man right fast."

We had to wait ten minutes, then the sheriff opened the doors to both holding rooms and the corridor was filled with people, laughing and talking in Spanish. A deputy unlocked one of the cells set back in the wall, and Mojo stepped out barefoot in the light, blinking his red eyes, with his stringless shoes in his hands.

"What happened?" he said. "The Man get tired of us already?"

A Mexican man put his arm around Mojo's shoulders and pulled him into the crowd walking towards the stairwell. The Mexican spoke no English, but he pointed his thumb into his mouth in a drinking motion.

"There you go, brother," Mojo said.

The sheriff glared at us all, the red knots on his face tight against the skin.

I came up behind Rie and slipped my arm around her waist, and kissed the cool smoothness of her cheek. She turned her face up to me and I kissed her again and ran my hand through her hair.

"How did you do it, babe?" she said.

"I want you to meet R.C. Richardson," I said.

R.C. lifted off his Stetson with a slow, exact motion and let it rest against his pants leg, and bent forward with a slight bow and his best look of southern deference to womanhood on his face. He pulled in his stomach and stiffened his shoulders, and for just a moment you didn't notice the bolo tie and the yellow cowboy boots.

"I'm proud to meet you, miss," he said.

"Rie Velasquez," she said, and her eyes smiled at him.

"I was just telling Hack I didn't have time to eat

breakfast this morning, so why don't we go across
the street to the cafe and see if we can get a steak?"

His eyes were looking over Rie's face, and I knew
that it took everything in him to prevent them from
going further. He stepped aside and let us walk in
front of him as we followed the crowd upstairs.
R.C. was about to begin one of his performances.
He had several roles, and he did each of them well:
good-natured oil man when he was buying leases;
humble Kiwanian and patriot; friend-of-the-boys
with a wallet full of unlisted telephone numbers.
But now he was a gentleman rancher, somebody's
father, an older friend with his fingers on all the
right buttons when you were in trouble. We had
to wait for the deputy to find the brown envelopes
with our wallets, change, and belts in them. He was
young and evidently new to his job, and he had
difficulty reading the handwriting of the people
who had booked us.

"Snap it up, boy," R.C. said. "We don't want to
grow no older in this place."

"R.C., we still have about seventy-five feet to go
to the door," I said.

"You either do a job or you don't," he said.
"That's what's wrong all over this country. Like that
little bondsman back there. He don't spit without
sitting down and thinking about it first."

We signed for our possessions, and R.C. slipped his slicker over Rie's shoulders. It was still raining hard outside. It came down in curving sheets that swept across the flooded courthouse lawn. Some of the oaks were almost bare, and the leaves floated up against the trunks in islands. Cars and trucks were stalled in the street, the headlight beams weak in the driving rain, and somewhere a horn was stuck and blowing. The neon sign over the cafe and tavern looked like colored smoke in the wet, diffused light.

R.C. opened up a big umbrella over our heads and we splashed down the sidewalk towards the cafe. The air smelled clean and cool, and even the rain, slanting under the umbrella and burning against the skin, felt like an absolution after the day and night in jail. There's no smell exactly like that of a jail, and when you can leave it behind you and walk out into a rain storm you feel that the other experience was never really there.

The water in the street was up to our knees, and R.C. held Rie by one arm and covered our heads with the umbrella while exposing his own. The rain sluiced off the brim of his pearl-gray Stetson, his western suit was drenched, his shirt had popped open more above his belt and his stomach winked out like a roll of wet dough. He was an old crook and a lecher, but I liked him in a strange way—

maybe because he had no malice towards anyone,
and even in his dishonesty he was faithful to the
corrupt system that he served, and his buffoonery
lent a little humor to it. Possibly that's an odd reason to like someone, but I had known much worse
men in the oil business than R.C. Richardson.

He opened the door for us, and we went inside
with the rain swirling through the screen. Men in
cowboy boots and bluejeans were drinking bottles
of Pearl and Jax at the counter, a Negro was racking
pool balls in back under an electric bulb with a tin
shade around it, and the jukebox, with cracks all
over the plastic casing, was playing a lament about
lost women and the wild side of life. R.C. took off
Rie's slicker and held the chair for her at one of the
tables with oilcloth covers tacked around the sides.
In his politeness he was awkward, like a man who
had been put together with bad hinges, but it was
seldom that he was called upon to show manners
above those practiced in the Dallas Petroleum Club.

"R.C., you're not a sonofabitch, after all," I said.

He looked at me strangely, his thick hands on
the table top.

"Well, I hope your brother was wearing his
brown britches when he watched the late news last
night," he said, then blinked at Rie, his smooth face
uncertain. "Excuse me. I forget I ain't in the oil field
sometime."

She smiled at him, and he took in his breath and opened his fingers. We hadn't eaten at the jail that morning, and I could smell the pork chops and slices of ham frying on the stove. We ordered steaks and scrambled eggs, with side orders of hash-browns and tomatoes.

"You must have put your fist plumb up to the elbow in that man's stomach," R.C. said. "I've never seen a man dump over that hard. I thought he was going to strangle right there on the ground."

"The local news boys must have done a good job," I said.

"They sure as hell did. They got it all. You smil-ing with handcuffs on and them two cops holding you by each arm. I bet Bailey needed a respirator if he seen that." R.C. laughed and lit a cigar. "God-damn, if I wouldn't mark off all that bail money just to see him trying to get to the phone."

The waiter brought our steaks and eggs, and set a pot of coffee on a napkin in the center of the table. I cut a piece of steak and ate it with a slice of peppered tomato. R.C. was still laughing with the cigar in his mouth.

"You reckon he's already called the mental ward in Austin?" he said.

"I think it's been a good morning for you," I said.

"Hack, you and him have been giving me hell all

these years, and by God I don't get many chances
to bail my lawyer out of jail."

"How bad is it going to be, Hack?" Rie said.

"I don't know."

The door opened and the rain swept across the
floor. I felt the cool air against my neck.

"Miz Rie, don't worry about Hack losing in court,
because he don't."

"It might be a little more difficult this time," I
said.

"I remember once I was almost chopping cotton
on Sugarland farm, and you had the case dismissed
in a week."

I remembered it also—painfully. Four years ago
R.C. had drilled into a state-owned oil pool and
had bribed three state officials, one of whom went
to the penitentiary.

"He walks into court with that white suit, and it
don't take him five minutes to have everybody in
the jury box watching him."

Rie looked at me, and I dropped my eyes.

"Once he got a colored man off for raping a
white woman, and I swear to God the jury never
even knew why they let him go."

"It's almost noon. Let's have a beer," I said.

"You know you ain't going to get any time. Why
you let this girl worry?"

"Order some beers."

"You really think they're going to put somebody from your family in the penitentiary?"

"Would you shut up, R.C.?"

His face was hurt and embarrassed, and Rie touched my hand under the table.

"You're giving away all his secrets," she said. "He hates to admit that he's anything but a left-handed country lawyer."

He looked at her eyes, and his face mended as though a breeze had blown across it. He was in love with her, and if I hadn't been at the table his performance would have grown to absurd proportions.

We finished eating, and R.C. paid the check and left a three-dollar tip on the table. We walked across the flooded street in the rain to his Mercedes, and he opened the car door for Rie and held the umbrella over her head while she got in. The inside panels were covered with yellow, rolled leather, and the black seats were stitched with a gold longhorn design, and on top of the dashboard there was an empty whiskey glass and a compass inside a plastic bubble. We drove slowly out of town while the water washed back in waves over the curbs, and R.C. pulled a pint of Four Roses from his coat pocket and offered it to us.

"Well, that's the first time I ever seen you turn

one down," he said, and he drank from the bottle as though it contained soda water.

The county road that led to the cannery had collapsed in places along the edges from the overflow of ditch water, and the rows in the fields had been beaten almost flat by the rain or washed into humps of mud. The gusts of wind covered the brown water with curls and lines like puckered skin, and the torn cotton and leaves turned in eddies around the cedar fence posts. In the distance I saw a cow trying to lift her flanks out of the mud.

A great section of the cannery roof had been blown away in the storm. The metal was ripped upward in a ragged slash, like a row of twisted knives, and there was a huge black hole where the rest of the roof had been. Picket signs were strewn over the ground by my automobile, and the rain drummed down in a roar on the tin building, the loading platform, and the freight cars. R.C. parked as close as he could to the Cadillac and went around to Rie's side with the umbrella. His western pants were splattered with mud up to the knees, and drops of water ran down his soft face. He closed the door after her and walked around to the driver's side with me, the rain thudding on the umbrella.

"Look, Hack, it's going to take some money to beat this thing," he said. "I know you got plenty of it, but if you need any more you only got to call. Another thing. You take care of that girl, hear?"

"All right, R.C."

"One more thing, by God. I think you flushed your political career down the hole, but I felt right proud of you out there. That boy looked like he had muscles in his shit till you come off the ground. I always told Bailey you was crazy but you're still a goddamn good man."

He slammed the door and splashed through the mud to his automobile, his face bent downwards against the rain. We followed him out through the cannery gate onto the county road, and I saw the empty whiskey bottle sail from his window into the irrigation ditch. Then he floored the Mercedes and sped away from us in a shower of mud and brown water.

"He's a wonderful man," Rie said.

"I believe he liked you a little bit, too."

"Where's he going?"

"Back to his motel room and get sentimentally drunk in his underwear. Then about dark he'll drive across the border and try to buy a whole brothel."

"Couldn't we ask him over?"

"He'd feel better with the morning intact the way it is. In fact, it would hurt him if he had to continue."

The collapsed places along the edges of the road

were beaded with gravel, and cut back into deepening sink holes in the center. I could feel the soft ground break under my wheels.

"Was he straight about nobody from your family going to the penitentiary?" she said.

"The deputy already has my civil rights charge against him, and if those camera boys were any good they filmed his knee in my eye, and I can make a hard case against the cops. But there's a good chance I'll get disbarred."

"Oh, Hack."

I put my arm around her wet shoulders and pulled her close to me.

"Stop worrying about it, babe. My grandfather knocked John Wesley Hardin on his ass with a rifle stock, and Hardin was a lot tougher than the Texas Bar Association."

"I kept making fun of you about picket lines and the union, and now you might get burned worse than any of us."

Her back was cold under my arm. I kissed the corner of her eye and squeezed her into me.

"Don't you know that real gunfighters never lose?" I said.

She put her hand on my chest, and I could feel my heart beat against her palm. She looked up at me once, then pressed her cheek against my shoulder the rest of the way back to town.

The dirt yards in the poor district were covered with water up to the front porches, and the waves from my automobile washed through the chicken-wire fences and rolled against the houses. Tin cans, garbage, and half-submerged tree limbs floated in the ditches, and a dead dog, his skin scalded pink by the rain, lay entangled in an island of trash around the base of a telephone pole. Some of the shingles had been stripped by the wind from the union headquarters roof, and the building itself leaned at an angle on the foundation. I took off my boots, and we waded through the water to the porch.

Mojo and a Mexican man were sitting at the table in the front room with a half-gallon bottle of yellow wine between them. They had melted a candle to the table, and Mojo was heating his glass of wine over the flame. The smoke curled in a black scorch around the glass. His eyes were small and red in the light.

"My brother here is teaching me how to put some fire in that spodiodi," he said. "You can see it climb up right inside the color. That's what I been doing wrong all these years. Drinking without no style."

He drank the glass down slowly, and poured it full again. I could smell the wine all the way across the room.

"This telegram was in the door when I got back from the jail, and a man come by in a taxicab looking for you," he said. "He didn't leave no name, but he looked just like you. Except for a minute I thought he had to go to the bathroom real bad."

I tore open the envelope and read the telegram, dated late last night.

I DON'T KNOW IF YOU WILL RECEIVE THIS. I GUESS I DON'T CARE WHETHER YOU DO OR NOT. CALL VERISA IF YOU FEEL LIKE IT. OR SIMPLY TEAR THIS UP.

Bailey didn't bother to sign his name.

"What did the man say?" I said.

"He was going up to the cafe, and then he was coming back," Mojo said. "He give me a dollar so I'd be sure to tell you."

Good old perceptive Bailey, I thought.

"I think we ought to buy that man a glass of this mellow heat when he comes back. He needs it," Mojo said.

"He needs a new mind," I said.

Rie went into the back to change clothes. I looked in the ice box for a beer, and then drove the Cadillac down to the tavern and bought a dozen bottles of Jax and a block of ice. I found a tin bucket in the kitchen, and chipped the ice over the bottles. Rie came out of the bedroom dressed in a pair of white ducks, sandals, and a flowered shirt. She had brushed back her gold-tipped hair and had put on her hoop earrings and an Indian bead necklace.

"Hey, good-looking," I said, and put my arms around her. She pressed her whole body against me, with her arms around my neck, and I kissed her on the mouth, then along her cheek and ear. I could smell the rain in her hair.

"Do you have to leave with him?" she said.

"No."

"Are you sure, Hack?"

"We'll give him some of Mojo's sneaky pete. That's all he needs."

She ran her fingertips over the back of my neck and pressed her head hard against my chest.

"Don't feel that way, babe," I said. "I just have to talk to him."

She breathed through her mouth and held me tightly against her. I kissed her hair and turned her face up towards me. Her soldier's discipline was gone.

"I couldn't ever leave you, Rie," I said. "Bailey is down here out of his own compulsion. That's all there is to it."

I hadn't lied to her before, and it didn't feel good. I picked up the bucket of beer and cracked ice by

the bail, and we walked onto the porch and sat in
two wicker chairs away from the rain slanting under
the eaves. The solid gray of the sky had broken
into drifting clouds, and I could see the faint,
brown outline of the hills in the distance. The Rio
Grande was high and swirling with mud, the surface
dimpled with rain, and the tall bank on the Mexican side of the river had started to crumble into
the water. I opened two beers and raked the ice off
the bottles with my palm.

It had been a long time since I had enjoyed the
rain so much. The wind was cool and smelled of
the wet land and the dripping trees, and I remembered the times as a boy when I used to sit on the
back porch and watch the rain fall on the short
cotton. In the distance I could see Cappie's gray
cabin framed in the mist by the river, and even
though I couldn't see the river itself I knew the bass
were rising to the surface to feed on the caterpillars
that had been washed out of the willows.

"Is he really like you describe him?" Rie said.

"I don't know. Maybe I'm unfair to him. After our
father died he had to take care of the practical
things while I played baseball at Baylor, and then
I quit college to join the Navy, and he had to finish
law school and run the ranch at the same time. He
can't think in any terms now except finances and
safe people, and he usually makes bad choices with

both of them. Sometimes I'm afraid that if he ever
finds out where he's invested most of his life he'll
shoot himself."

I drank out of the beer and leaned my chair back
against the porch wall. Inside, I could hear Mojo
singing, "Hey, hey, baby, take a whiff on me."

"Do you think that's why people shoot themselves?" she said.

"I never thought there was anything so bad that
it could make a man take his life in seconds. But I
do know there are other ways to do it to yourself
over long periods of time."

"Bailey sounds like a sad man."

"He gets some satisfaction from his tragic view.
His comparison of himself with me lets him feel
correct all the time."

"Hey, hey, everybody take a whiff on me," Mojo
sang inside.

I saw a taxicab turn into the flooded street and
drive towards us, the yellow sides splattered with
mud. The floating garbage and tin cans rolled in
the car's wake.

"Do you want me to go for a drive?" she said.

"No. I want you to meet him. It will be the best
thing that's happened to him in a long time."

"I feel like I shouldn't be here, Hack."

"Who the hell lives here, anyway? He doesn't,
and I sure didn't ask him down."

I squeezed her hand, but I saw it made her uncomfortable. The waves from the taxi washed up
through the yard and hit against the porch steps.
Bailey paid the driver and stepped out the back
door into the water. His brown windbreaker was
spotted with rain, and the lines in his brow and
around his eyes had deepened with lack of sleep.
The rims of his eyes were red. In fact, his whole
face looked middle-aged, as though he had worked
hard to make it that way. He walked up through
the water with his head lowered slightly and his
mouth in a tight line.

"How you doing, brother?" I said, and took a sip
out of the beer.

"I have a plane at the county airport," he said.
He looked straight at me and never turned his head
towards Rie.

"Get out of the rain and meet someone and have
a beer."

"We'll leave your car there. You can fly back and
get it later," he said. His voice had a quiet and determined righteousness to it, the kind of tone which
he reserved for particularly tragic occasions, and it
had always infuriated me. But I was resolved this time.

"It's bad weather for a flight, Bailey. You should
have waited a day or so," I said. I was surprised that
he had flown at all, because he was terrified of airplanes.

"Do you have anything inside?" he said.

"Not a thing."

"Then we can be going."

He was making it hard.

"Would you sit down a minute, for God's sake?" I said. "Or at least not stand under the eave with rain dripping on your head."

He stepped up on the porch and wiped his forehead with his palm. He still refused to recognize Rie. I carried a chair over from the other side of the porch and pulled another beer from the ice bucket.

"There. Sit," I said. "This is Rie Velasquez. She's the coordinator for the union."

"How do you do, ma'am?" He looked at her for the first time, and his eyes lingered longer on her face than he had probably wanted them to. She smiled at him, and momentarily he forgot that he was supposed to be a somber man with a purpose.

I opened the bottle of beer and handed it to him. The chips of ice slid down the neck. He started to put the bottle on the porch railing.

"Drink the beer, Bailey. If you had some more of that stuff, you wouldn't have ulcers."

"The Senator and John Williams are at the house."

"John Williams. What's that bastard doing in my home?"

"He was spending the weekend with the Senator, and he drove down with him this morning."

"You know the old man wouldn't let an asshole like that in our back door."

"He told me he would still like to contribute money to the campaign."

"You'd better get him out of my house."

"Why don't you take care of it yourself? This is my last errand."

"Do you think we could get that in writing?" I said.

"You don't know the lengths other people go to for your benefit. The Senator is going to stay with you, and so is Verisa, and I wouldn't be here if I didn't feel an obligation to her."

"What obligation is that, Bailey?" I said.

"I'm going to fix lunch," Rie said.

"No, stay. I want to hear about this feeling of obligation. What is it exactly, brother?"

His eyes looked quickly at Rie, and he drank out of the beer.

"Don't worry about decorum or people's feelings," I said. "Dump it out on the porch and let's look at it. You're doing a swell job so far."

"I'll be inside, Hack," Rie said.

"No, goddamn. Let Bailey finish. He's saved this up in his head through every airpocket between here and Austin."

"All right," he said. "For the seven years of disappointment you've given her and the alcoholism and the apologies she's had to make to people all over the state. A lesser woman would have taken you into court years ago and pulled out your fingernails. Right now she's under sedation, but that will probably slide past you like everything else in your life does."

"What do you mean, sedation?" I said.

"She called me up drunk an hour after the television broadcast, and I had to go over to the house with a doctor from Yoakum."

Rie lit a cigarette and looked out into the rain. Her suntanned cheeks were pale and her eyes bright. I didn't know why I had forced her to sit through it, and it was too late to change anything now. The wind blew the rain against the bottom of Bailey's chair.

"How is she now?" I said.

"What do you think? She drank a half bottle of your whiskey, and the doctor had to give her an injection to get her in bed."

The bottle of beer felt thick in my hand. I wondered what doctor would give anyone an intravenous sedative on top of alcohol.

"She threw away her pills this morning and tried to fix breakfast for the Senator and Williams," Bai-

ley said. "She almost fell down in the kitchen and
I put her to bed again and refilled her prescription."

"Don't you know better than to give drugs to
people with alcohol in their system?" I said. But he
didn't. His face was a confession of moral earnest-
ness with no awareness of its consequence.

"Go back with him, Hack," Rie said.

"Bailey, why in the bloody hell do you bring on
things like this?" I said.

"Don't you have it confused?" he said.

"No. You have this talent for turning the simple
into a derelict's hangover."

"I think you're shouting at the wrong person."

"You've always got all kinds of cool when you
do it, too. Think about it. Isn't it in moments like
these that you're happiest?"

"I don't need to listen to this."

"Hell, no, you don't. You just dump the hand
grenades out on the porch and let other people kick
them around."

"I told you I'm through with this crap, Hack."

"You've been peddling my ass by the chunk to
all buyers and bitching about it at the same time,
and now you're through. Is that right, buddy?
Frankly, you make me so goddamn mad I could
knock you flat out into the yard."

"Stop it, Hack. Go on back with him," Rie said.

Her face was flushed, and her fingers were trembling on the arm of the wicker chair.

"Should I run a foot race with him down to the airport? Or maybe Bailey can import the whole bunch down here and we can sit on the porch and find out what a sonofabitch I am."

Rie put her fingers on her brow and dropped her eyes, but I could see the wetness on her eyelashes. None of us spoke. The rain drummed flatly on the shingled roof and ran off the eaves, swinging into the wind. My face was perspiring, and I wiped my forehead on my sleeve and drank the foam out of the bottle. I looked at her again and I felt miserable.

"I'm sorry, babe," I said.

She turned her head away from Bailey and put an unlit cigarette in her mouth.

"Call me tonight at the beer joint. Somebody will come down for me," she said.

The wind blew the curls on the back of her neck, and I could see her shoulders shaking. But there was nothing to do or say with Bailey there, and I went inside the screen and asked Mojo to stay with her until I called. When I came back out Bailey was still on the porch.

"I didn't get out the back door on you," I said.

But he didn't understand; he stood against the railing, with the rain blowing across his slacks, as though his physical proximity was necessary to

draw me into the automobile. I started to tell him
to get in the car and read a road map and not raise
his eyes until he heard me open the door, but he
would have had something to say about that and
we would start back into it all over again. When
we drove away Rie was still looking out into the
rain with the unlit cigarette in her fingers.

We didn't speak on the way to the airport. The
air conditioner stopped working, and the windows
fogged with humidity and the sweat rolled down
my face and neck into my shirt. I felt a black anger
towards Bailey that you can only feel towards
someone you grew up with, and as the heat became
more intense in the car I resented every motion that
he made. He opened the window and let the rain
blow across the leather seats, then he closed it and
tried to pull off his windbreaker by the cuffs and
hit me against the arm. I turned on the radio and
we both listened to a Christian crusade evangelist
rant about the communist antichrist in Viet Nam.

The two-engine plane was parked at the end of
the runway in three inches of water. The rain beat
against the silver, riveted plates of the fuselage, and
the wind out of the hills was still strong enough to
push the plane's weight against the anchor blocks
around the wheels. In the distance the hills looked
as brown and smooth as clay.

The cabin had three metal seats in it, spot-

welded to the bulkhead, with old military safety
straps, and when the pilot turned the ignition, the
electric starter on the port engine wouldn't take
hold. Then the propeller flipped over stiffly several
times, black exhaust blew back across the wing, and
the whole plane vibrated with the engines' roar.
The backwash from the propellers blew the concrete dry around the plane, and the pilot taxied out
slowly on the runway with the nose into the wind.
Bailey kept wiping the rain water and perspiration
back through his hair, and his other hand was
clenched tightly on his thigh.

"I'm going to jump it up fast," the pilot said over
his shoulder. "There's bad down drafts over those
hills."

Bailey reached under his seat and took out a half-
pint bottle of sloe gin in a paper sack. He didn't
look at me while he drank. The plane gained speed,
the brown water blowing off the sides of the runway, and the wet fields and the few silver hangars
flashed by the windows, then we lifted off abruptly
into the gray light, the plane shaking against the
wind and the strain of its own engines. The crest
of the hills swept by below us, and in moments I
could see the whole Rio Grande Valley flatten out
through the window. The fields were divided into
great, brown squares of water, the orchards that
hadn't been destroyed by the storm were dark

green against the land, and the river had almost covered the willow trees along its banks. There were dead cattle and horses in the fields, their stiff legs turned out of the water, and the barbed-wire fences had been bent down even with the road. Milking barns had been crushed over sideways, and some farmhouses had lost their roofs, and from the air I felt that I was looking down into something private, an arrangement of kitchens and bedrooms and family eating tables, which I had been unfairly allowed to see.

Bailey's face was white, and he pulled on the bottle again and coughed. He hated for me to see him drink, but his terror of the plane was greater than any feeling he had about personal image or even his ulcerated stomach.

"We'll be there in an hour," I said. "He's above any bad currents now."

Bailey was rigid in the metal seat, the safety belt strapped across his stomach. His fingers were pressed tight across the flat side of the bottle, and the perspiration was still rolling down his face.

"I don't know what kind of agreement you'll come to with Verisa and the Senator, but you and I are going to have one with our practice," he said. His voice was dry, and his accent had deepened with his fear.

"Why do I have to come to an agreement with

anyone?" I knew all the answers he had, but he wanted to talk or do anything to forget the plane and the distance from the ground.

"Because you're holding a big I.O.U. to other people," he said.

"Did it ever strike you that the Senator is a bad man who never did anything for anyone unless his own ass was buttered first? That for thirty years he's served every bad cause in this country? Or maybe that he needs me much more than I needed him?"

He sipped out of the sloe gin, and the cap rattled on the bottle neck when he tried to screw it back on.

"I've already told you, you say it to him," he said. "I don't give a goddamn where your paranoia takes you this time, because tomorrow I'm going to write a check for your half of the practice."

"Okay, Bailey," I said, and watched him hold in all his anger and bent ideas about a correct world and the correct people who should live in it.

I had thought we would land at one of the small airstrips in Yoakum or Cuero, but Bailey had told the pilot to put the plane down in the empty pasture behind my house. The land was flat and cleared of stones, and ten feet above the riverbed, but even from the air I could see the pools of water that had collected in the Bermuda grass. We circled over the ranch once, the wings tilting in the wind currents, and I tapped the pilot's shoulder and leaned against the back of his seat.

"There's armadillo sinkholes and a lot of soft dirt in that field," I shouted over the noise of the engines.

He turned sideways briefly and nodded, then began his approach over the river. The fields of corn, tomatoes, and cotton rushed towards us, the stalks and green plants pressed into the earth by the wind, and I saw the natural gas wells pumping up and down and the windmill ginning like a flash of light in the thin rain, the gray roof of the stable and the weathered smokehouse leaning into the depression where we put the oak logs, and then the white house itself with the latticework verandah and the rose bushes and poplar trees along the front lane. We dipped suddenly over the post oaks by Cappie's cabin and hit the pasture in a spray of mud and grass across the front windows. The wheels went deep into the wet ground, the tail lifted momentarily into the air, and the pilot gunned the engines to keep us in a straight line across the pasture, although he couldn't see anything in front of him. Water and mud streaked across the side windows, then one wheel sunk in a soft spot and we spun in a sliding half circle, with one engine feathered, against the white fence that separated my side lawn and the pasture.

The pilot feathered the other engine and wiped his face on his sleeve. Bailey had spilled the bottle of sloe gin over his slacks.

"Do you have a hard drink inside?" the pilot said.

"If you drink Jack Daniels," I said.

I opened the cabin door, and the rain blew into our faces. We climbed over the white fence and ran across the lawn through the oak trees to the front porch. The Senator's limousine with the tinted windows was parked on the gravel lane. The poplar trees were arched in the wind, and magnolia leaves and rose petals were scattered across the grass. One of Verisa's large earthen flowerpots had fallen from the upstairs verandah, and the soft dirt and cracked pottery lay in a pile on the front steps. It seemed a long time since I had been home; maybe the house looked strange to me because the Senator's car was parked in front, but even the worn vertical line of bullet holes in the porch column seemed new, as though Wes Hardin had drilled them there only yesterday.

I took the pilot through the front hall into my library and opened a bottle of bourbon for him and filled a silver bucket with ice cubes. He sat in my leather chair, his wet cigarette still in his mouth, and poured the glass half full without water.

"I usually stay on a formal basis with my passengers," he said, his face fatigued over the raised glass, "but are you guys on a kamikaze mission or something?"

I closed the door behind me without answering, and walked into the living room. The Senator was sitting in the deer-hide chair by the bar, dressed in blue slacks and a gray golf shirt with a highball balanced on his crossed knee (the whiskey was just enough to color the water). His tan was darker than when I had seen him last, and his mowed, white hair moved slightly in the soft current from the air conditioner. John Williams leaned against the bar with his sunglasses on, tall, the face pale and as unnatural-looking as smooth rubber, and his tan suit hung on him without a line or crease in it. Verisa sat on the couch in a sundress she had bought three weeks ago at Neiman-Marcus, and if she had a hangover from the alcohol or the sedation she had done a wonderful job of burying it inside her. Her auburn hair was brushed back against her shoulders, the makeup on her face made her look fresh and cool, and she lay back comfortably against the cushions with the stem of her wineglass between her fingers as though she were at a D.A.R. cocktail party. But there was also a quick glint in her eyes when I walked into the room, and I knew she was looking forward to a painful retribution on my part.

The Senator rose from his chair and shook hands

with me. His blue eyes wrinkled at the corners when he smiled, and his hand was as square and hard as a bricklayer's.

"You've had an eventful weekend," he said.

"It was probably exaggerated by the television boys," I said.

"I don't believe there was any camera distortion there. Do you?" The acetylene-blue eyes wrinkled again so that it was impossible to read them. "But, anyway, you know John Williams."

"Mr. Holland," Williams said, and raised his glass.

"Hi."

"I'm enjoying your taste in bourbon."

"Help yourself to a bucket of it," I said.

"Thank you. I think I will," he said, and smiled somewhere behind his sunglasses.

"In fact, take a case with you. I have a crate of limes on the back porch to go with it."

The room was silent a moment. Bailey looked at the floor, his brown windbreaker dark with rain, then went behind the bar and raked a mint julep glass through the ice bin.

"You want water in it, Hack?" he said.

"Give it to Mr. Williams. I'm changing my taste in bourbon."

"Maybe I had better wait on the porch," Williams said.

"There's no need for that," the Senator said, and his blue eyes moved onto my face again.

"Hell, no," I said. "That's a real storm out there, Mr. Williams. Enough to short out all the electric circuits on an ICBM."

I despised him and what he represented, and I let him have a good look at the anger I felt towards his presence in my home. He finished his drink and clicked his glass on the bar.

"I think it's better, Allen," he said.

"Fix John another drink," the Senator said to Bailey.

"Get some limes, too, Bailey," I said.

"For one afternoon would you talk without your histrionics?" Verisa said.

"I haven't had much of a chance to talk today. Bailey has spent the last two hours giving me the south Texas sonofabitch award."

"This doesn't have to be unpleasant, Hack," the Senator said.

"Talking reasonably is beyond him," Verisa said. "It violates some confirmed principle he has about offending other people."

"Give Mr. Williams a drink, Bailey," I said. "See about the pilot, too. I think he's getting plowed."

"Well, we won't drag it out then, Hack," the Senator said. "The state committee called last night and asked me if we should drop you and run a boy from

Gonzales. I told them that we would still carry the district no matter who runs, and I want you in the House in January."

"That's good of you, Senator, but I wonder why we all have this intense commitment to my career," and I looked right through the wrinkled light in his eyes.

"Because I feel an obligation to your father, who was a good friend to me. I think what you've done is irresponsible, but with time you'll probably make a fine congressman."

"I'm afraid that I'm through with political fortunes."

"That's a lovely attitude at this point," Verisa said.

"I believe Hack is still a little angry with Rio Grande policemen," the Senator said. "Actually, we may have picked up more of the union vote, and your arrest won't hurt you with the Negroes and the Mexicans. The important factor is that we make use of it before the Republican gentleman does."

"Sorry. I think that boy from Gonzales would be a better bet."

"You're everything I expected today," Verisa said.

"How about the car planted against the fence?"

"You're lovely just as you are. It couldn't have been more anticipated," she said.

"I want to finish this, Hack," the Senator said. "I

plan to talk to the committee this afternoon and give them your assurance about the rest of the campaign."

"I don't think you should do that, Senator."

"The assault charge can be taken care of," he said. "It will probably involve a small appointment in Austin, but it's a simple matter."

He had still chosen not to hear me, and I felt the anger rising inside me.

"Don't you realize what's being done for you?" Bailey said from behind the bar. "Try to think about it a minute. You committed a felony yesterday that could get you disbarred or even sent to jail."

"No, I don't realize a damn thing, because I have an idea that all this investment in me isn't out of good will and old friendships. What do you think, Mr. Williams?"

He sipped from his fresh drink with a sprig of mint leaves in it, rested his arm on the bar, and looked at me from behind his sunglasses. The texture of his skin was the most unnatural I had ever seen on a human being.

"I think it would save time if the case were explained to you a little more candidly," he said.

The Senator looked at Williams, and momentarily I saw the same uncomfortable flicker in his eyes that I had seen on the trip to Washington when I had realized that predators came in various sizes.

He paused a moment, then turned back to me before Williams could speak again, his fingers pressed on the highball glass.

"Possibly your alternatives aren't as clear or easy as you might believe, Hack," he said. "I've made some commitments in this election that I intend to see honored."

"It's a matter of votes on a House bill to rescind the oil-depletion allowance, Mr. Holland. Although Allen doesn't run again for two years, it's been necessary to promise several oil companies that the right people will be on a committee to prevent anyone from lowering the twenty-seven-and-a-half-percent allowance that we now have. As you know, it involves a great deal, and so a few people have pressed Allen rather hard on winning support."

Williams was enjoying the Senator's discomfort, but I didn't care about either of them then. I felt light inside, like a high school athlete who had been told he was needed to pick up the towels in the locker room.

"Did you know about this shit, Bailey?" I said.

"No."

"You sold my ass all over the state and you never guessed what it was about."

"I didn't know, Hack."

"Well, you saw me coming, Senator," I said.

"Are we going to enjoy a melodrama about it now?" Verisa said.

"No, I think I just finished the ninth inning, and you can have the whole goddamn ball park."

"I believe you're being overly serious about this. The oil-depletion allowance is in the interest of the state," the Senator said. "Also, every holder of office pays some kind of personal price to represent his constituency."

"I'd call that boy in Gonzales. Let me have a beer, Bailey."

"Maybe you should tell Mr. Holland about the rest of his alternative now," Williams said. He raised his drink slowly to his mouth.

"I thought you'd been saving something special out," I said. Bailey handed me the beer in a glass, and I took a cigar from the oakwood box on the coffee table. The Senator sat down in the deer-hide chair and crossed his legs with his highball in his hand, but his eyes didn't look at me.

"I don't like to do this, but there's a man named Lester Dixon in Kansas City and he's made a deposition about the time he spent with you in a North Korean prison camp," he said. His eyes looked at the end of his shoe, thoughtful, as though he were considering a delicate premise before he spoke again.

Verisa took a cigarette from her pack and put it

in her mouth. Her arm lay back against the couch, and her breasts swelled against her sundress when she breathed.

I lit my cigar and stared into the Senator's face.

"What did Airman First Class Dixon have to say?" I said.

"I don't believe we have to talk about all of it here," he said.

"I think you should, Senator. I imagine that Lester's deposition was very expensive."

"Two men from your shack were executed after they were informed upon." He raised his eyes into my face and tried to hold them there, but I stared back hard at him and he took a drink from his glass.

"Did he tell you how it was done?" I said.

"I never met him."

"He's an interesting person. I helped send him to prison for five years."

"The statement is twenty pages long, and it's witnessed by two attorneys," he said. "It's been compared for accuracy with the transcript from his court-martial, and I don't think you'll be able to contest what he says about your complicity in the deaths of two defenseless men."

"The telephone is in the hall, Senator. Next to it is a list of numbers, one of which is the *Austin American*. No, instead finish your drink and let Verisa get the city desk for you."

"It will be done more subtly than that. Possibly a leak from someone on the state committee, a small rumor at first, and then a reporter will be given the whole thing."

"You probably have ways I've never dreamed about."

"That's true, but the outcome will be the same in this case."

"Then I guess we can all say good-day to each other."

"No, there's one more thing," he said, and his eyes took on the same expression they had before he drove the tennis ball into my nose. "Right now you're enjoying your virtue. With an impetuous decision you've become a Spartan lying on his shield, and I'm sure you'll need this image for yourself during the next few weeks. But I want to correct a couple of your ideas about integrity in political office. Negotiation and compromise are part of any politician's career, and your father learned that lesson his first term in Congress."

"What do you mean?"

"He accepted a fifteen-thousand-dollar contribution to sponsor the sale of public land to a wildcat company in Dallas. The land sold for fifty dollars an acre."

"Bailey, do you want to tell these men to get out, or you want to wait on me?"

He looked down at the bar, his forehead white.

"Bailey," I said.

The balding spot on his head was perspiring, and I could see the raised veins in the backs of his hands.

"Just look at me," I said.

"I'm sorry, Hack. I didn't know they were going to do this."

"Then you tell them to get out."

He leaned on his arms, his face still turned downwards, and I felt my head begin to grow light, as though there were no oxygen in my blood.

"Goddamn it, you're not going to bring these men into my home to do this, and then stare at the bar," I said.

"He was going to lose the ranch, Hack. He knew heart disease was killing him, and he was afraid he'd die and leave us nothing."

The rain blew against the windows, and I could hear the oak branches sweeping heavily back and forth on the roof. Outside, the light was gray in the trees, and the stripped leaves stuck wetly against the trunks. My dead cigar felt like a stick between my fingers.

"You and this man will leave now, Senator," I said.

"Thank you for the drink, Mr. Holland," Williams said, and set his glass on the bar. "You have a nice home here."

"Thank you, too, Verisa," the Senator said. "I'm sorry if we've made the day a little hard for you."

The three of them rose and walked together to the front hall. They could have been people saying good-bye after a Sunday dinner. Verisa's sundress fit tightly against her smooth back, and she had a way of holding herself at a door that made her look like a little girl. Williams raised his hand once to me, backwards, the way a European would, and smiled again somewhere behind those black-green glasses.

"Good-bye, Hack," the Senator said.

I lit my cigar and didn't look back at him, then I heard the door click shut as I stared down into the flame.

"I'm sorry," Bailey said.

"Forget it and give me one hard one."

"I wouldn't have brought you back for this."

"I know that. Just make it about three inches and a little water."

He poured into a tall shot glass and let the whiskey run over the edge. He started to wipe off the counter with a towel, and then knocked the glass into the sink.

"Christ, Hack," he said.

"I'm all right," I said, and poured the shot glass full myself and drank it down neat.

"You goddamn fool," Verisa said.

"Leave him alone," Bailey said.

"You're going to pay for it with every stick and nail in this house," she said.

I walked away from them towards the hall. The hum of the air conditioners and the heavy sweep of the oaks against the eaves were loud in my head, and the boards in the floor seemed to bend under my boots. I could feel something important begin to roll loose inside, in the way that you pull out a brick from the bottom of a wall. I opened the door to my library and took the cigar out of my mouth. The pilot still sat in my leather chair with the half-empty bottle of Jack Daniels in his lap. His face was colorless, and he had dropped a lighted cigarette on the rug.

"Do you think you can get it up again today?" I said.

"Yeah, buddy, if you don't mind flying drunk," he said.

We walked out into the rain, crossed the lawn, and climbed over the fence to the plane. The air was sweet with the smell of the wet land and the dripping trees and the ruined tomatoes that had been pounded into the furrows. The chain on the windmill had broken and the water was spilling

white over the lip of the trough into the horse lot.
I could see the willows on the river bank bending
against the sky, and the deep cut of the drainages
on the distant hills and the thin line of sunlight on
the horizon's edge. My two oil wells glistened
blackly in the rain, pumping up and down with
their obscene motion, and the weathered shacks of
the Negro and Mexican farm workers stood out
against the washed land like matchboxes that had
been dropped from the sky at an odd angle.

The pilot wiped the plane's windows clean of
mud and grass with his windbreaker, and we took
off across the pasture in a shower of water from the
backdraft of the propellers. Just before we reached
the river the pilot pulled back on the stick and gave
the engines everything they would take, and we
lifted over the trees into the sky and turned into
the wind. The river, the willows, the post oaks and
Cappie's cabin dropped away below us, and then
the house and the deep tire imprints of the Senator's limousine on my gravel lane, and finally the
small whitewashed markers in the Holland family
cemetery.

EPILOGUE

No one won the strike, not the growers or the farm companies or the field workers, because the storm didn't leave anything to win. After the water had drained from the fields, the ruined citrus lay on the ground and rotted under the humid sun until the air was heavy with the smell of the cantaloupe, watermelon, and grapefruit that dried into cysts and then burst apart. The cotton rows were washed flat and the sweep of mud through the fields baked out hard and smooth in the late August heat as though nothing had ever been planted there.

I withdrew from the election, and one of the Senator's aides released Lester Dixon's deposition to a state news service, but no one was particularly interested in it. A reporter from the *Austin American* telephoned me and asked if I had seen it, would I

like him to read it to me over the phone, and I
answered that I wouldn't and would he do several
things with it of his choosing, and I never heard
about it again. Since then I've come to believe that
one's crimes and private guilt, those obsessions that
we hide like that ugly black diamond in the soft
tissue of the mind, are really not very important to
other people.

Bailey acted as my defense lawyer at my hearing
in Pueblo Verde, and had the assault charge
dropped after he promised the district attorney we
would file our own charges against the sheriff's department (there were several lovely frames in the
news film that showed the deputy's khaki knee
bending upward into my eye). I was even proud of
Bailey. He was a better criminal lawyer than I had
thought, or at least he was that day, and even
though the court was hostile to us and the judge
stared hotly at Bailey when he addressed the bench,
he was determined that I wouldn't get any time and
he made the county prosecutor stumble in his
wording and contradict himself. I was given a year's
probation for resisting arrest and disturbing the
peace, and we went across the street to an outdoor
barbecue stand and drank beer for three hours in
the warm shade of an oak tree. Two weeks later I
received a letter of reprimand from someone in the
Texas Bar Association, and I refolded it in the en-

velope and returned it with a pass to the Houston livestock show.

Verisa divorced me and took the Cadillac, eighty acres I owned up in Comal County, and the two natural gas wells, but I held on to the ranch and the house and my thoroughbred horses. She went to Europe for six months, and occasionally her name was mentioned on the society pages of the *New York Times* (a reception at the American embassy in London, dancing with a member of the Kennedy entourage in a Paris nightclub), then she returned to Dallas, where she had been born, and bought a penthouse apartment overlooking the city's skyline and the green hills beyond. She entertained everyone, and from time to time I heard stories about what a radiant hostess she was and how many unusual and interesting people she managed to have at her parties. She sent me an invitation to her wedding, and at first I didn't recognize the groom's name, then I remembered meeting him once at a Democratic cocktail party in San Antonio. He had inherited the controlling stock in a newspaper, and he had turned the paper's editorial page into a right-wing invective against everything liberal in the state. But I remembered him most for the fact that he didn't drink and his cleancut chin was always at an upward angle when he turned his profile to you. I sent them a silver service with a

one-line note of best wishes on a card inside. Four
months later he was killed with another woman in
an automobile accident on the Fort Worth highway. Verisa inherited the newspaper, and after a
period of mourning the parties began again at the
penthouse and her picture appeared regularly on
the society pages with a young district attorney
who rumor said might run for governor in two
years.

Rie and I were married right after the divorce,
and the next fall we had twin boys. They were both
big for twins, and I named one Sam for my father
and the other Hackberry, since I felt there should
always be one gunfighter in the Holland family.
Bailey bought out my half of the law practice, although he argued against it in his emotional way
and wanted to continue the partnership, but I was
through with the R.C. Richardson account and
dealing with oil company executives. I didn't practice for seven months, and spent the winter and
early spring working on the ranch. I dug fence
holes and strung new wire on the pasture, reshin-
gled the barn roof that had been stripped by the
storm, put a new water well down, and plowed and
seeded sixty-five acres of corn and tomatoes. And
each time I twisted the posthole digger in the
ground or drove a six-penny nail down flat in the
wood, I could feel the last drops of Jack Daniels

sweat out through my pores and dry in the wind, and a new resilience in my body that I hadn't felt since I pitched at Baylor. I worked hard each morning, with the sun low over the willows on the river bank, and through the day until late evening when the shadow from the tractor fell out across the rows and the purple light drew away over the horizon. And when I had pulled the seed drill over the last furrows against the back fence I could already smell the land beginning to take hold of new life, and after the next shower small green plants would bud one morning in long, even lines.

Rie and I took my best three-year-old up to Lexington that spring and raced him at Keeneland. Each afternoon we sat in the sun with mint juleps and watched the horses break from the starting gate on the far side of the field, with the jockeys like toy men on their backs, and move in a tight formation down the back stretch, the lead horses pushing hard for the rail, then into the far turn as the roar of their hooves grew louder, their bodies glistening with sweat, and Rie would be on her feet with her arms wrapped tightly in mine, the quirts whipping down into the horses' flanks and the sod flying into the air, and then there was that heart-beating rush when they came down the home-stretch with the jockeys pouring it into them, and the thunder against the turf was louder than the shouting of the crowd. We won a thirty-five-hundred-dollar purse in one race, and placed in two others, and the evening before we left for Texas I took Rie on a long drive through the bluegrass and the Cumberland Mountains. The limestone cliffs rose straight up out of the hollows, and the tops of the white oaks and beech trees were covered with the sun's last light. I was tired and quiet inside after the two weeks of racing, and the rolling hills stretched away towards Virginia in a violet haze, but a sense of time and its ephemeral quality began to weigh on me, as when you give yourself too long a period of restoring things that you hurt through indifference or cynicism in the first place.

Two days after we returned home I drove to San Antonio and became a trial lawyer for the A.C.L.U.

It's summer again now, and the corn is green against the brown rows in the fields, and I irrigated my cotton acreage from the water well I put down and the bolls have started to come out white in the leaves. In the evening I can smell the dampness of the earth in the breeze off the river, and the wet sweetness of the Bermuda grass in the horse pasture, and just before dusk the wind flattens out the smoke from Cappie's cabin and there's just a hint in the warm air of oak logs burning in a wood stove. I built a large, circular crib around a chinaberry tree in the side yard for the boys to play in,